A GIRL'S BEST FRIEND

A GIRL'S BEST FRIEND

MOONLIGHT DETECTIVE AGENCY™ BOOK THREE

ISOBELLA CROWLEY   ELL LEIGH CLARKE
MICHAEL ANDERLE

DISRUPTIVE IMAGINATION

LMBPN Publishing
PMB 196, 2540 South Maryland Pkwy
Las Vegas, NV 89109

First US edition, November 2019
eBook ISBN: 978-1-64202-593-4
Print ISBN: 978-1-64202-594-1

THE A GIRL'S BEST FRIEND TEAM

Thanks to the JIT Readers

Dave Hicks
Kelly O'Donnell
Dorothy Lloyd
John Ashmore
Micky Cocker
Charles Tillman
Jackey Hankard-Brodie
Jeff Eaton
Deb Mader
Misty Roa
Nicole Emens
Jeff Goode
Larry Omans

If I've missed anyone, please let me know!

Editor
The Skyhunter Editing Team

To Family, Friends and
Those Who Love
to Read.
May We All Enjoy Grace
to Live the Life We Are
Called.

PROLOGUE

Scalion Vampire Coven, Flushing, New York

Not far from the Queens Botanical Garden, a secret passage under the street could be located if one knew where to look. It was the only entrance that led directly to the vampire coven's audience chamber from the surface. Half a dozen other tunnels, however, also led to it from other points underground.

Scalion himself now sat on his high-backed oak chair within the chamber, the other four vampires within his sphere of influence seated a little below him, two on the far side of the table and one at each end. Their thralls gathered in the shadowy open space behind them.

One of the four, a svelte, dour-faced woman with reddish-bronze hair wearing a flowing white dress, looked at their leader.

"Scalion," she inquired, "why, exactly, are we here? Is this about the messages?"

He smiled grimly. "Of course it is, Ravenna. There are a few other housekeeping matters to discuss, routine things of minimal consequence. Let us get those out of the way first. Then we'll serve red salt tea and talk of this...person who seems to think she is our long-lost ruler."

Contemptuous chortles and half-snorts of derision went around the table. It had been a long time since anyone had dared to threaten them. The last time it had happened, the fool who'd uttered the threats had lived barely long enough to regret his hubris.

The vampire leader ran a hand through his black hair that he wore slicked back behind his ears in what he liked to think was the traditional fashion. "The nerve of these little foreign upstarts," he muttered.

The thralls stood, waiting, as he began the meeting. "First, in addition to a minor slip-up in which a human witness may require a mindwipe, our blood bank has experienced slight overdraft issues lately—"

Gazes wandered upward and around as he spoke. Long before, the chamber had been a crypt in service to one of the first European families to inhabit this land. Scalion had taken it over not long after that. He'd ensured that it was kept separate from New York's collective basement-labyrinth of sewers and subway tunnels, while also connected it to places of interest to himself, not least his own estate.

His thralls, abetted by the occasional human hireling, had expanded and improved upon the chamber until it resembled the black fane of a deconsecrated church. The ceiling of the space almost passed for vaulted arches and scarlet hangings of finest silk and velvet.

Here, he and his underlings could forget the crassness that went on daily above their heads.

The dull, prosaic matters passed through the discussion quickly enough. Once they'd all come to satisfactory agreements, they moved on to the subject that truly interested them.

"Now, then," Scalion proclaimed, "let us elaborate on the matter of the oh so polite letters which, as I understand it, each of us received at home. We will compare them to ensure they are identical, but I suspect we all were sent the same message."

The four nodded.

Smirking, he proceeded. "And I suspect our mysterious friend will receive five resounding answers of 'no,' of course."

Behind them, before any could answer, a voice echoed. All their heads snapped toward the sound.

"Thank you," the newcomer intoned, "for your prompt reply."

It was a woman, tall and curvy, with square-cut black hair that stopped above her shoulders, a dusky complexion, and large, almond-like eyes. She wore a reddish-brown dress and a gold necklace. Her sonorous voice was somehow both full and dusty sounding and thick with a curious accent, vaguely Middle Eastern.

Silence reigned in the chamber for a moment as their visitor scanned the scene before her slowly. Those gathered there simply stared in response.

Scalion spoke first. "You must be Moswen Neith," he stated.

Slowly, her lips smiled but the expression didn't reach her eyes. "Yes."

Ravenna scrutinized the woman, half-squinting and her

mouth twisted in a sneer. "Hah! You do not look so imposing and magnificent as your arrogant missive seemed to suggest. Are we to suppose that now, we should quake with fear because you snuck in to stand before us while we spoke?"

"Of course," Moswen replied. "Unless, of course, you heed my offer." She stood utterly still and watched them.

The other woman looked at her leader.

He sat and glowered at his uninvited guest, his demeanor cool, haughty, and almost bored. Finally, he snorted.

"None of us," he began, "have even heard of you, Ms Neith. Your pretentious offer was the kind of thing we might expect from a celebrity or a ranking member of the Vampiric Order. It would seem you are a medium-sized fish used to ruling a small pond. Here, suddenly, you find yourself in the sea, surrounded by sharks. I advise you to go home."

An almost lazy wave of his hand capped off this recommendation as if shooing her off.

But beneath this veneer of arrogance, he was not entirely certain if Ms Neith would be dismissed so easily. A cold tension seemed to have wound into his gut and something in the air itself seemed off, somehow, like the shifting of charges that preceded a powerful storm.

She took two steps closer.

The thralls, two dozen in all, roiled like masses of heated liquid and fell back from the dark woman, yet poised themselves for action at the same time.

Scalion watched them and his jaw clenched. They were intimidated by her, he concluded. They would attack if ordered to do so, but they were unused to such casual defiance of their master by someone who, just maybe, was not an utter fool.

He raised his hand again, now with a firm motion and his palm outward. "Stop," he commanded and put the full force of his preternatural abilities into the word. Humans on the receiving end of such a command would have frozen instantly in their tracks and most lesser vampires would have stalled.

Instead, Moswen strolled two more steps before she came to a halt. Even then, it appeared to be entirely of her own will as though she'd thought it over and paused simply to humor him.

"Scalion." Her voice had grown husky. "I am not here to waste time posturing. My ultimatum was clear, and it extends to all of you. Join me and serve me or die."

Ravenna had stared intently at the interloper but now, she turned to look sharply at her leader, her frown deeper than usual and her eyes blazing. Cold fury was there, but something else as well—fear.

Scalion made up his mind to sic the thralls onto their new friend. From the sides and behind, they could take her and distract and immobilize her, while the five vampires closed in from the front.

But first, he intended to have the last word.

"Ms Neith," he jeered and trailed off into a brief chuckle as her dark eyes fixed on him, "congratulations on having demonstrated a basic degree of competence in being able to resist a command. But I'm afraid your little exercise in poorly thought-out swagger has come to an—"

Suddenly, she was airborne.

He bolted from his chair and found his feet, his vampiric reflexes overcoming his shock. In the same moment, the four seated below him darted up too. They yelled protests as their hands twisted into claws.

The henna-and-golden streak pounded into him and through him before he could even so much as raise his hands.

Shouts turned to screams, flesh rent, and wood snapped and tumbled against stone.

Choking and sputtering, Scalion stumbled back into the space where his would-be throne had been. Moswen had toppled it as she passed. There was also a gaping, bloody crevice under his chin where his throat had been.

He collapsed to his knees, his hands clasped over the blood-gushing hole. His vision blurred and dimmed and he knew with a cold fear that he would not be able to regenerate a wound like this before she finished him off.

Unless his followers could kill her first.

Pandemonium had already erupted. The interloper was perched on the far wall behind him like a spider, and Ravenna and the other three already began to race toward her in a bestial rage while the thralls moved forward to engage the intruder.

In the next moment, Moswen was behind him. Her hand ripped through what remained of his neck. His head tumbled behind his body to land atop the debris of his chair.

His followers attacked. Ravenna and one of the other men vaulted toward the walls and maneuvered around and above the intruder, while the other two attacked her directly from the front.

The thralls moved to join the action and were only a few paces from the empty table, but the battle between preternaturals was unfolding so fast that they might not have time to play a role in it.

Moswen and a bald male vampire met each other in mid-air, and it was the latter who fell back as both plummeted to land hard. The dark woman's hand had punched all the way through his chest to emerge with his heart clutched in her fist.

A few of the thralls in the front rank hesitated and stumbled, their programmed loyalty momentarily overridden by sheer horror and terror.

Forms flashed and darted, screams echoed, and blood sprayed. In the space of a few eyeblinks, the foreign vampire had ripped the others to shreds. The entire alcove where Scalion's chair had stood was spattered with the pieces and fluids of the slain.

The thralls stopped. Those who had possessed them as masters were now dead. In slack-jawed silence, they watched as Moswen crawled out of the carnage and arrayed five heads on the table—Scalion's in the center and two of the others' on each side.

The vampire stood before the uneasy throng. She licked the blood from her lips, raised a hand with her fingers spread, and felt for the thralls' brands.

All two dozen of the slaves clenched as pain suffused their bodies. The markings over their hearts placed there by their deceased lords and ladies glowed with the light of various different colors. All quickly transformed to the same amber-golden hue which flashed from her eyes.

They were hers now.

Moswen's consciousness expanded. Her terrible will extruded into the feeble minds of her new slaves and she drank of their fear and submission, finding it almost as satisfying as blood. They, the lowly, would serve the exalted, as was their destiny.

The power of her mind enfolded the thralls, drew them closer to her, and secured them. That accomplished, it reached still farther outward.

Like a bird of prey gliding over a desolate wilderness in search of a hapless wounded rodent to descend upon, the vampire's will hunted. There was one particular rodent she sought and she was certain he was still in New York City.

She sensed him only dimly at first, a small point of mortal heat in a cold landscape that pulsed faintly with the residues of her own power as well as the stink of enemy influence. The man called Alexander Thomas, her traitorous former servant.

"Good," she whispered.

Moswen retracted the power of her mind and brought it to bear upon the thralls in Scalion's chamber. At her insistence, half of them shuffled down one of the branching corridors toward his estate and she strode behind them. The other half of the throng fell in at her rear to guard her passage.

Alex still lingered in this city as the new lackey of Taylor Steele, exactly as she had expected. If she found him, she would find her foe.

The vampire was more powerful than Scalion had been, but she felt no fear of her. She, too, would be eliminated like the pretender she was. And then, Moswen Neith would be the sole ruler of what was, in this present age, the greatest city on Earth.

As for Alex, she merely hoped that he knew she was coming for him. In the shadows of the tunnel, the corners of her mouth turned upward and the fangs showed beneath her lips.

CHAPTER ONE

<u>*Moonlight Detective Agency Offices, Bushwick, Brooklyn,*</u>
<u>*New York*</u>

"Bullshit!" the client bellowed and pounded his fist on the desk. A few papers dislodged from their piles and fluttered like giant confetti. The overturned coffee mug also rattled and threatened to fall and shatter on the floor.

David Remington, who worked under the pseudonym Remington Davis, adjusted his tie and kept his attention fixed on the hulking troll all the while. On the desk in front of him, only a few inches from the client's club-like hand, was a scan of the incriminating photograph.

"It's the truth. You know how women are sometimes. Can't live with 'em, can't, uh…"

The huge bluish humanoid made a choking sound and his eyes appeared to be turning red. *I must have said something wrong*, Remy surmised. *And I only attempted to be empathetic.*

They'd received the present client, a Mr. Shauckburn, in the back office with a curtain drawn to divide them from the front reception area. It wouldn't do to have human clients traipse in and potentially glimpse a preternatural creature out of his disguise.

"Can't what? I can't what?" the troll demanded.

The door opened behind him and Taylor stepped in. "Excuse me," she said in her soft voice, "is something wrong?"

"Wrong?" their customer raged and flung his heavy blue-green arms up over his head. "Did you hear what this son of a bitch said? He said I can't live with my wife. And anyway, that photo could be doctored."

Remy tried to think of a clever response to the ridiculous accusation, but it took a second. During that time, Taylor glared at him with her black eyes, turned toward the troll, and spoke first.

"Mr. Shauckburn, first, let me apologize for my colleague's clumsy usage of a human expression that is unlikely to make sense to members of your community. He's lapsed back into a bad habit I've tried to cure him of."

"Nonsense," Remy retorted sharply when he found his voice again, "I have no bad habits whatsoever." That's, uh, not entirely true, though, he admitted inwardly.

She ignored him and continued to talk to their client while she rested a pale, red-nailed hand gently on his thick arm. "I am terribly sorry about the news of your wife's infidelity. However, we have no reason to doctor a photograph. First of all, that kind of unprofessional dishonesty would damage our excellent reputation."

The troll grunted and fidgeted in place, but at least she seemed to hold his attention.

"And second," she went on, "during an infidelity case,

this kind of clear and definite proof is usually the point at which our services are no longer required. An unscrupulous agency that simply wanted to bill you would therefore try to disguise clear proof so they could collect further fees for continuing the investigation."

Remy snapped his fingers and transformed the motion into pointing at her. "Right, exactly. That's precisely what I was about to say."

Shauckburn growled, squeezed his eyes shut, and brought his clenched fists up toward his chest as he struggled to bring his emotions under control.

"I still can't fucking believe it!" he grunted. "We've been married for sixteen years. Who is this guy? He's even uglier than my brother."

He swiped a hand toward the photo, where his spouse was locked in a highly intimate embrace with a young man with puffy cheeks, bristly hair, and an upturned nose.

"He's a wereboar, apparently." Remy shrugged. "I didn't even know there were wereboars. Werecats are bad enough. Yeah, he's fairly hideous, but he also looks younger than you, so maybe that has something to do with it. Women sometimes get to that point where they want to pretend they're back in college or whatever."

The troll's eyes bulged as he stared at the investigator, and he began to literally tremble with barely suppressed wrath. "I'm not old!" he roared.

Remy would have shrunk back a step or two, but he was still seated in his chair behind the desk. *Crap. It looks like I still don't have the whole 'tact' thing down as well as I ought to.*

He cleared his throat and tried to ignore the sweat

forming on his palms. A quick glance at Taylor for help suggested that he was on his own. She'd leaned back against the wall, her arms folded over her chest, and now regarded him with an aloof expression of mild annoyance.

That definitely meant he was on his own.

"Uh," he stammered, "pardon. I forgot that you guys age slower than humans, right? In mortal years, you'd be old, but you're definitely not in troll years. Aging like a fine wine, as they say."

Shauckburn made a low barking noise. "I'll...smash you like a...wine!" He sounded like he was choking on his own anger at this point.

And here I am, Remy lamented, *at least trying to be nice to this guy.*

Something beeped and the voice of Bobby, the receptionist, sounded in the office, barely audible over the snarls of their client.

"Ms Steele, Mr Remington," she said, "the New York City Chief of Police is here. He...uh, demands to speak to you right away. Should I let him through?"

Remy kept his eyes on Shauckburn and raised both palms in a gesture of placation. He wracked his brain for some other way to calm the troll while Taylor answered the message.

"Bobby," she snapped, "do not let him back here no matter what. Understood? We'll be out directly along with Mr Shauckburn."

"Yes, ma'am." The receptionist's voice fell silent, although Remy thought he could hear her talking to someone out in the lobby. As he recalled, she wore a lacy, low-cut blouse, so he had faith in her ability to keep the chief distracted for a while.

He focused on the troll. "Sir, if you would kindly please calm down and put your disguise on, I will offer you a ten percent discount on our services, paid out of my own pocket. How does that sound?"

"Ten?" Shauckburn all but bellowed. "It should be more like—"

Taylor clamped a hand on his shoulder and offered him the thin, enchanted mask and gloves he wore to give himself the appearance of normal human skin tone. For some reason, undisguised trolls were easier for normal people to see than most other preternaturals.

"Your disguise," she said briskly. "Please put it back on, Mr Shauckburn."

For another two or three minutes, they argued with the inconsolable troll. Finally, Taylor grasped him around the upper arms and shoulders—he knocked over a side table, which made a fair amount of racket—and refused to release him until he cooperated.

Remy then had the honor of trying to put the mask on his face. Fortunately, Shauckburn mostly growled and stared, rather than attempting to bite his hand off.

"There," the investigator said, "your mask is mostly on. You might as well complete the ensemble with the gloves, now that you've come this far."

The troll finally agreed. Remy noticed, though, that the mask didn't stick to his face properly. Either Shauckburn would need to fix it himself or they'd simply have to hope that the Police Chief outside didn't look too closely at the tall angry guy.

All three exited the office and moved toward the lobby and the front door beyond.

Remy walked out in front so he could partially block the huge, saggy-faced troll, not to mention the fact that Taylor held said troll's arm in her deceptively powerful grip and guided him as she moved.

Shauckburn muttered again, "This is still bullshit. This isn't over!"

A balding man of medium height with a dark-blue overcoat draped over his shoulders stood before the reception desk. The chief was perfectly positioned to witness their disgruntled client's exit.

The investigator took a deep breath and tried to think of how best to explain the shouting plus the crash of Shauckburn knocking over the side table. Hopefully, he wouldn't have to mention the fact that the troll's face looked rather like it was melting on the left side.

To everyone's surprise, however, the chief offered only the briefest of sidelong glances as the trio, including the large angry troll, passed behind him and through the doors. He seemed completely enraptured by Bobby. She prattled about something or other and more importantly, her blouse was indeed low-cut.

They stepped outside.

"Again," Taylor said, "we apologize. And of course, Remington will make good on his offer of a ten percent reimbursement discount. Please try to have a good rest of your evening, Mr Shauckburn."

A tremble of rage went through the troll as he loped off toward his truck. "Too fucking late, but thanks." Finally, he was gone.

The young man and the vampire stepped back toward the door, paused a moment in the chilly January air, and examined the policeman through the glass.

Taylor patted a slim hand on his arm. "Nicely done," she said.

He grinned and mentally prepared a comment to acknowledge how well he'd handled the Shauckburn situation, but Taylor interrupted him. "Hiring Ms Diaz to be our receptionist, I mean. It seems she's working out even better than expected."

Remy shrugged, then nodded. He would take what compliments he could get. Besides, the first time he'd seen that cleavage, he knew he was looking at a potential business asset.

The two pushed through the door and stood behind the chief. The man spared another quick glance toward them but returned his gaze to Bobby's chest as he opened his mouth to speak.

"So, hi," he began. "I'm here to follow up on that incident from five or six weeks ago. The disturbance."

The investigator nodded and maintained a vaguely pleasant smile—the kind of expression he always used for Public Relations. Of course, he knew exactly what the man was referring to, but both he and Taylor waited to hear more before they offered their two cents' worth.

The chief cleared his throat. "Your neighbors complained of a loud, violent confrontation—considerable shouting, crashing and things breaking, and even gunshots. They thought it was a goddamn gang war or possibly a terrorist attack. Police responders arrived on the scene to find your office trashed. I'm sure you remember—"

"Yes," Taylor answered and kept her voice mild. "We filed a report."

"Yeah." The man dragged his gaze away from the receptionist long enough to produce a manila folder from under his coat. He set it on the desk, opened it, and made a show of leafing through a few papers within.

Remy squinted at the documents. *What the hell are those, warrants for our arrest?*

The chief cleared his throat. "So, according to this, you said teenagers broke into the place after hours and used it to throw a party, trashed the place, and then got into an altercation with one or two junkies passing through the area and someone pulled a gun. Which led to further trashing."

He raised his gaze to meet Taylor's. "Is that correct?"

She nodded. "It is, to the best of our knowledge. Our people did not arrive until the damage had already been done."

Watching the cop, Remy noticed the steady, narrow-eyed gaze and the slight pucker of distaste around the mouth. Clearly, he thought they were hiding something and he seemed highly interested in finding out exactly what.

"You know," the man countered, "we canvassed the area, interviewed the locals, and checked some of the security feeds and all that, and a funny thing turned up. No one seems able to remember any teenagers hanging around the neighborhood that night."

Taylor raised her left eyebrow and shrugged. "They must have come from another neighborhood nearby and been sneaky about it."

"The thing is," the chief responded almost instantly, "what a coupla people did claim to see was some people in dark suits skulking around. Being real sneaky like professionals. They weren't sure exactly where these individuals were going but it was in this vicinity." He waved his index finger in a circle while he pointed it at the floor.

Remy pretended to look surprised, even though the man had focused most of his attention on the vampire. The man was referring, of course, to Agent Kendra Gilmore's team, who'd staked out a building down the street to help capture Moswen Neith's servant, Alex.

The fact that he seemingly had no idea who they were meant that, as planned, the FBI still hadn't bothered to share its information with the NYPD. Gilmore had kept her word.

Taylor made a show of pondering this supposedly new information. "I see," she commented finally.

"And," the chief went on, "that doesn't seem the slightest suspicious to you? Like it contradicts some of the finer points of your statement? You didn't neglect to report anything like, say, a well-organized squad targeting a safe box in your office that might have held something you wouldn't want to talk about?"

She placed a finger over her lips. "Hmm…well, no. I'll concede that the detail about the black-suited persons is disturbing. However, we're really quite backed up with cases right now, which makes it difficult to do our own investigation. So, if you're unable to do your own job and want me to look into it, I'll have to charge you our standard fee for a private case."

He snorted and seemed almost to bristle as he stuffed

the report papers into the folder and took a step back. "That'll be the day." He grunted.

As he turned and marched toward the door, Remy saw a short, broad figure coming in from the opposite direction.

The man ignored the newcomer and said over his shoulder, "It's a good thing the Guggenheim Museum was able to recover that stolen idol." Then, he was gone.

Remy sighed. "It was a fake, anyway," he muttered.

The man who now entered the office brushed shoulders with the departing cop as he stepped into the lobby. It was Surrly, the dwarf. Even by the standards of his species, he was squat and broad.

"Oblivious humans," he grumbled. "You'd think I'd be unusual enough to warrant the dignity of a second glance."

Remy waved. "Hi, Surrly! How goes the rocks business?"

"Rocks!" The dwarf snorted. "Your kind are as oblivious to mineral value as you are to the existence of differences between sentient peoples."

Bobby started to ask their guest if he was related to Andrew Volz, their tech specialist, but Taylor stepped forward to greet him before she could finish.

"Surrly, nice to see you again. What brings you here this evening?" She extended a slim white hand.

He smiled beneath his iron-colored mustache and extended a hugely thick arm. It looked as though he might crush her hand or snap her forearm with his grip, but she displayed no sign of discomfort.

The visitor opened with a grunt. "I have another job for

you. Not so much an investigation, but it is something I'm sure you could handle."

Remy thought of how he'd exchanged some of Surrly's "rocks"—uncut gems—for cash by trading them to a certain werecat. It was probably something like that, he concluded.

Taylor spread her hands. "Go on. I don't believe you've ever come to see me yourself while requesting my services before, so I am intrigued."

When he studied her, Remy noticed a slight tension and skepticism. She had a hell of a poker face but then again, he was a hell of a poker player.

The dwarf took a few more steps in and seated himself on one of the lobby's chairs.

Bobby caught his attention. "Do you want any coffee, Mr...uh, Surrly?" she asked.

He raised a blocky hand. "No, thank you. I'll not be here for too long."

"Okay. Let me know if you need anything."

The receptionist leaned back and buried her face in the latest issue of The New England Inquirer, a disreputable gossip sheet which often attempted to report on the preternatural but usually failed miserably at it. Remy had featured in quite a few of their stories. When neither of her two bosses made a move to escort the client through to the inner office, she set her reading matter aside and wandered off, presumably to give them space or perhaps simply to make herself coffee.

Remy hung back, leaned against the reception desk, and folded his arms over his chest while Taylor sat in another chair across from the dwarf.

"Now," Surrly began, "what I'd like your help with is in granting me certain assurances. You see, my cartel is moving in a certain amount of extra merchandise lately."

He seemed to pause for a second to consider his words, but before he could go on, Taylor interrupted him.

"What is the merchandise?" Her tone was still mostly soft, but Remy noticed the underlying edge to it.

The dwarf bristled. "My client has requested privacy on the matter, so I am not at liberty to divulge that information. Suffice to say that, as with everything I deal, it is of great value."

"Avocados?" the investigator guessed.

Surrly shot him a death glare and his busy unibrow angled downward in the middle. "No."

Taylor ignored her partner and pressed on with another question. "And what kind of assurances are you talking about?"

He turned back to the woman. "I wish to be assured that my merchandise will be safe. After the shenanigans six weeks ago, one can't be too careful. Not to mention, all that nonsense drew undue attention to my operations. Vultures have begun to circle. From what I hear, newer and bigger vultures."

Remy filed that intriguing detail away in his mind. Later, it might be wise to determine if their visitor knew anything about Moswen Neith.

The stout man went on. "Everything I know suggests that you would be the one to stop anyone from interfering with the shipments. Few in this city are stupid enough to cross you."

Something in the energy she gave off grew cooler, harder. "No," she stated flatly.

"What?" Surrly straightened, shocked by her response.

She did not react. "You've come to request security from a firm that performs investigations. We're private detectives, not hired muscle. Anytime we flex our muscle, it is only in response to someone egregiously flaunting the rules or threatening us directly. We are not a 'show of force' to be rented for the purpose of intimidating your rivals."

Scoffing and muttering under his beard, the dwarf heaved himself to his feet. "I would not have expected this kind of treatment from you of all people."

An average-looking, thirtyish blond man stumbled into the lobby from somewhere deeper in the office.

"Uh, does our guest want any coffee?" he asked in an Australian accent. He squinted at the client and seemed to recognize him, immediately went pale, and backed away slowly. Fortunately, the dwarf paid him no heed.

"No," Remy called after him, "Bobby already asked about that. Thanks for being such a good intern, though."

Surrly, ignoring the interruption, had pivoted away from them and was about to leave. Taylor and Remy watched as he stormed toward the door, paused a few feet before it, and half-turned toward them.

"I may have to rethink our business relationship," he said over his shoulder. "Clearly, you care more about technicalities or your reputation than you do about actually helping your customers."

"Not necessarily," Taylor replied calmly. "Cool down a

little and perhaps you can contact us again at another time."

Shaking his head, he shoved angrily through the doors and disappeared out into the night.

Remy sighed. "It's a shame. He's actually a charming fellow to work with, aside from being a total asshole and all. Plus, I'm a tad disappointed that we weren't able to introduce him to Alex as 'the guy who killed your guys.'"

Thinking back on the horrid scene of half a dozen of Surrly's dwarves torn apart in a sewer tunnel, he almost immediately regretted his own attempt at humor. The image still haunted his nightmares. And while Alex had been rendered harmless, the creature who'd driven him to do that was still on the loose.

Taylor's eyes had gone distant, and she drummed her red nails on the armrest of her chair.

"It's strange," she muttered finally. "What could Surrly's cartel possibly be shipping that's so valuable that he would look for outside help to protect it? That's not like them at all. Dwarves usually like their privacy and prefer to work within their own circles. And it's not as if the diamonds and such he dealt in before were exactly worthless."

He almost answered but realized he'd already blown his "avocados" comment and didn't have a Plan B.

She looked at him. "Remington, I'd say that sounds like a job for you. Tomorrow, I want you to start trawling for rumors that might shed light on this matter."

"Wait," he countered. "You turned down a paid job offer from him, but now we'll actually investigate what he's up to anyway for free?"

"Don't pretend to be dense," the vampire snapped. "Any

suspicious activity involving New York's preternatural community is, ultimately, our business. Paid or not."

The investigator thought back to all the lingering debts he still had—and to how far he still was from being truly rich again, enough so to get his family speaking to him once more. The personal discount he'd offered to Mr Shauckburn certainly wouldn't help.

"Well," he shrugged, "at least I'm on hourly."

CHAPTER TWO

Park Avenue Shopping District, New York City

Remy was not the kind of person who was prone to fear, but by now, he had begun to learn that fear had its uses.

As such, he decided that if he had to plunge into another potentially dangerous investigation, it would be wise to have backup. Magical backup, preferably. The kind that could do handy things like deflect bullets, make cars invisible, and track suspects all across town by their smell.

He knew exactly the woman for the job. It was only a question of finding her.

Usually, Riley—a member of the Fair Folk from the Fluttershire Colony under the George Washington Bridge —arrived for work quite reliably whenever he had paid the colony for her services. But lately—within the last few days —she'd been mysteriously AWOL.

And he was reasonably sure he knew why. Something about her had changed after the day, a little over a month before, when he'd taken her on a date to the New York Botanical Gardens in the Bronx.

Now, he drove his Lincoln slowly through Midtown Manhattan toward Park Avenue and took his time to do visual scans of the streams of pedestrians.

Someone behind him honked. "Hey!" the driver yelled out of a rolled-down window. "It's clear, asshole."

The man then proceeded to wheel his Honda around to the left, cutting someone else off, and glared at him as he passed.

"Oh, gosh," Remy drawled. "Heaven forbid I drive within the speed limit for once. Ugh, that probably means he thinks I'm a tourist, though. Or from upstate."

Other cars sang similar songs of rage with their horns as he puttered along the avenue and scrutinized the post-Christmas shoppers. Many people received gift cards or even simply cash from distant cousins and parents who no longer knew how to buy things for their adult children. There was thus always a second surge in commerce in the weeks after the holiday, so the throngs really were nothing out of the ordinary.

After perhaps twenty minutes of trawling the shopping district, he found what he was looking for—a couple, one of whom could only be Riley. The other was...a guy. Who he was didn't necessarily matter.

The fairy, as he'd expected, had taken the form of a human. She stood about five foot three, a noticeable increase from her natural height of five inches. Her body was at once slender and curvy in all the right places, and she wore a striking if rather weird and garish dress which accentuated it.

The garment was made to resemble a tiger's fur. She also had a matching pull-over cap and plain orange gloves and boots. Some of her hair, a radiant platinum color that was almost more white than blonde, spilled out from under the hat.

From this angle, her back was to him, but he knew it was her. And although he couldn't see her face, he knew it complemented the rest of her. Whether fairy-sized or human-sized, she was stunningly beautiful, although it was easier to notice in the latter case.

Much, much easier. And since that day at the gardens, he was far from the only one who'd noticed.

The man she was with turned his head to say something to her and allowed the investigator to glimpse his face briefly. He was almost a full foot taller than her but otherwise unremarkable except in being rather generically handsome—the type of guy who came straight off the assembly line at certain universities. Without a doubt, he'd probably been kicked out of at least one of them.

He was also well-dressed, to an extent that stopped barely short of being flashy. It didn't quite look like he was showing off but no one who saw him in public would assume he was anything other than rich.

"Well," he said to himself and thought of his own bank account, "maybe not that rich."

Remy immediately assumed that Riley had picked up on the man's assumed prosperity and had probably registered it as a bonus when selecting him as her temporary companion. Since the two of them were positively loaded with purchases, this seemed a likely possibility.

The man held no fewer than four bags, two in each

hand, all of which bulged with gifts and clothes and probably expensive chocolates or other such things. At his height, he probably had the strength to manage but it still looked like his arms were under strain by now.

The fairy, meanwhile, held exactly one similar bag, although it probably weighed less than the others by a good five or ten pounds.

"God," he muttered, "it's like she's trying way too hard to be a human woman. Sooner or later, others will notice and start asking her for lessons on how to get men to buy that much shit for them."

Despite his words, though, he felt his stomach clench with worry. She did not seem to appreciate how much potential danger she was in.

While in human form, she lost the ability to use her other fae powers. Her attractiveness might inspire men to protect her but otherwise, she was as helpless as any other mortal.

And this at a time when a terrifyingly powerful vampire might well be tracking her. Taylor had mentioned the fact that Moswen Neith might know that Riley had aided them.

There was another thing, too, that concerned him. He'd seen her in this neighborhood three or four times previously on different days throughout the last month. The man she was with now was not the same man she'd been with last time.

And it had been someone different the time before that.

Not that it was his place to judge other peoples' lifestyles—especially given some of the crap he'd done—but he didn't think Riley realized that human men were almost as strange and excitable as human women. Some of them didn't take it well when a lovely young woman flirted with them and disappeared off the face of the earth a week later, only to be seen thereafter in the arms of another man.

An open parking space along the street suddenly manifested itself. Remy pulled his car into it and got out hastily, almost forgetting to lock it as he merged with the pedestrian traffic along the sidewalk.

He followed Riley and her date at a consistent distance of about fifteen to twenty feet. There were enough people on the street that this kept him fairly inconspicuous but he could still overhear most of their conversation.

He would also be able to leap into the fray if something should happen.

"Oh, ha!" the stuffed shirt exclaimed, probably in response to some corny joke the oversized fairy had told. "You really do have a sense of humor, don't you? I don't meet all that many girls who do."

With distaste, he noted that the man was practically swooning. He must not have known a heartbreaker when he saw one.

She's making a habit of this. Next week, she'll be back out here with some other moderately wealthy, oblivious dude. Anything to keep them lavishing attention on her.

To his embarrassment, the next thing that crossed his mind was the memory of how desperately she used to want his attention and only his. She hadn't yet discovered other men.

The lovebirds slowed near an intersection, and it

sounded like their date was about to end the same way her previous ones had.

"Sorry," Riley said in her cute, girlish voice, "but I'm so tired. Especially after carrying this." She held up the single, light bag. "Do you think you could call a cab for me?"

"Aww," the guy responded, "I'm sorry to hear you're having trouble. Of course. Let me...uh, set this stuff down, and I think I can reach my phone..."

Remy ducked into the nearest store for a minute, then emerged and walked back the way he'd come. Riley would undoubtedly head home and he intended to meet her there.

Fluttershire Fairy Colony, Fort Washington Park, New York City

"How many times," Remy wondered aloud, "have I driven to this damn place and parked in this exact spot—or the one right next to it, if necessary—over these last few months?"

Riley and he were together so often, much of the time, that it would make more sense for her to have simply moved into the agency's office by now. It wasn't like she took up very much room.

He shut his car off, retrieved his purchase from the passenger seat, and stepped out. When he'd remote-locked the vehicle, he set out across the frosty grass of the park on foot. He held the item he'd brought with him behind his back.

It was a cold day and not many people were out. Still,

there were always a few dedicated joggers or glumly dutiful dog owners taking Fido out for his daily bout of fresh air, defecation, exercise, and barking at nothing in particular.

One such woman wore a puffy white coat and walked a puffy white poodle and tried to flag him down.

"Excuse me," she called out in a nasal voice, "do you know what time it is? I forgot my watch."

Remy slowed but did not stop. "You don't have a cell phone? Shit, suddenly I'm nostalgic for the nineties again. Uh, it was about 11:05 when I left my car a couple of minutes ago."

"Thaaaanks," the woman drawled, and she and her canine companion pranced off.

After glancing around for a moment to make sure no one else was too close—or, at least, paying too close attention—he strolled toward the two earthen mounds that lay beneath the shadow of the George Washington Bridge.

New Yorkers were fairly desensitized to eccentric behavior but having a full and detailed conversation with people who appeared not to exist might still draw more attention than he'd like.

Better that, though, than someone actually seeing who he was speaking to. But this was unlikely. Most people could not perceive the preternatural at all.

He stood where he was for a moment and did nothing whatsoever.

When that didn't work, he looked around again, coughed, and said, "Well, it's me, Remy. Hello?" The fae must have been getting especially fat and sluggish lately on all the honey he'd brought them in addition to their weekly raids on the dumpsters next to pizza places.

A minute or two later, flickers of movement caught his eyes from both the left and the right.

"Hey!" yelled a tiny voice, high-pitched and indignant. "How dare you stand there on our grass."

"Yeah!" added another. "It's all crusted with frost and probably broke under your bulging, oversized feet."

With a sigh, Remy waited for the guards to come closer and exchange the usual unpleasantries.

As always, there were two of them, one from each of the two nests. Both were humanoids about five or six inches tall—they could have lain in his hand like a hammock—with iridescent wings like a dragonfly's and eyes that sparkled with brilliant light. The one to his left had skin tinged with azure and cerulean, whereas the one on the right exhibited a peachy-amber hue.

"You—Remy!" the blue one exclaimed and pointed at him. "We know who you are. You're the one who talked Riley into bringing all this...this, this garbage to our sanctuary."

"Yes," agreed the orange one. "We've been worried sick about how often she's gone, these days, and how exhausted she is from the tribulations you lay upon her. Not to mention, there's no way we can fit all this stuff in our hole." He flourished a tiny hand.

His gaze followed the motion and for the first time, he noticed a huge pile of crumpled bags and empty boxes that had accumulated in a small depression in the earth near the nests, half-hidden by trees.

"What the hell?" he sputtered.

It was obviously the spoils of Riley's previous shopping trips. However, the clothes and jewelry and candy and gadgets seemed to be gone—the local bums had probably discovered the stash rather quickly and picked over it like locusts descending upon a crop field.

"Man," Remy went on, "this really is getting out of hand, isn't it?"

"For once," shrieked the blue guard, "you speak the truth."

The orange one chimed in with, "Not that we need you to speak anymore. Begone from here."

He shook his head and pinched his nose. The Fair Folk were notoriously fickle, and for such long-lived creatures, they had curiously short memories. Riley was a little different, but every time he encountered the others, they seemed to have forgotten how splendidly they'd gotten along the last time he'd given them a gift.

Until, of course, the next gift appeared in front of them.

"So," he began, in defiance of Orange's request that he shut up, "Riley has been gone because she's helping me again—as previously agreed, and as I already paid you for with two pounds of nice, unfiltered honey—and everything is fine. After this is over, she'll have more than enough time to hang out and...I don't know, dance on an icicle or whatever it is you guys do in the winter."

"Silence!" howled Blue. "Your promises ring hollow."

Judging by their facial expressions, they didn't really even comprehend what he was talking about. They probably only heard something like, *blah blah blah human stuff blah blah blah*, he guessed.

There was one thing they did understand, though.

"I have something for you." He produced the object he'd hidden behind his back.

"Oh!" Orange gasped. "Oh—is that—"

"Yeppers," he confirmed. "A sixteen-ounce jar of honey-roasted peanuts. Enough for the entire colony, I think. I know you guys like nuts and these nuts..." He paused for dramatic effect. "Were roasted in honey."

Squealing in near hysteria, the two guards summoned another dozen fairies, blue and orange both, from the dual holes. The whole swarm descended in a fluttering mass upon the jar, seized it with their twenty-six tiny hands, and carried it off toward a spot halfway between the two openings.

Remy wondered if a fight might break out over whether it went to the blue hole or the orange hole first, but he supposed they could simply unscrew the cap and distribute the individual peanuts accordingly.

A couple of the fae shouted over their shoulders.

"Thanks so much, Remy," said one.

"You're the best," cooed another. "We love you."

Before he could observe a potential tug-of-war between color factions, though, he heard a car draw up in the parking lot behind him and very close to where he'd left his own vehicle.

He turned quickly to what he realized was a taxi. A pretty young woman stepped out and the driver, a man who looked rather smitten, helped her unload her five bags. The two of them carried the merchandise a few yards out into the grass before Riley waved the man off. Reluctantly, he returned to his cab and drove away.

Remy debated whether he should rush over and help

her with her baggage or mediate a potential dispute amongst her people. He glanced back. The fairies had, indeed, thought to unscrew the cap. It probably helped that he had loosened it himself beforehand in case of exactly such a contingency.

When he looked toward Riley, though, she was gone.

"Shit," he muttered and jogged toward the pile of her bags.

He'd barely taken a few steps when all five of them levitated into the air, flashed slightly with silvery light, and began to waft toward the colony.

His eyes bulged. "Shit. Even more so." He quickened his pace to a sprint.

She had transformed into her usual size and shape and now used her magic to carry her own bags—in a public place. Normally, her judgment was better than that, but she had said she was tired.

The investigator glanced around as he ran. No one was in the immediate vicinity but someone might appear at any moment. Even if they couldn't see the fairy herself, they sure as shit would see the mysterious floating packages.

The tiny form became visible when the first bag was almost within arm's reach. "Oh! Remy!" she blurted.

"I'll take your bags," he instructed. "Here...uh, set them down. Now." He snatched the first one out of the air.

The other four dropped to the earth in unison. He scrambled to grab them all and succeeded in virtually the same moment that a jogger in a shiny jumpsuit appeared at the corner of his eye. The man paid him no heed as he ran past. Still, Remy almost collapsed from sheer relief. Taylor would not have had time to hunt random park-goers and mindwipe them.

He struggled to carry the fivefold load back toward the nests as the fairy hovered lazily in the air over his shoulder. She didn't seem up for much conversation.

A little distracted, he realized also that her coat, hat, gloves, and boots had fallen off her when she'd transformed and still lay in the grass behind him but opted to leave them there. By New York standards, a matching tiger-print outfit languishing in a park wasn't that strange.

"Riley." He grunted and shifted his weight to adjust for the motion as he heaved the bags along. "We have a job. I need you."

She released a soft and lengthy sigh. "I'm so tired," she complained. "I can't right now. I need to rest, Remy."

"Okay," he allowed, "that's fine, but I need you at the office first thing tomorrow morning, then. Can you do that?"

"Yes." She rubbed her eyes. "I think so."

"Good." He examined her as they continued their slow, awkward procession toward her home. She did look tired, but there was something else, too. She almost seemed...depressed?

He maneuvered the fairy's ill-gotten haul toward the pile where the remains of the previous troves lay. "I'll...uh, set these down here for now." Breathing heavily, he dropped the bags into the mess and wondered which lucky vagrant or bored twelve-year-old would be first to find them.

Riley didn't seem to care. She drifted past him and fluttered slowly down into the blue faction's hole.

Remy rubbed his chin as he watched her.

It's definitely time for an intervention. I need to have a talk with her about the dangers of manipulating random men and basing her happiness on the amount of bullshit they buy for her.

As soon as they were alone, of course. He hoped she got some rest in the meantime.

CHAPTER THREE

Sally's Café, Astoria, New York City

"So." Remy sighed and frowned. "It's come to this."

With him having to wait overnight for Riley, he needed something constructive to do with his time. Taylor's orders were to start the snooping today.

Unfortunately, he couldn't think of much under the circumstances. Finally, he'd descended all the way to the bottom of the proverbial barrel and decided to talk to the press.

"Yeah…I'm really getting desperate." He dodged a Vietnamese couple arguing as they walked their schnauzer and rounded the corner. His destination was in sight.

As he ambled toward Sally's Café with his hands stuffed into his pockets, he consoled himself with the proviso that The New England Inquirer barely qualified as "the press," anyway.

He slipped his phone out of his pocket and glanced at the screen. He'd received nothing from Don Gannon, which meant that there were probably no problems and the old geezer would show up on time.

Don hated to miss out on a potential story, after all. Although as journalists went, he was a decent enough guy, really.

It was approaching late afternoon by now. The café appeared to be moderately busy, and by the time his business there was done, the early rush hour would be underway.

At least this was all happening on one of his "off" nights. After how badly Alex had kicked his ass, Remy had finally enrolled at a mixed martial arts gym to get himself back in shape and learn to fight properly. He'd shown up for every class.

At first, he hadn't been able to do much—he was still recovering from a couple of broken ribs, which limited his mobility—but they'd started him with basic exercises to improve his strength and flexibility. From there, they'd drilled the fundamentals of movement, balance, timing, and a few basic moves into him.

Finally, things were starting to get interesting. He was now healed up well enough that they'd been able to demonstrate a Brazilian Jiu-Jitsu takedown without putting him in the hospital, not to mention a couple of elementary Muay Thai strikes.

"And," he mumbled to himself, "the bastards seemed to enjoy throwing me on my ass. I'd say that's all the motivation I need to do it to someone else should they unwisely decide to fuck with me."

Of course, they'd also advised him not to get into any fights. Not only to avoid legal entanglements but, furthermore, because he'd need more training to put the moves together with the balance and timing necessary and fully understand the nuances of everything he was doing.

But what did they know?

He opened the door, stepped into the café, and scanned it quickly. It looked like a nice little place. There was a *Please Seat Yourself* sign, handwritten on one of those mounted blackboards. This was fortuitous since he also located Don Gannon seated at one of the booths in the far corner, steadily drinking coffee and facing the door. A few other patrons gradually consumed coffee and sandwiches at a table alongside the man.

Remy walked toward the reporter and his mind ambushed him with something he'd seen in a couple of really cool spy movies—he couldn't recall the titles—a few years before.

Two clandestine agents had met in a café much like this one, seated in different booths with their backs to one another, and had made seemingly random comments into the air as a way of communicating with one another via code. Plus, no one could honestly say they ever saw the two men "sitting together," and the noise provided by the other customers conveniently interfered with their comments, anyway.

He decided to give it a try. He and Gannon were there to discuss sensitive matters, after all.

Remy sat in the seat directly against the reporter's back and pretended to ignore the squinty, puzzled stare the man gave him as he passed.

As he settled, he made a loud half-grunt and half-sigh, stretched his arms, and picked the menu up. "Ahh…" he began, speaking to no one specifically, "now I'll have to inquire as to how the coffee is here. I really could use something to blast me back to full attention, like...uh, a double-barreled Remington."

One of the dowdy-looking old ladies at the table next to Don shot him a cockeyed glance. Behind him, the man's raspy voice intoned, "What the hell?"

The waitress, a nice Chinese American girl, approached and asked how he was and what he'd like to get started.

"Coffee," he told her, "with a dash of cream on the side, please. I'll probably have food also, but it will take me a few minutes."

"No problem," she responded. "I'll be right back with your coffee."

After she departed, he waited for an upsurge in the ambient noise before his next attempt at surreptitious communication.

"It sure is a nice day," he began and directed his voice vaguely upward, "at least for January. Who knows where the weather will lead us next, though?"

Don uttered a ragged, exasperated sigh. His coat rustled and he stepped around to the booth and slid into the seat across from him.

"Hey," Remy said, "do I...uh, know you?"

The reporter pursed his lips and glanced briefly at his mug. "This was from a movie, wasn't it? Some spy crap. Well, it works a hell of a lot better if both parties actually have a code agreed to beforehand. Wouldn't you think?"

"I suppose." He pouted.

"In any event," the man continued, "nobody really gives a crap about either of us being here."

The waitress returned and placed a steaming mug, plus a tiny container of creamer, before the investigator. She did a brief double-take when she realized Mr Gannon had switched booths but turned it seamlessly into a promise to refill his cup directly.

"Thanks," the reporter quipped.

Remy added quickly, "And I'll need a couple more minutes."

"That's quite all right." The girl turned to attend to the old ladies' table.

He looked across at his contact. Don was a tall man, although he tended to stoop a little. He was close to the end of middle age with long, rangy limbs and an equally long, careworn face. His somewhat shaggy hair and short, bristly beard were streaked with silver. Today, like every other day Remy had seen him, he wore a brown trench coat that probably qualified as a golden oldie.

"That was clever," the aged man rasped and paused to cough, "but this isn't East Germany before the Wall fell, for God's sake. I thought you were old enough to know that two men who look nothing alike meeting for coffee and talking about weird shit was not exactly cause for alarm in our city."

"Well—" he started to protest.

"And not even that weird, really. It isn't as though anything we have to discuss is much different than a contractor asking his buddy in real estate about any properties about to be developed, or a wannabe homewrecker asking how someone's marriage problems are coming along. Is it?"

Remy shrugged. "Fair enough. Did you have a nice Christmas?"

"Splendid," Don returned at once. "I always was more partial to New Year's, though. There's a real American holiday."

He wasn't about to argue with that. "It does seem like they spike the eggnog more heavily."

Their waitress returned and asked if he was prepared to order food yet. Feeling self-indulgent, he requested a Monte Cristo sandwich, confident he could eliminate the calories within the next day or two.

"Sounds good," the young woman remarked. "That'll be out in a few minutes." She took his menu and hurried off into the surrounding bustle.

"So," Remy started to ask the older man but paused to sip at his coffee now that it was no longer liable to create heat blisters on the roof of his mouth. "Have you heard anything lately about...uh, strange things coming into the city?"

He fixed Don with a carefully innocent look and waited for a reply.

The old man sighed and looked somewhere toward the ceiling.

"You'll have to be more specific than that. All kinds of rumors make their way to the Inquirer's staff. Do you have any idea of some of the crap that reaches our ears? Everything from Unidentified Flying Objects sighted over JFK International to mind-control cotton candy surreptitiously produced by the Deep State and then distributed at Coney Island."

Remy swished his coffee in its cup. "Touché. I haven't

been to Coney Island in a couple of decades, so I'm afraid I can't comment. But, yes. What I'm looking for, more precisely, is any stories pertaining to odd things, merchandise or what have you, coming into New York by boat and being unloaded by little men." He took another sip of coffee as Don leaned back and thought. "Well, short men," he clarified as the man still looked confused. "Some of them are about as wide as they are tall."

The reporter furrowed his heavy brow. "I can't say I've heard anything about ships," he related, "but there is one rumor that might be of use to you. 'The Seven Dwarves are looking for Snow White in Harlem,' so it goes. People love stories of fairy tales coming to life in one way or another. Does that mean anything to you?"

"It might." He scratched behind his ear. "At least that narrows the search down to Harlem. Last I checked, New York was kind of big."

His sandwich arrived and he dug in and carved away at the fried and sugared bread and its contents with gleeful abandon. Don took the opportunity to ramble for a few minutes about his joint pain and his dislike of digital journalism. The younger man at least tried to listen and nodded politely about every five or ten seconds.

As Remy paused near the end of his meal, the older man half-smiled around his cup as he took a long swig. "Now, then, per our arrangement...what do you have for me?"

Before he could answer, their waitress suddenly appeared. "Will you gentlemen have anything else tonight? Dessert, maybe?"

Don shook his head.

Remy looked at the young woman. "Mm...no, thanks. We'll head out in five minutes or so."

"Okay, I'll be right back with your checks. Separate?"

He gave her a thumbs-up and she hurried off as he returned his attention to Mr Gannon.

"Well, Don, I can't tell you all the salacious details, due to there being an ongoing investigation and whatnot," he said, "but I can point you in the right direction."

The reporter's eyes took on an almost hungry look. "I'm all ears."

"The feds," he continued, "are concerned that an Israeli-Egyptian crime syndicate may be trying to expand its operations to our fair city, and that it may be involved with certain experimental substances they stole from the IDF. Possibly. That's the word on the street, anyway. It ought to be tons of fun, reporting on something like that."

"Hmm." The journalist rubbed his hands together. "Yessir, that's some juicy material. Potentially. The kind of thing I can write about in such a way as to leave the door open for all the conspiracy theorists to run hog-wild but without exactly saying anything too authoritative. Plausible deniability for us, you see."

Remy pantomimed shock and allowed his mouth to fall open. "Are you trying to suggest that the Inquirer is afraid of lawsuits? That would almost imply that you're worth suing."

"Hey, now," Don wheezed, "I don't insult your line of work."

True. I need to stop pushing people's buttons simply because they look easy to push. It's another bad habit from the old days that needs to go.

Before he could apologize, though, Don continued.

"Maybe you're turning things around with your little errands for this agency, but prior to that, I'd heard you were arrested in Times Square again after reverting to your old ways."

His mouth almost puckered as if he'd bitten into an expired lemon. "That was part of the investigation we were conducting. I used myself as bait."

That phrase "old ways" was what particularly bothered him. Sometimes, it seemed like half the entire New York Metropolitan Area still remembered—and might always remember—the stupid, irresponsible, drunken, drug-addled playboy known as David Remington.

"Whatever you say," Gannon conceded with a shrug of his hunched shoulders. "I imagine it worked." He didn't sound like he was being sarcastic.

The waitress returned with their checks and they thanked her, paid, and tipped within reason. Both stood and Remy put his coat on as Don slid his hands into the pockets of his own.

"Mr Gannon," he commented, "thanks again for your time and your suggestions. This is a fairly nice place, too. They have decent enough coffee. Anyway, I hope you find something interesting to report on." He paused. "But don't report on me, okay? I haven't been in your publication much lately—Jenny Ocren must have found a new hobby or something—and I'm perfectly happy to keep it that way."

Don smiled and extended his hand. "I shall do my best."

Remy took the hand and shook it. "I'll accept that

answer. Have a nice…uh, Valentine's Day, in a few more weeks."

They stepped out the door almost in unison, and the reporter turned right and vanished quickly down the street into the thick of the city.

The investigator hesitated as he considered his next move. En route to the café, he had deliberately taken the longer route to give Mr Gannon more time to reach the location. He'd kept to the major streets and lost himself in the crowds, waited at pedestrian crossings, and all those fun things.

On the way back to his car, he opted to take a shortcut through a back road. It ought to save him three, perhaps even four minutes. That way, he would have the fun of plunging into the first wave of rush hour traffic even sooner.

From the café's door, he turned left instead of right and ducked down the street.

It was narrow and quiet, more of a glorified alley than anything else and sheltered from the winter breeze. Although he had always thought that Astoria was one of the nicer parts of Queens, this almost-forgotten little route was grimy enough to have character.

He passed a block through it quietly, crossed the street, and continued on the other side. Here, both the buildings and the trees were a little taller, which left the narrow lane in relative gloom beneath the weak, cloud-covered winter sun.

Someone stepped out in front of him.

"Whoa," Remy said and tensed reflexively. His senses rose to peak alertness when he also heard someone else move behind him. "I don't have a cigarette. Let's get that out the way right off the bat."

In the second or two it took for his brain to process everything it had seen and heard, however, he quickly reached the conclusion that these guys were after more than a smoke.

The one ahead of him hadn't so much as stepped out as pounced—and from behind a dumpster, at that. He was light-complexioned with shoulder-length brown hair that looked wispy and tattered.

The man behind him had seemingly dropped into the street from a roof or tree branch. He was a round-faced South Asian man with a shaved head.

Both were about twelve or fifteen feet away. Something about them—the look in their eyes, mainly—was instantly disturbing, not least because it looked familiar. It was a crazed expression of desperation, mingled fear, and anger like a cornered animal about to fight back, even though it was they who had cornered him.

Alex had looked exactly the same way when he'd been under Moswen's control.

"Oh, crap," he muttered.

The two men snarled with bestial fury and attacked. Each wove slightly in a different direction but otherwise, seemed to hurl themselves toward him with total, lunatic abandon.

Remy hadn't had much martial arts training yet, but what little he'd drilled into himself and what little he could remember kicked in. These were bolstered by the lessons he'd learned during these past months with the agency when he'd been in a disproportionately large number of fights, some of them to the death.

He surged toward the one who'd come at him from the front and attempted to engage him first and eliminate the chance that both thralls would be able to attack him at the same time.

Reflex and memory intertwined to remind him of his lessons on movement. He pivoted to the side as the ragged man made a powerful but clumsy swipe at his face with a hand twisted like a claw.

The one behind was almost on top of them but Remy moved around the first one and aimed a fast kick at the back of the man's knee. It connected, although not as straight or hard as he would have liked. Still, it was enough to make the bastard's leg buckle, and his own forward momentum made him stumble forward and land on his knees.

The investigator spun barely in time as the second attacker attempted to leap over his fallen comrade and barely succeeded. The man landed hard and needed a second to regain his balance.

That was all the time Remy needed to fumble in the dumpster the first assailant had hunkered behind and seized the neck of a nice seven-hundred-and-fifty-milliliter liquor bottle. Sadly, it was empty.

The South Asian guy, who seemed to gargle his own breath in a way that almost sounded like he was choking, threw himself at his quarry and tried to overwhelm him with sheer force, speed, and fury.

For the blink of an eye, the investigator was afraid, but something dawned on him. These two were weaker than

Alex had been and probably barely stronger than ordinary humans. Still, there were two of them, and they were pissed.

He did an instant calculation of the trajectory of the man's fist, and he swung out and upward with the bottle. It passed between his opponent's arms and shattered against the left side of his jaw. One of the fists diverted off course, thumped him in the chest, and drove him back.

A tremor went through the bald guy's whole body as he wavered from the bottle blow and slumped against the dumpster. Remy gasped, the punch having knocked the wind out of him. But he was still standing and his adversary was not.

By now, the long-haired white guy had already sprung to his feet and looked almost like he was about to foam at the mouth. The investigator settled into a basic combat stance with his right hand holding the broken neck of the bottle facing his enemy.

Rather than try another broad swipe, though, the man thrust his fingers at his quarry's face. He flinched and cursed as the guy's other hand descended on his wrist and clawed at it.

Remy let the bottle fragment go, backpedaled, and slipped away before his attacker could seize hold of him. But already, his foe was winding up another attack.

This is the takedown. It looks like a golden opportunity to—

The strike came so fast and hard and at such a strange angle that the golden opportunity quickly decayed first to silver and then to bronze. That was still a medal, though.

He inserted himself into the man's space and pulled on his arm and shoulder while he pushed against his legs with his own. It wasn't the identical move he'd learned in class, but the basic principles were the same. The objective was to interfere with the opponent's balance and use inertia against them.

His assailant tumbled forward and tripped over the legs of his partner.

"Hah!" He laughed, only to realize that the bastard would find his feet in another second and he might not be able to outrun him. Quickly, he looked around for another weapon.

A large section of pavement was cracked and loose. High on adrenaline, he pounced on it and lifted it, broke it off, and hoisted it over his head. It probably weighed a good twenty pounds.

Remy hastened to the side of the man he'd thrown and hurled the concrete chunk at his leg. It landed on his ankle with a satisfying crunch, and the man screamed, partially pinned to the ground. The weight might not have held him under other circumstances, but it was different with a broken bone.

That was his cue to sprint past the assassin and keep running. He slowed only a little when he reached the next street at the end of the block. There, he turned right and detoured slightly to get off the same course and lose himself in the nearest crowd if he could find one.

A few people seemed to sense something was amiss and veered away from him as he hurried between them. He drew in a deep breath and tried to look normal.

After a moment, he glanced down and saw that his wrist was bleeding slightly where the man had snatched at him. Frowning, he put his gloves on and pulled his sleeves down over their ends to cover the wound.

"Well," he said quietly enough to be barely audible, "it looks like the training has already paid off. That Egyptian bitch will have to do better than that if she thinks she can beat us."

Remy almost burst out laughing, suddenly giddy with the rush of victory, but stopped himself with a few more measured inhalations.

In the next moment, he froze in place as a thought descended from on high to strike him.

If Moswen's henchmen had attacked him, they might also have tried to strike at Taylor. And she needed to sleep during the day—for at least the next ninety minutes and maybe two hours, she was almost helpless.

"Shit," he muttered and broke into a run. "Shit shit shit shit shit—"

Recalling also that his attackers hadn't been permanently eliminated, he increased his run to a sprint. A few people yelled or swore at him as he tried to dodge around them.

He could be back at his car in only a few moments. But from there, it would take a bare minimum of forty-five minutes to reach her estate in Harrison and he'd have to pay the goddamn toll.

His only hope was that Presley, her butler, felt on the ball today. If not, he might already be too late.

CHAPTER FOUR

Taylor's House, Harrison, Westchester County, New York

For Christmas, Taylor had finally given Remington a remote device that would open the gate at the front of her property. In the past, he'd always had to stop, get out, press the button, and wait for Presley—or occasionally, Taylor herself—to buzz him in.

Well, except for the time the gate lay busted and hanging on its hinges after the vampire Gabriel attempted a coup d'état and sent his minions to steal her coffin.

Of course, she'd given him a stern admonishment that he was not to abuse the privilege of free access to her mansion and its grounds, and he'd agreed, smiling, happy to be free of the inconvenience.

Now, he felt like he hadn't thanked her enough.

"Okay," he mumbled and pressed his thumb against the device's button, "come on, come on..."

The gate opened, seemingly far too slowly, as his car sped up the drive toward it. Gritting his teeth, he was forced to actually apply the brakes for a second to slow down enough so as not to sideswipe the iron lattice in his haste.

He supposed it was a good sign that the gate wasn't broken again, at least. But Moswen's thralls, with their preternaturally augmented strength and agility, could have simply scrambled over it.

No one had answered the phone on any of the three times he'd called, either. He'd tried once as soon as he got into his car, once in Manhattan, and once when he crossed the Westchester county line.

Speeding past the gate, he fishtailed a little around the uphill section of the driveway until the house itself came into sight.

"It's about time," he grunted. His rear bumper knocked over a stone birdbath and the bowl separated from the column to spill cold water and half-formed ice over the dying grass.

He ignored it, confident that he could repair the damn thing later if need be.

Stamping on his brakes sufficiently hard to make the tires squeal, he turned the steering wheel in such a way that his car spun in the broad paved area in front of Taylor's massive garage and came to a stop with his driver's side door conveniently pointed toward her front walk.

"So far"—he gasped, threw off his seatbelt, and shoved the door open—"so good." Nothing looked too suspicious.

Still, even with the century-old trees that surrounded her estate blocking out most of the sky, he could see fading blue sky and reddening sunlight overhead. Taylor was still sleeping, oblivious to what might be coming for her.

He jogged down the walkway and jumped over the steps to land on the broad stone porch. The wooden double doors remained shut. Usually, Presley opened them as soon as he knew he was coming.

"Come on, Jeeves," he protested quietly, "don't make me break through a window. I will if I have to, but—"

Remy delivered three rapid knocks on the wooden surface and tried the handle. The door was unlocked. It clicked open and he dashed over the threshold, feeling suddenly vulnerable with the realization that he didn't have a weapon. Right now, he'd feel much better holding something like, say, an AK-47. Or perhaps a flamethrower.

He darted a few steps in, his shoes thudding on the massive rug, and stopped.

The butler stood in the hallway beyond the edge of the foyer, wiping his hands with a rag.

"Presley!" he exclaimed, suddenly seized by multiple simultaneous emotions. "Jesus. Are you okay?"

The man half-turned toward him. He looked every inch the elderly, old-fashioned English gentleman he was, with a reserved and dignified demeanor and an air of strength that seemingly contradicted his advanced age.

Given this, Remy had been more than a little surprised to discover that the old man was a lycanthrope, or so Taylor had said. He'd never seen him change into his wolf form.

"Oh," the butler drawled, "quite all right, sir, thank you."

Remy shuffled forward a few more steps. His eyes adjusted to the dim light of Taylor's creaking and anti-quated mansion and he took a closer look at the butler and his surroundings.

His tuxedo was a tad ruffled but otherwise unmarked. The piece of cloth with which he cleaned his hands, however, was mottled with deep splotches of rusty-red and bright crimson stains were still smeared across the insides of his fingers and parts of his wrists.

The investigator gaped. "What the hell happened?"

With a few more brisk rubs and wipes, the old man finished his task. There was still a trace of residual ruddiness to his hands, but at least he wouldn't wipe blood on whatever he touched at this point.

"We had a few unexpected visitors, I'm afraid," the old man stated. "A somewhat disturbing development although fortunately, not a serious problem. As I was engaged in greeting them and seeing to their needs, I'm afraid I was unable to get the door. I'm dreadfully sorry about that."

Remy clapped a hand to his face. The tension had begun to drain from him, replaced mostly by relief although, to some extent, also annoyance.

"I really, really," he began, "do not give a crap about the goddamn door. As long as you and Taylor are all right. Some pricks attacked me while I was in Astoria picking up a lead on our current investigation. I'd be very surprised if they weren't Moswen's people."

Presley nodded curtly. "Mm, yes, so would I. Undoubtedly, Ms Steele will be interested in discussing the matter when she awakens. Might I persuade you to stay until nightfall?"

Breathing out, he collapsed into his usual chair. "No persuasion is necessary."

Usually, when he arrived at Taylor's house, he went out of his way to make fun of the butler. The old man's buttoned-down formality and old-world politeness made him such an easy target that he simply couldn't help himself.

Now, though, while still worried about his business partner's continued existence and with Presley scrubbing literal blood from his hands, it somehow did not seem like such a good idea.

The man disappeared somewhere into the rear of the mansion and it sounded like he exited through a back door.

Remy sat and listened. While waiting for the sun to set, he grew increasingly disturbed. The noises sounded like someone dragged something oblong and heavy, followed by what could only be digging out near the rocky hill which blocked the estate's grounds from the sight of the neighbors.

"Well," he muttered under his breath, "I guess this means the old boy was on the ball today."

He recalled his own experiences with lycanthropes. They were nothing to be fucked around with. He'd killed one himself, a South Carolinian named Tucker who was old enough to personally remember the last days of the Confederacy. But despite Remy's bravado after the fact, it hadn't exactly been easy.

Without Riley and a little fortuitously placed silver, he might not have prevailed at all. His various brushes with death since he started work at Moonlight Detective Agency had gradually begun to humble him.

Time passed and while he waited, he took a leak in the downstairs toilet and, feeling fatigued, wished he'd drunk a second cup of coffee at Sally's, even if it did threaten his sleep. He sensed he would need a fair amount of energy for the coming talk with both Taylor and her butler.

Presley walked in, seemingly from nowhere. The man—werewolf—could move with one hell of a soft, sneaky step, Remy had to admit.

"It's now dusk, sir," the old man pointed out. "Please excuse me as I prepare Ms Steele's tea. She'll likely wish to drink it before she engages you in conversation."

"That's quite all right, Jeeves," Remy said absentmindedly and waved a hand. "I used to know a few of those people who effectively turned into were-monsters themselves when they woke up and only became human again after a cup of coffee. Or, in some cases, coffee followed by a trip to the bathroom."

Nodding, the butler strolled off. "My name is Presley, though, sir. Do please remember."

"Oh. Right. I completely forgot." Plus, even he had to admit the joke was getting old by now. Besides which, Presley had been nothing but good to him, really.

He stretched and mentally replayed the backstreet attack in his mind, the better to describe it to Taylor in detail.

Something shifted and scraped in the basement. Footsteps, so smooth and gentle as to be almost inaudible, worked their way up the staircase. A door opened and a slim, dark silhouette stood in the hallway near the door to the kitchen, barely in sight of where Remy sat in the foyer.

The vampire nodded her head. "Hello, Remington. Whatever the bad news is, you can tell me in a few minutes."

He gave her a thumbs-up, and she walked into the kitchen to greet Presley and receive her red salt tea.

With a shudder, the investigator wondered if it had been made, as usual, with their humanely-obtained stores from the blood bank or whether it had been stretched somewhat with the au natural stuff which Moswen's thralls had generously provided. He cut that line of thought off and instead, turned his consideration to where he and Riley would look for clues tomorrow.

Four or five minutes passed. Taylor emerged from the kitchen, sipping the last of her tea from a cup with a rusty-stained interior, and allowed her black eyes to settle on him. She wore, as usual, a thin black silken night robe that greatly flattered her svelte figure.

"Now," she began, "it seems both of us had unwelcome guests a couple of hours ago. I want both you and Presley to describe your respective experiences so you can compare similarities between your accounts. Let's all relocate to the sitting room, shall we?"

Remy trailed behind her but in front of the butler.

The sitting room was, like the rest of the house, furnished in a somewhat outdated style but nonetheless tasteful and elegant. They arranged their chairs so they faced one another in a circle.

Presley cleared his throat. "If I may begin, Ms Steele, I shall recount what happened here, and we'll move on to Mr Remington's story."

The vampire drained the last of her cup and motioned for the old man to begin.

"About two hours before you awoke," he related, "someone tripped the silent alarm and on the security cameras, I saw three figures trespassing on the estate. Two came over the wall in front, and a third snuck up from the back, climbed around the base of the hill..."

He went on to explain how, in order to minimize damage to the house, he had left a window open for the flanker and placed a trap for him to fall into, although he did not specify what kind of trap. In the interim, he personally went out on the front lawn to engage the two who attempted a frontal assault.

"They were clearly branded," Presley pointed out, "very likely by Ms Neith, I would assume. Their abilities were noticeably more formidable than those of average humans although still nothing to warrant intense concern."

Hearing that, Remy felt his gut tighten. No matter how tough he thought he'd become, the preternaturals still always seemed to find ways to casually dismiss the competence of mere mortals.

Taylor nodded. "I see. Moswen probably knew she couldn't expect to overwhelm us with only three of her thralls, even with me asleep. This was a feint of sorts to test our strength. When her lackeys do not return, she'll know what she needed to know. Which means"—she sighed—"that her next move will be far more decisive and far more dangerous."

"My thoughts also, madam," the butler agreed. "I had planned to save the last of them for interrogation, but it seems he did away with himself out of fear before I could get to him. I've already hidden the bodies and you may decide how best to dispose of them at your convenience."

The vampire smiled grimly. "Thank you."

She turned her face toward Remy. "Now, what kind of

trouble did you get yourself into? And, in all fairness, out of."

"Fairness is right," he remarked. "I didn't require the slightest help to deal with the situation personally."

"Oh, of course not." She looked like she wanted to glance askew at a corner of the ceiling but had managed to stop herself. Her self-control was admirable.

Remington went on to describe his encounter in as much detail as he could recall. He tried not to embellish the parts that made him sound kickass, but it was difficult. After all, he'd won the fight single-handed.

"I see." She set her empty cup down along with its saucer and drummed her fingertips rhythmically upon the end table. "Did you happen to see which direction they fled in?"

He cursed himself silently. "Uh, no, sorry about that. As soon as the battle turned in my favor, all I could think about was whether or not you were okay." He shrugged.

Taylor smiled in a subtle but gentle way. "I appreciate that and I'm being quite honest. However, we have, unfortunately, learned nothing except that Moswen now has enough pawns that she can afford to sacrifice a few. Which means she's preparing to turn the heat up."

The vampire's face shifted into an equally subtle frown. "What I don't know is whether she'll simply launch a bigger attack against us or wait for us to react and try to draw us into a trap. The former option may be cruder, but if she has enough strength—be it in numbers, firepower, or anything else—it's as viable as the latter. We have friends, but not an army."

Remy allowed his hands to flap up from the armrests. "So, what do we do next?"

"Well," she replied, "first of all, I'll have to talk to Alex. As he still bears the residues of Moswen's brand, he should have...felt or sensed something coming. He is close enough to us that Moswen directing her will in our direction ought to have tripped the alarm, so to speak."

"By all means." He snorted. "Talk to him, then. At least he's backed off a little lately with the smart-ass remarks. I suppose it's finally sunk in that we saved his ass instead of simply letting Moswen kill him. He's not completely stupid."

Taylor agreed and asked a question of her own. "And what have you discovered thus far?"

He adjusted his position and took a deep breath.

Presley, at that moment, raised a hand. "Would you like some tea, sir?"

"No thanks," he replied. "Something alcoholic might be nice, though. Only one drink, of course."

"Certainly." The butler stood and headed to the kitchen.

Remy looked at the vampire. "In all honesty, nothing yet, although a few proverbial little birds have pointed me in the right direction."

"That's a terrible mixed metaphor, Remy," she observed. "The expression has to do with little birds telling a person something, not pointing them in a direction."

He pretended to ignore her and went on. "Tomorrow, I'll follow up on a lead in Harlem. A few rumors seem to have emerged from the neighborhood of late. There's nothing too specific, but it sounds like dwarves are involved so it could get us closer to whatever Surrly is so concerned with."

"Good," the woman said, "but that could be hazardous. Not least because we know that Moswen is finally out for blood. Sending three of her servants after Presley and me could not have possibly been intended as a real assault but sending two after a lone human suggests that she legitimately intended to kill or at least capture you."

Remy swallowed and wiped the palms of his hands on his pant legs. "The thought had occurred to me, yeah."

"I don't want you out there without backup. She knows who you are and probably has ways to track at least some of your movements." Judging by her tone of voice, she did try to express honest concern but also hinted that she had no patience for arguments right now.

He twisted his neck and it responded with a satisfying crack before he retorted, "Yes, yes. I'll bring Riley with me. She'll be available again in the morning."

Presley's soft footsteps moved back toward the sitting room as Taylor leaned forward in her chair and drew Remy's gaze back to hers.

"I'm afraid that's not good enough this time, Remington. When you were hunting Alex, Riley was barely able to keep you alive. Something extra is required."

He started to protest but she cut him off with a raised hand and a sharp increase in volume.

"Don't squabble with me over this," she snapped and put the preternatural power of command into her voice. For an instant, he felt as if his larynx were paralyzed.

The vampire continued. "I know that you learned a few things from that experience and that you've availed yourself of a month or so's worth of basic martial arts training since then. Well and good. However, for your own safety, we'll get you a little extra help, and it's to your benefit to be accommodating."

Presley stood in the doorway until she finished. He approached and handed Remy a short glass with barely enough brandy to cover a pair of ice cubes. "Your drink, sir."

"Thanks, Jeeves." He sighed.

Taylor caught the butler's attention. "Presley, we need to make a phone call."

CHAPTER FIVE

Taylor's House, Harrison, Westchester County, New York

Three hours had passed. Taylor had insisted that Remington remain at her home while the individual they'd called readied himself and traveled to meet them.

On the plus side, the delay meant he could get away with having a second drink. He had, of course, snuck a third, which he prepared himself when Presley wasn't looking since she had advised against it.

"You know," he said a little too loudly to the butler, "I still don't see the point of this nonsense. I've been in this business for, like, about five months already and none of these big, scary, supernatural—sorry, preternatural—creatures has killed me yet. That has to count for something."

Presley, who attempted to clean the kitchen counters before their guest arrived, cleared his throat. "It does count for something, sir. But not for everything. Luck has always been a factor in your case, and luck has an unfortunate way of running out at inconvenient times. We're only trying to stack the odds more in your favor."

"Odds?" he marveled. "Do you have any idea how good I am at poker? I beat a whole room full of mobster card sharks that one time. Fair enough, I wasn't positive that I'd win, but I had a good feeling about it, dammit. Besides, maybe luck is, itself, a preternatural ability. See? I'm really one of you guys."

"Splendid, sir," the old man murmured. "You didn't exceed your two-drink limit during a moment of inattention on my part, did you?"

"That's immaterial," Remy sputtered and somehow pronounced the word correctly. Still, he was a little embarrassed that he felt drunk after a measly three glasses of brandy. It had been a while since he'd had more than a single drink within the span of a single night. And even then, he only drank about two nights per week.

Things had certainly changed.

Taylor stepped into the kitchen. "Remington, stop pestering Presley. He has work to do. The kitchen looks reasonably nice as is, but I won't object to it being spic and span. Go sit in the foyer and wait. Conrad will be here any minute."

He sighed. "Fiiiiine. Who the hell is this Conrad guy, anyway? Some ex-Spetsnaz dude who owes you a favor or something?" He took two halfhearted backward steps toward the doorway out of the kitchen.

"No," she answered and planted her small white fists on her hips. "And I cannot believe that your alcohol tolerance has decayed to the point where only two drinks would have this effect. Did you sneak a third while Presley was distracted?"

Remy wagged a finger. "Before I answer that, I need to

remember whether or not you have magical powers of lie detection. I'm fairly sure you do."

The vampire looked toward the ceiling and beyond, perhaps for guidance. "For God's sake. Sit in the foyer. In a moment, I'll bring you a glass of water and a cup of coffee. Fortunately, we'll have things to discuss before you're expected to drive home, although if all else fails, you can pay for your own Uber and reimburse us for the gas it will take to drive your car to the office tomorrow."

He trudged toward his usual chair. "Yeah, yeah, whatever." Thoroughly disgruntled, he slumped into the seat and brooded.

After all the progress he'd made since he joined the agency, she still thought that, on some level, he wasn't capable of handling himself—like a little kid. And she thought, therefore, that he needed a babysitter.

The vampire herself, now dressed in black slacks and a black blouse, emerged from the kitchen after a few minutes and ordered him to drink an entire eight-ounce glass of water, which, begrudgingly, he did. She placed a steaming cup of coffee beside him.

"Drink that over the course of the next half-hour or so," she instructed. "Presley can get you a sleeping pill for the road if you're concerned about your ability to drowse off later this evening. For now, though, it's more important that you sober up."

"Yes, Mother," he grumbled.

She ignored the remark and took the empty glass to the kitchen.

Another five minutes passed before a car pulled into the

driveway. Its headlights made the curtains glow and white light spilled around their edges.

Presley emerged almost instantly. About three heart-beats after the lights died and the car's engine shut off, he unlocked and opened the door.

"Conrad," he proclaimed. "Welcome. So good to see you again."

It took a few seconds for Remy's brain—which was not operating quite at one hundred percent functionality—to register the fact that Presley had called the new arrival by his first name. Normally, he addressed everyone as Mr This or Ms That.

Taylor materialized at the back of the foyer at the same time as a sharply dressed young man stepped through the door. He had dark-brown hair and a neat goatee of the same color, which accentuated rather than hid his strong jawline.

"Good evening," their guest said. Like Remy, he spoke with a slight Mid-Atlantic accent that suggested a back-ground among the high-society families of the American east coast. Officially, this accent, a relic of the old Social Register days, wasn't used much anymore but traces of it remained if one knew where to listen for it.

Conrad's voice was a little deeper and smoother than Remy's, though.

He also appeared to be about the investigator's age or perhaps slightly younger—at least twenty-seven but no older than thirty-two. Unless, of course, he knew and could afford an exceedingly good plastic surgeon.

Furthermore, compared to Remy, he was approxi-mately one inch taller.

The vampire stepped forward. "Good evening, Conrad. Thank you for coming on such short notice. We apologize for the inconvenience, but matters have grown serious. Besides, this ought to be a great opportunity for you."

The dapper fellow smiled. His face lit up in a way that was pleasantly amiable but also a tad smug.

"It's quite all right. I'm glad to be here, truth be told. And you're right about that. I look forward to being of service."

Remy groaned inwardly. *Christ, this guy is a complete Boy Scout. I bet he's a vegetarian and a teetotaler as well. And he looks like a goddamn jeans model.*

Not to mention that he is most likely still welcome in high society.

Something on his cheeks and the back of his neck felt hot, almost stinging.

Presley smiled and placed a hand on the man's broad shoulder. "You will be, have no fear." He closed the door.

So, they know each other. Taylor did say once that Presley had many friends in interesting places.

Taylor turned to the side. "Remington, please stand and introduce yourself to our guest. Feel free to have another sip of coffee first, if necessary." There was a noticeably sharp-edged undertone to her voice.

He did exactly as she'd requested and took a long, slow drink from his mug before he hoisted himself gradually from his chair. Rather than move, however, he remained in place, extended his hand, and smiled.

Conrad looked a little surprised but returned the smile and walked the four steps it took to be within range of his handshake.

"Hello, sir," the newcomer opened. "You must be Remington Davis. It's a pleasure to meet you."

His hand wrapped around the one proffered, and although he didn't squeeze much, it was impossible not to notice that he had a hell of a powerful grip.

Remy shook the hand and released it. "The one and only. You, meanwhile, must be Conrad, since that's the word Taylor and Presley used to refer to you, whoever you are."

The vampire shot him a blood-curdling death-glare, but Conrad merely laughed it off. "Yes, sir, quite correct. Conrad Warfield, at your service."

"Awesome," he drawled. "Wait, are you human?"

Conrad seemed to register the significance of this question with a strategic raising of his eyebrows. "Most of the time," he replied. "I take it you've been...ah, initiated into certain facts about our world."

"Well," he said, "if that's your overly coy way of referring to vampires, werewolves, ghosts, goblins, fairies, and so forth, then yeah, I have."

The man laughed again, although it seemed to require a little more effort this time. "Good, that will simplify matters. I'm a lycanthrope. Clearly, you've met Presley. Let's simply say that both he and I were educated within the same tradition and aim to fulfill similar roles in society."

Remy widened his eyes in mock surprise and looked over the man's shoulder at Taylor. "Wow, you got me a butler for Christmas. It's a little late, but still. Thanks, Taylor. You're the best."

Presley had folded his hands behind his back and

turned to stone, although he almost looked amused. The vampire, on the other hand, did not appear amused in the slightest.

"That's enough, Remy," she snapped. "Conrad will act as your bodyguard. Provided, of course, that you don't scare him off with your obnoxious and immature behavior before I can finish negotiating a contract with him."

She paused and turned to speak to their guest. "Conrad, I can assure you that Remington is not, in fact, like this all the time. He was actually improving for a month or so there, but the recent stresses drove him back toward bad old habits. Which, hopefully, his liver ought to clear from his system come morning."

"I see." Conrad nodded but his expression and body language betrayed the slightest awkwardness. All things considered, though, he did a rather good job of maintaining his affected balance between proper, high-class behavior and affable relaxation.

Presley stepped forward and cleared his throat again. "All right, then, if you'd all like to have a seat, I can bring drinks—within certain limits—to anyone who'd like them."

Remy ignored the offer. Taylor said she was fine, and Conrad requested tea. The old man nodded and strode away to the kitchen.

"Now," Taylor said, "let us negotiate a workable short-term contract."

Without bothering to ask for Remy's feedback, the vampire and the young werewolf engaged in a polite exchange over exactly what the responsibilities would be. The gist was that he would protect the investigator for at least the next two weeks or until otherwise noted during the investigations to come during the hours of daylight, at least.

"I'm flexible," the young man stated, "but as a freelancer, I do have to insist on not getting locked into anything too firmly, too quickly, or for too long. Of course, if all goes well, I'd likely be happy to renew our contract or negotiate a new one."

Presley appeared and handed a cup of tea, with saucer, to his fellow lycanthrope, who sipped it with one pinky extended.

"Of course." Taylor drummed her fingernails on the armrest of her chair. "The nature of our work makes it difficult to give ironclad assurances, but we will be happy to update you on any changes in the situation as soon as we ourselves are aware of them. Mostly, we merely need to be certain that Remy will have proper backup if his assignment takes him into dangerous places in the near future. Which may indeed be the case."

They continued to, essentially, restate what they'd already said for the next several minutes. Remy realized he was already tired of listening to them.

"Okay," he blurted, "there's something else you should know, Conrad. I own the company. No, really. Taylor runs it, but in point of fact, I own a majority of its shares, so when you come right down to it, whatever she agrees to pay you is my money. And frankly, I don't think I really need a babysitter. I already have a fairy. And I kicked those two thralls' asses this afternoon."

The vampire looked directly at Remington, while the two werewolves exchanged a glance. "David, since you have also been doing the lion's share of our accounting, you of all people should know that our business expenses have repeatedly been ameliorated by infusions of cash from my personal fortune."

"Right," he muttered. "I forgot about that."

"And," she went on, "you needn't act as though this is all some kind of insult to your abilities. You've proven yourself far more capable than I ever would have expected. We're simply bringing Conrad on due to the magnitude of the threat we face. You ought to appreciate the fact that we are simply trying to keep you alive."

Remy sighed. "Fine."

It wasn't only his abilities that felt insulted, though. Somehow, his brain had projected onto the clean-cut lycanthrope every single one of the Ivy-Leaguers who'd washed their hands of him over the years.

He leaned forward, locked eyes with Conrad, and extended the index finger of his right hand over the spread palm of his left. "But," he went on, "you're still our employee, which is another way of saying that we have the power to fire you, and so forth. So let's lay out some ground rules. My rules, to be specific."

Conrad nodded innocently, although Remy wasn't sure he liked the vague hint of swaggering humor he detected beneath the man's professional façade.

"First," he began and allowed his right index finger to descend upon his left, "I'm in charge. I call the shots, always. Is that clear?"

"Of course, sir, perfectly clear."

"Right." He mimicked the man's nod and moved his right index to his left middle finger. "Second, I'm the one who decides where we go. No backseat driving, whether in the car or on foot or even in a frickin' helicopter if by some chance we end up in one of those, I guess."

"Yes, sir, of course."

"Third, anytime we encounter anyone, you let me do all the talking unless I specifically ask you to contribute or ask you a question."

"Absolutely, sir, yes."

He continued to respond with polite nods and the faint shadow of a smirk. Something about it made Remy's stomach clench, and he wondered if the over-polished bastard really meant what he said.

Taylor stepped in. "Conrad, the rules that I have established and the terms of our formal contract trump Remington's personal stipulations any time there is conflict between the two."

Soon, the vampire had finished ironing out the financial and administrative specifics of their arrangement.

Conrad and Taylor rose from their chairs in perfect unison, and Remy struggled somewhat to join them. The combination of all the excitement yesterday, the bruise on his chest from where the South Asian guy had punched him, and his unexpected drunkenness had taken a toll that he could not quite hide.

The young werewolf looked at each of them in turn. "Well, then, it's been a pleasure." He smiled again. "I'll take my leave now and meet you, Remington, at the Brooklyn office tomorrow morning, at nine o'clock sharp."

The vampire returned the smile and shook the man's hand. "Thanks again, Conrad. And, once more, I promise that Remy will be in a better state in the morning. His current condition is a direct result of...well, the same things that inspired us to hire you."

"I understand." He said his final goodbyes, turned, and left, with Presley holding the door for him and then closing it.

Remy sighed. "Such a nice young man," he quipped.

"He is," Taylor stated. "Don't abuse the privilege of having someone so well-mannered at your beck and call. And make sure you sleep well tonight since I don't want you to behave the same way tomorrow that you did tonight. That would make me a liar."

She glared at him and he adjusted his tie to hide the sudden urge to swallow saliva.

"I'll be fine," was all he said. "Goodnight, Taylor. Oh, and you too, Presley. Thanks."

He turned and walked toward the door.

Taylor was suddenly at his side. "Remy. One more thing."

"What?" He turned to face her, exhaled slowly, and allowed his shoulders to slump. It had been a long day.

The vampire looked into his eyes and drew him into the black pools of her own.

"It's not safe for you to stay at your own home right now, not with Moswen on the move. You might be able to get away with it tonight while she reviews the results of her feint and decides what to do next, but starting tomorrow night, I feel that you should begin staying at my house. Presley and I can protect you here when Conrad isn't available. You'd never be without preternatural aid."

Remy rubbed his eyes and forehead. "All this talk of protection and how much I need it." He groaned. "I suppose I appreciate that you care about my safety, but is all this really necessary? Besides, I don't like the idea of giving up my independence. The whole reason I started working for the agency was to forge my own way after mooching off my family for far too long—"

Taylor had tried to be nice with him but now, her eyes narrowed a little. "Everything is not about your ego, you know," she chided. "Everyone needs help at times. Including me."

"Okay, great," he countered, "but I'm not on board with...ugh, it would almost be like moving back in with my parents. No offense, but I'd rather find a way to make my apartment more secure. Set up a collection of booby traps or something."

She frowned. "Please think it over. I refuse to force you to do the smart thing."

He nodded, waved his hand, and opened the door. "I'll...consider it," he said and stepped out into the darkness.

CHAPTER SIX

Abandoned Warehouse, Harlem, New York City

"Why?" Remington groaned. "Dear God, why did I pick last night, of all nights, to get drunk?"

Riley frowned a little. "Umm…I don't know. Why are you asking me that?"

He rubbed his eyes. "It was a rhetorical question. Besides, I wasn't asking you. I was asking God."

"Oh." She seemed confused.

The investigator brought his gaze down from his hands and hoped his face wasn't flushed with embarrassment. If it was, he could probably claim it was only the cold making the blood rush to his face, but still.

The truth was that he could not believe that three drinks—three— had given him a hangover. Not only was his tolerance shot all to hell, but this might indicate that he was starting to get old. His thirty-second birthday wasn't too far off. The thirtieth had been bad enough.

As they strolled toward the warehouse sequestered in one of the more godforsaken corners of Harlem, Remy glanced over his shoulder. "Wait, I changed my mind. I hereby declare that it wasn't a rhetorical question. What do you think, Wonder Boy?"

Conrad smiled innocently. "Me, sir? And, does this mean that—as per your rules—you are giving me permission to speak and offer commentary on the situation?"

"Yes," he stated in a monotone.

"Very well." The well-groomed werewolf had trailed behind him but now, he picked up his pace to walk alongside.

"I think, sir, that you over-drank due to stress and trepidation over the potential difficulties that we knew we'd face today. People do that kind of thing all the time, you see. The discipline of Psychology refers to it as the Self-Handicapping Effect."

Remy had only paid attention to the parts of his Psych classes that dealt with sexuality and had used various hallucinogens to forget the rest, so he waited for the man to explain.

"You see," the lycanthrope went on, "an individual is afraid that, if put to the test, he might fail. So, to save face, he deliberately sabotages himself by doing something highly stupid—like, for example, getting drunk right before an important event—thus all but guaranteeing his failure. But, critically, he can then blame the failure on the alcohol, rather than having to face the prospect of failing even when operating at the top of his abilities."

The investigator almost missed a step but forced himself to continue his stroll.

"Very nice, Conrad," he said in a low voice. "No one asked your opinion. 'Look at me, I'm Conrad. I know psychological stuff, wooo...'" He raised his hands and wiggled his fingers.

"Wait," Riley pointed out and looked even more befuddled, "you actually did ask his opinion."

Remy took a deep breath to keep from plunging his own head directly into the nearest snowdrift. "Don't explain the joke, Riley."

She shrugged. "Sorry. You've made even less sense than usual lately, I guess."

Conrad shot her a gentle, sympathetic smile. "It's all right, Riley," he assured her, "he's having a bad day."

Something in his new bodyguard's tone was ever so slightly patronizing and Remy's teeth ground and scraped against each other. Still, they had work to do, so he forced himself to keep his mouth shut for the moment. Perhaps they'd get along better once the hangover dissipated.

They'd been on the case for almost two hours, not counting prep time at the office or travel time thereafter. And although, finally, they were on the verge of finding something noteworthy, he already felt as though he'd worked a full shift.

At nine in the morning, they had all congregated in Bushwick. Everyone had arrived on time, except for Remy, who was one minute late. Riley had appeared in human form for the benefit of Bobby, the receptionist, who still hadn't been properly initiated into the whole "preternatural" side of things.

Thereafter, they'd spent time quickly outlining their—Remy's—brilliant plan, which was to park at the north edge of Central Park, have Riley enchant the car to protect it, and walk randomly around Harlem all day, asking anyone they met where they could find 'Snow White.'

Once he had explained the plan, Conrad had raised a hand like a schoolboy requesting permission to speak but he had ignored him.

When they were in the car and headed toward Manhattan, though, he had permitted the werewolf the use of his mouth and asked him for the capsule version of his life story.

"Well," Conrad had begun, "first of all, would you like to know how old I am?"

"Sure," he had agreed. "I would assume you'll be able to legally drink within the month."

Of course, the man had laughed at that. "Oh, I'm flattered, but you're a little off. I was born in 1946. I'm a Baby Boomer."

"Wow," Remy had reacted, his voice monotone. "That's...uh, great. Baby Boomer. You must be proud. Did you drop much acid in the sixties?"

Another canned chuckle followed and Conrad had replied in the negative before he continued with the surprisingly boring tale of his normal, upper-middle-class upbringing, and how proud his parents were to be able to send him to Harvard—in time to miss out on the Vietnam War, too. Of course, college was where he had been bitten by an extremely large dog one fateful night.

The investigator's mind had begun to wander during the anecdote. Specifically, it wandered toward Riley. He still wanted to have that intervention talk with her, but his bodyguard was a late addition to their plans. Having a heart to heart with a female fairy would have been strangely awkward with a goateed male werewolf listening.

Eventually, Conrad finished relating his life story. They'd driven the rest of the way in relative silence before finally arriving at the edge of Harlem.

Once they had eventually found a parking space, Remy had maneuvered the Lincoln into it, waved Riley and Conrad out, and shut and locked the doors. A quickly performed magic spell from the fairy had ensured that no one would steal or damage it while they searched the neighborhood.

Unfortunately, not many locals had been out and about. It had snowed overnight, and, he had noticed, the day wasn't much warmer than the Ninth Level of Hell. Cocytus, the cold one. He did remember some things from school.

"Hey," Riley had said after they'd already walked for twenty minutes or so, "there's a person."

They were tramping through a residential area and a fortyish black man wearing a heavy parka lugged a second trash receptacle out to the curb alongside the first. He'd only shoveled enough snow to make room for two, so there probably wouldn't be a third.

Remy guided his companions toward the fellow. "Excuse me," he called, raised a hand, and tried to make eye contact.

The man squinted at him with a reserved skepticism

that stopped only slightly short of hostility. "What you want, man?"

"So..." The investigator continued until he moved within five feet. He stopped and glanced from side to side as he put his hands in his pockets. Conrad hung back behind his shoulder. He lowered his voice. "Nice morning, huh? So I was wondering—and don't take this the wrong way—but would you happen to know where I can find Snow White?" He allowed his eye to twinkle mischievously.

The stranger's eyes, on the other hand, bulged with sudden fury. "Motherfucker, this ain't that kind of neighborhood," he ranted and flung his hands up. "Get the fuck out my face. Gentrifying-ass motherfuckers."

He spun on a heel and stormed back to his house, snowpack crunching under his boots.

"Huh," said Riley. "That didn't work."

Remy frowned, followed by a sigh. "Well, at least we narrowed it down."

"True," said Conrad, "we have eliminated a single address within Harlem from consideration." Even though there was no such noise, Remington somehow thought he could hear him laughing.

His head snapped toward the werewolf. "Yes, Conrad, thanks. But it's not what I meant."

Riley flew around in front of his face. "What, then?"

"More importantly," he explained, "we now know for sure that whoever Snow White is, she's illegal. It might be an individual—say, a prostitute—or might be the name of an underground brothel or gambling house. Or it could be the street name of a drug or something like that. Possibly even code for some asshole who could point us in the direction of any of the above, plus maybe black-market weapons. It's definitely something that law-abiding citizens such as this gentleman"—he gestured toward the house—"don't want to be involved with."

Harlem, like New York City in general, had far less crime than it used to. Still, there ought to be someone who could point them in the right direction.

As they started down the street in search of more citizens, Conrad raised a hand. "Is our man Surrly usually involved with illegal contraband?"

Remy shrugged. "He mostly ships rocks. Uncut gems and such, which can go either way depending on exactly how and where he got them."

They obtained nothing of value from their next three attempts to question the locals, either. A tired-looking woman and two teenagers, when asked, shrugged and said they had no idea what Remy was talking about, although the woman looked suspicious.

Annoyingly, Conrad also received appreciative looks from a couple of college-aged girls, and the investigator motioned for them to keep moving.

They moved gradually into a less-reputable part of the neighborhood, where they saw a man in his twenties getting out of his car in a lot beside a large housing complex.

"Excuse me," Remy had said while he attempted to flag the guy down.

He'd taken one look at them and immediately bolted into a run, vanished across the lot, vaulted a fence, and disappeared somewhere into the snow.

Riley was confused. "What was his problem? I don't think he saw me. And you don't look scary."

He pondered that last statement for a moment. "Actually, Conrad and I are wearing rather nice coats and our ties are poking out near the collar. I should have thought of this and had us wear something cheap and casual."

The thought hadn't occurred to him before. He never really wore cheap casual clothes, but it wouldn't be the first time he'd had to make sacrifices for the job.

"As is," he went on, "either that guy has a warrant out and assumed we were cops, or he pissed off the wrong people and thought we were mob enforcers."

"Ohhh," the fairy acceded. She'd always struck him as more cognizant of human culture than most fae and she was learning more all the time.

Finally, they had encountered an attractive young lady who had both known what the hell they were referring to and been willing to help.

She stood with her arms folded, glowered in a self-protective way, and frowned before she spoke.

"Yeah," she said, "I don't have no involvement with that ratchety shit, but if you looking for Snow White, you go down this street, take a left, and go all the way to that old warehouse. But don't mention me."

Remy flashed her a conspicuous grin of reassurance. "Have no fear, we won't. Besides, we don't even know who you are. In any event, thanks. Go inside and have a warm mug of cocoa or something."

In response, she stared at him as though a leprechaun were dancing on his head, shook her head, and backed slowly away as they strode off in the direction she'd indicated.

"Interesting," he told his entourage as they'd advanced into a desolate, non-residential zone. "She specifically used the phrase 'that shit.' I'm leaning toward it being a drug."

Having said that, his smile immediately slid off his face as his brain sank back into memories.

It had been so, so long since he'd been high.

And I don't miss it, he'd told himself, forcefully. *Really, I don't.*

That train of thought, however, simply made him remember the night before and once again, he felt the full force of his embarrassing hangover weighing down on him.

Now, they were almost at their destination. The warehouse was in sight.

"Wait," Riley commented, "that place doesn't look like anyone is using it. I sense something strange up there, but it looks…"

Remy finished for her. "Abandoned, yes. Junkies like to congregate in places where no one will bother them. Or occasionally in swanky penthouses."

He immediately cursed himself for that last statement. Conrad might file it away to use against him later.

The location was half-hidden from the street by a combination of a defunct gas station and a concrete half-wall, with a dilapidated and rusty chain-link fence encircling the rest of its grounds. Aside from the three or four places where it had fallen, of course, which allowed for easy access.

The building itself looked about ready to be condemned.

Remy glanced at Conrad and the fairy. "I say we go right in. Quietly and carefully, yes, but I don't feel like staking the place out all day, especially not in this weather."

The werewolf looked like he was about to say something but he only nodded. He must have remembered the "I'm in charge" rule.

Riley flew up to perform aerial scout duty as the other two found the fence gap that looked the easiest to get through. No other people were around. A single car drove past but the occupants ignored them.

They climbed through the hole and approached the building itself. A side door hung slightly ajar. The fairy descended and hovered between the heads of the two men before they advanced.

"There are people in there," she informed them. "They remind me of some of the people who sleep near my colony."

Remy nodded. "That sounds about right. How many?"

"Four."

Whether that was bad news or neutral news, he knew, depended on the nature of the druggies and, more importantly, the nature of the drug.

Snow crunched slightly under their boots but otherwise, they made little noise as they approached the side door.

"I'll go in first," he whispered to his companions. "Come in about thirty seconds after me unless I come back and tell you otherwise."

Without waiting to see how Conrad might respond, he eased the door open and stepped through.

It was mostly dark within, although pale winter sunlight filtered through the boarded-up windows and some cracks in the ceiling to keep the place from being pitch black. A few rusted shelves of cheap metal and old, battered crates and boxes were piled around but otherwise, the warehouse was effectively empty.

In the center of the floor, four persons sat around a crude makeshift campfire, its edges ringed by scrap metal. They were bundled in torn and ragged clothes, still damp in places from the snow outside. All had the characteristic look of the chemically addicted homeless.

Two of them held syringes. Remy blinked. Within the plastic cylinders was a brilliant liquid the color of fresh milk, and it gave off a faint luminescence. He'd never seen anything like it before.

It looks like we found Snow White.

Conrad's soft steps came up behind him, and he felt rather than saw Riley float near his shoulder as well. The three of them, half-hidden by a stack of crates, watched as the two junkies with syringes inserted the needles into their arms and slowly shot up.

A sudden wave of nausea hit Remy—he'd done the same thing far too many times—but he forced it away with a deep breath. He turned to his companions.

"I'll simply ask them where they got that shit. It's the simplest method," he told them. "If it leads back to Surrly, we'll know that the reason he wanted extra protection is because he's branched out into crap he really shouldn't be dealing in."

The lycanthrope raised a hand again. "Ah, sir, I would advise against that."

Hearing the werewolf say that only made him want to do it even more, although part of his mind knew it was stupid. He spun toward the druggies, also ignored Riley's sudden look of worry, and stepped out toward their little bonfire.

"Hi," he greeted them and walked slowly to make his approach nice and obvious so as not to startle them. "Someone told me this was the place to find Snow White. Is there any chance you boys know where…" He trailed off.

The four—three men and one woman—had not even acknowledged his presence. The other two must have already shot up a moment earlier. Remy watched them as they languished in bliss-faced oblivion.

Fuck, it looks like they're having a good time. I wonder how long it lasts. Usually, street people can only afford the cheap stuff that's over and done with after a few minutes.

The two who'd shot up first twitched. Actually, jumped might almost have been a better term.

Remy squinted at them. "What the heck? Are you guys—"

The two who'd jerked in place began to spasm and splits appeared in their clothes. A few seconds later, the other two followed suit.

"Uh…" Remy gasped. "Oh, shit."

Their bodies swelled and muscles puffed outwards. Veins became starkly visible and pulsed with soft white light and their skin and flesh turned a chalky color. In the next moment, they began to make ape-like grunting and snorting noises, leapt up and down, and smacked their own heads with their fists.

The investigator took two steps back in an attempt to avoid detection and regroup with the fairy and the were-wolf before the three of them fled out into the snow. As he began to take his third step, one of the mutating junkies saw him.

His blood went cold at the mindless, crazed anger in the man's eyes, not to mention the literal foam that formed around the edge of his mouth. Riley screamed somewhere behind him.

In a heartbeat, the first two had attacked him. Their distended limbs clawed and thrashed toward his face while their teeth gnashed around guttural cries of primitive rage.

Remy's reflexes kicked in and bypassed the lingering effects of his hangover as he ducked under the first one's attack. It was fast but clumsy and unbalanced, and he shoved at the man's back while he launched a kick at his leg. His assailant sprawled into the nearest stack of crates.

Conrad, who stood behind those same crates, took a couple of neat steps to the side to avoid the collision. Otherwise, he did nothing and only watched.

Riley had already entered the fray by the time the second mutant was within arm's reach of the investigator. She shouted something in her strange native tongue, gestured at the monstrous woman, and glowing sparks, bluish-silver in color, leapt toward her target.

The woman moved in virtual slow motion as if she'd plunged into a tank filled with invisible molasses. Remy had enough time to get around her to the side but immediately stood face to face with the third of the mutants.

"Christ!" he snapped and lunged with his fist to strike the man hard in the jaw and distract him for a split-second. The delay was enough for him to stumble back, away from the augmented junkies and toward his supposed bodyguard.

"Conrad!" he shouted, "do you plan to actually do something?"

He flung himself away and rolled to evade the bum-rush of the next mutant, only to take a powerful knee to the stomach and barely duck under the grasping of four hands. Riley threw another spell to slow the two who tried to seize him.

"Oh," Conrad replied, "sorry. You had instructed me to stand back and let you take the lead in all matters. However, if you'd like to specifically ask for my help, I'd be happy to oblige."

The first man to attack had recovered by now and began another charge. Remy seized him under the arm, thrust his hip against the man's side, and hurled him across the floor.

Before he could even fully draw breath, the woman broke free of Riley's spell and punched him in the side of the face. He allowed the blow to drive him back and pedaled rearwards to stay clear of the next few blows while he struggled to control the pain and dizziness.

The fairy tried something else and a few more sparkles flashed in the dim air. "I can't put them to sleep," she cried. "That stuff they put into themselves is blocking it."

He snatched an empty wooden crate and thumped it directly into the face of the advancing mutated woman. She howled and toppled backward. The other three, having recovered and overcome the slow spell, were only a few feet away and gaining.

"Okay, fine," he yelled to Conrad through gritted teeth. "Help me. I kinda need it."

Saying that stung almost as much as his cheek did but it was true.

Remy tossed the crate at the other mutants and cursed when one of them shattered it with a swipe of his arm. Out of the corner of his eye, he saw Conrad rapidly stripping clothes off while his form seemed to distort and elongate. Dark hair now bristled from his flesh.

A black shape streaked between the investigator and his assailants, and the one in the lead who'd destroyed the crate fell back, gurgling and thrashing. His throat had been ripped out and deep gashes had clawed through his chest.

"Hah!" Remy scoffed, suddenly surging with both relief and confidence. He stepped forward, but it was unnecessary.

In the space of about five seconds, Conrad annihilated the remaining three attackers to scatter limbs and chunks across the floor and leave what remained as little more than twitching, bloody heaps.

The investigator's jaw hung open as the lupine beast, mostly black or very dark brown, panted and snarled over the corpses. Then, seeming to remember who he was, Conrad darted toward the pile of his clothes while his fur already began to thin and retract.

Riley flew over. "Remy! Are you okay?"

He put a hand on his cheek. It was bruised and there was a chance he might have a slight fracture to his cheekbone, but the woman in her crazed state hadn't hit him hard enough or directly enough to do severe damage.

"Mostly." He gasped. "Thanks."

Off to the side, the werewolf stood, dressed again, and brushed himself off.

"Right," Remy said, "yeah, okay. I am hereby altering my rules. In general, you stand back and let me deal with things. But if you see me having my ass kicked or about to have my ass kicked, then…" He hesitated for a second. "Please help me."

Conrad smiled and nodded. "Of course, sir, understood."

The investigator knelt and examined the carnage. He didn't want to look very hard at the poor bastards mutated by the drug, especially now that they'd been ripped to shreds.

One of the syringes caught his eye, though. There was still a trace of the glowing white liquid left in one of them. He knelt, picked it up, and carefully avoided the needle or any of the residual drug.

"Hmm." He placed the syringe inside a ragged fanny-pack that one of the junkies had dropped. "Well, at least now I know where we need to go next."

CHAPTER SEVEN

Farmers' Market, Tuxedo, New York

"Conrad," Remy said and projected his voice toward the backseat without looking at its inhabitant. His eyes were focused on finding the correct road. "How long ago was it that I popped those allergy pills?"

The goateed young man glanced at the clock. "Twenty-five, perhaps twenty-six minutes ago, sir."

"Good job." He raised his right hand in a thumbs-up gesture where his rear passenger could see it.

Riley, meanwhile, sat on the passenger seat. Remy had thought it appropriate to allow her to ride shotgun as a nod to her seniority, rather than force her to make do with the dashboard while Conrad rode in her rightful place.

They were driving out of the actual town of Tuxedo, a little upstate from Metro NYC, and into the rural area where the market was held. At this time of year, it was much smaller and slower than in the summer and autumn, but a quick phone call had assured Remy that it hadn't shut down completely.

Under his breath, he muttered, "We'll have to hope Maps hasn't packed up and curled in front of a fireplace or something."

"Ah," Conrad began, "may I ask who Maps is? And what are we looking for at this farmer's market?"

The investigator sniffed, mostly to make sure his nose wasn't clogging up. "A farmer," he stated. That answered both questions, really.

"Oh," said the other man.

Remy caught sight of the correct turn—a small dirt road, partially covered with packed snow—and turned the Lincoln slowly onto it. He glanced at the foot area of the passenger's seat, where the fanny-pack lay inconspicuously jammed into the pocket of the door.

A short drive ahead brought them to the field where the market was held. One of the sellers had cleared the snow with a plow attached to a pickup truck. He noticed that he'd only bothered to plow about a third of the field since that was about how many of the marketeers showed up in winter.

Seven or eight customer vehicles stood in a line near the edge of the field. He parked beside them when he found enough room to squeeze the car in without having to step into snow en route to the market itself. He got out, permitted Conrad to follow him, and opened the door for Riley to retrieve the satchel before locking the vehicle with the remote.

The werewolf frowned as he looked at the covered stands and the few heavily bundled people milling around. "Are these...humans?" he asked. He squinted and fidgeted like a man about to plunge into a crawlspace who suddenly realized it might be infested with bugs and spiders.

"Oh, not quite," he replied absently. He was distracted as his mind considered where the poor druggies had obtained their fatal dose of Snow White.

They walked quickly down the length of the field, passed most of the stands, and waved to the proprietors. A small, discreet table set up near the back was where Remy suspected the seller he was looking for could be found.

Oddly, everyone stared at them with expressions colder than the weather.

Conrad swallowed and fell in closer behind Remy's shoulder. He was sweating.

"Ah, sir," he inquired, "are these people...werecats?"

"Yeppers," the investigator replied cheerfully. "A whole commune of them. Vegetarians, too, interestingly enough. How did you guess? The smell or something?"

Saying this, he thought he felt his sinuses tingle, but it might have only been his imagination. So far, the allergy pills worked to fortify his nose against the dark forces of feline dander.

"Correct," the lycanthrope replied. "I...ah, really wish you had warned me. Our kinds do not get along. You might say werewolves and werecats are about as contentious as...well, dogs and cats."

He shrugged. "Damn. Well, I'm allergic to them myself —hence the pills—if that makes you feel any better. Don't worry, though, they're nice."

Ahead of them, a sleek, black-haired woman in a white parka "accidentally" knocked a large can of beets off her own table with an elbow and it rolled directly in front of

Conrad's feet. The werewolf tensed for a second but skipped over it easily, then paused to pick it up and hand it back to its owner.

"I'm sorry," he began, his tone mild, "it looks like you dropped this."

The woman pretended to ignore him as he set it on the table and hurried to catch up with Remy.

They passed two men who'd been having a conversation. Both stared briefly at the lycanthrope and returned to talking amongst themselves.

"You know," one of them said loudly, "a cousin of mine was murdered by a werewolf. It ran him up a tree, then reverted to human form, claimed to be the cat's owner, and flagged someone down to ask for help in getting his cat down. He didn't dare transform in front of a human, and the son of a bitch ate him as soon as the Good Samaritan left."

Conrad's face had gone completely stony, although he continued to nod politely to everyone he passed. Remy almost wondered if acting like a swaggering asshole might have been the better approach. He actually began to feel sorry for the guy.

The glares continued all the way to the far corner when at last, he caught sight of Ishmapps' distinctive market-stand.

Almost hidden behind a snowy bush, a thin man who appeared to be in his early forties sat behind a small table with a few examples of handmade bric-à-brac resting on its surface. Reddish hair fell to his shoulders and most of his face was covered by a scraggly beard of the same hue.

The knickknacks were mostly a distraction. His true

business lay in the all-natural herbal remedies which he dealt, quietly and carefully, from the locked case resting on the ground at his feet.

The man's head had begun to turn toward them and his nostrils flared so Remy, not wanting to give him the opportunity to escape, broke into a jog. After a second, he heard Conrad follow suit.

Ishmapps's yellowish-green eyes fixed on him. "What the shit?" he burst out and snapped to attention from his previous languor.

"Maps Cat!" Remy called and waved. "Look, guys, it's Maps Cat."

The werecat's lips drew back from his teeth. "Goddammit, I told you not to call me that. How many times now? Do you have Alzheimer's? Or do you seriously think it's still funny?"

The investigator came to a halt about two feet from the table. Steam formed in front of his mouth as he breathed more heavily from the brief jog and he smiled innocently. "Well, yeah."

Maps Cat bristled and seemed more like a feline than ever for a moment. "It isn't. Now, what do you want? And —wait, who the hell is this guy? Did you bring a fucking werewolf here?"

Remy glanced briefly over his shoulder and still pretended to be casually amused and unconcerned. "Oh, him? Yeah, Taylor made me bring him along. You know how she is." He chuckled and looked the werecat in the eye. "She always makes people do things whether they want to or not. Defying her is a bad idea, as we all know."

Ishmapps practically fumed. "What does she want this

time? What errand has she dispatched you on, errand boy?"
He shot a couple of death-glares at Conrad.

The werewolf, for his part, attempted to look neutral
and innocuous and failed dismally. In all fairness, this was
in part because a few other locals crept toward them, like
feral cats stalking a bird. It was the first time Remy had
seen his companion look flustered.

"Oh, ha," he chortled, "no one has ever called me an
errand boy before. It's funny because it's untrue." He
adjusted his tie. "But yeah, I'm conducting an investigation,
with Taylor's full support, and I kinda wanted you to have
a look at something. Can we talk in private?"

Ishmapps' eyes flicked toward Conrad. "Not with him
around. I refuse to go anywhere 'private' with a goddamn
lycanthrope. Their kind can't be trusted."

Remy shrugged. "Okay, fine, I'll leave him here and it
will be only you and me."

He looked at his bodyguard. "Hey, Conrad. Stay right
where you are, okay? I'll be back in a minute. We need to
have a talk. Everything will be cool."

"Ah…" the werewolf started and directed a nervous
glance from Remington to the approaching werecats, "that
might not be a good idea. Or if you must, please hurry, sir,
if you could."

"Oh, come on," he retorted and flapped a hand. "You'll
be fine. It's not like you guys have a Crips vs Bloods thing
going on."

Conrad coughed. "Actually…it kind of is like that. At
times."

One of the werecats closest to the goateed young man
licked his lips, perhaps disappointed to remember he didn't

have whiskers at the moment. "You," he said to Conrad, "don't smell like you belong here, boy."

Remy told Riley to keep an eye on things and left his two companions behind, taking the sulky Maps Cat to the edge of the woods with his ragged fanny pack in hand.

"So yeah," he began once they were out of sight and earshot of the general public, "I found some junkies in an old warehouse in Harlem shooting up with this." He opened the pack. "Do you know anything about it?"

Frowning, the werecat took the syringe out. He was smart enough to handle it gingerly and kept the needle away from both of them. His feline eyes lingered for a moment on the luminescent fluid.

The investigator told him the rest of the story, including how Surrly had come into the agency's office, seeking protection.

Maps Cat made a low sound, half-growl and half-sigh, in his throat. "I've heard a few rumors that some of the dwarves have been moseying into the preternatural drug trade lately. They're apparently importing and reselling crap that's far more dangerous than what I sell. Why you moronic humans made a medicinal herb illegal is beyond me."

Remy nodded and waited for more.

"In any event," the man continued, "I don't know any of the details. It's not really my business. But—" He tensed, and his eyes widened. "To be honest, I'm shocked that they would sell something like that to humans. In fact, I'm shocked that any drug could have that kind of an effect. It makes PCP sound like, well, cannabis. Whoever allowed mortals to get ahold of this shit made a big mistake and all of us might end up having to clean it up."

"Agreed," he said. "And cleaning up other people's mistakes is my and Taylor's specialty. You don't have to like us, but I think you're smart enough to grasp the wisdom of working with us on this."

Maps frowned but conceded. "Yes. Anything to keep the human authorities off our backs."

"Good." He glanced toward the stand. Violence had not yet broken out between the different species of were-people, so that was a good sign. He looked at Maps. "Let's share information, then. I'll tell you anything I hear that might be useful, and you do the same. Right now, if possible, but I'll give you the new office number and you can have Bobby patch you through to me or Taylor if need be."

The red-haired man scratched behind his ear and seemed to think about something. After a moment, he spoke again. "Tomorrow evening, there's a party, one where both preternaturals and humans will be. I sold a ton of product to the attendees. If the dwarves intend to try to compete with me by pushing this Snow White crap, that might be the place to look."

He produced a pen and a scrap of paper, wrote an address down, and handed it to Remy, who slipped it into his pocket.

The investigator patted Maps on the shoulder. "Gotcha," he told him. "Thanks, Maps Cat. Now, let's go rescue Conrad."

"Don't call me that!" Ishmapps snarled. For a moment, it looked like he might ball up and start hissing. "And that guy is yours to rescue. I don't care what happens to him."

Ignoring his attitude, Remy strode through the snow, the werecat trailing him.

Conrad appeared to be in the midst of a speech to try to pacify the humanoid felines who had all but surrounded him.

"...but really, catnip is no different from a pig's ear, when you stop and think about—"

"Pig's ear?" one of the werecats snarled. "Disgusting! Typical dog treat. And we're vegetarians."

Remy hurried up and put his arm around the werewolf's shoulder. "Ha, Conrad and his catnip. He loves the stuff, really, and that's only his way of making a joke. He's one of those people whose eye doesn't twinkle when he's being facetious. Pay him no heed. Anyway, we have to go. Enjoy the rest of this lovely winter's day."

He waved and led his companion through the narrowest gap between locals, noting that most of their faces had relaxed due to his intercession. Riley drifted along behind and above them.

Once they were out of claw's reach, Conrad, wiping sweat from his brow, gasped. "Thanks."

"For what?" he asked.

"You...well, you saved my ass, sir," the werewolf admitted. "I thought they were about to pounce on me."

"Oh." He removed his arm from the man's shoulder. "Well, an incident involving you dead and six werecats mauled would have caused problems I don't feel like dealing with. But you did save my ass at the warehouse, so you're welcome anyway."

The fairy floated downward. "I might have been able to handle some of them, but yeah, things were getting ugly."

Remy waved a hand. "Next time, I won't bring him. For now, though"—he turned to Conrad—"we need to get ready for a party. Tomorrow, but still."

"Certainly," the lycanthrope wheezed. "Anywhere but here. Oh, how are your allergies, by the way?"

He remembered to sniffle. "Fine."

CHAPTER EIGHT

Melrose, the Bronx, New York

It had taken a good twenty-four hours for Remy to get back into his party-boy persona from the bad old days.

Not only had it been necessary to call some of the stupidest of his friends—or, rather, people he used to consider friends—but he'd also needed to spend time getting back into the proper headspace. Moronic self-destruction, arrogance, and debauchery were things he had attempted to leave behind.

It was easier than he'd expected. After all, it had only been a few months. And he'd gone and gotten drunk only two nights prior.

Crammed into an Uber, they'd crossed the Harlem River. All four of them—Remington, Conrad, Justin, and Craig. The latter two were reliable types when it came to partying.

"Shit, ass, and fuck," Justin remarked. "I left my e-cigs in my room."

Craig piped up. "Driver! Do not go back under any

circumstances. I refuse to be seen in public in the company of some guy who vapes."

Justin extended his middle finger in front of his friend's face. "Shut up, Craig. You're simply pissed because you accidentally gave five dollars more to a charitable write-off than you meant to and were afraid someone would think you were a nice person."

The other man looked out the window at two women and made an obscene pantomime at them. "Aw, but I am a nice person," he protested.

The driver, for his part, merely chuckled in a slightly uncomfortable fashion and kept his hands on the wheel.

Remy smiled, laughed as needed, and offered commentary every few minutes. That was all it really took to fit in, for now. At some point, he would be expected to do something suitably ridiculous to live up to the David Remington legend, most likely, but the time was not yet right.

Conrad, meanwhile, had basically kept silent, aside from a few awkward smiles here and there. As Justin shifted to talking about scoring some Molly, heedless of how their driver might react, he turned and peered at the werewolf's face.

"Saaayyyyy," he drawled, poked the man in the chest, and tried not to smirk too hard, "you're not straight-edge, are you? If so, I have no idea what you're even doing here."

The lycanthrope cleared his throat. "I have a drink now and then but that's about it."

"Goddamn," Craig marveled. "An occasional drink. We have a baller here."

Remy wagged a finger. "Now, now. He's my chauffeur so I can't have him getting too fucked up. This is his night off, obviously, or he'd be driving, so he might end up having two drinks."

Conrad laughed it off and after a moment, Remy's friends grew bored with harassing him and moved on to talk about pills, escorts, and so forth.

The investigator glanced out the window and up. He thought he could barely make out a tiny, fluttering shadow moving through the corridors of light alongside the streets. He'd instructed Riley to follow their car discreetly but casually and regroup with them once they arrived at their destination.

As they drove through the South Bronx, their headlights illuminated long tracts of graffiti and the driver glanced at them before returning his attention to the road. "Say...uh, what is this place I'm taking you to, exactly? This isn't some kind of...um, illegal establishment, is it?"

Justin and Craig cracked up in snorting fits of laughter at that.

Remy had to be the responsible one in this instance. "It's only a party," he told the young man. "A...house party or block party, basically. Ignore these guys, they like being edgy."

"Hey!" Craig snapped. "I take offense to that."

He ignored the protest. "People go to parties all the time, do they not? What happens afterward is none of your business, so no need to worry."

The driver shrugged. "Okay, fair enough."

Moments later, they arrived. Although the neighborhood wasn't the best, the mostly empty apartment building in which the party would take place was surrounded by empty lots, so at least they'd have some privacy.

Only one of the attendees lived there. The party's orga-
nizer, Antony, simply rented several adjacent rooms. From
what Remy had gathered via the usual chatter, this wasn't
something the landlord would normally have agreed to,
but the man had greased his palm with a couple of
Benjamin Franklins on top of the "rental fee" and, therefore, made a convincing sales pitch.

Remy gestured to the nearest curb. "Drop us off right
here. There's no need to go to the door."

The man did so. They all piled out of the vehicle, final-
ized the transaction, and watched as the driver pulled
hastily out and sped off. The investigator also noticed the
fairy descend toward them, pleased that she hadn't fallen
behind or gotten lost. He knew Justin and Craig wouldn't
be able to see her, anyway.

"Right," Craig proclaimed, "let's go endanger the
integrity of our nervous systems."

"Fuckin' A," Justin agreed.

Light streamed from one of the side doors. Given how
cold it was, it was partially closed, but a doorman doubtless
stood within. The assumption was correct.

"Hi," he said as they stepped through and were immediately confronted by a grim-faced individual who, although
only of middling height, rippled with tattoos and muscles.
"We're on the guest list, don't worry."

After a couple of minutes of haggling, the doorman let
them in. Remy made sure to keep the door open long
enough for Riley to slip in while the man was checking
Justin out. Since this was a mixed-species party, he might
have been among the initiated and therefore able to actually see the fairy.

They proceeded down the hall and up the stairwell. Most of the action would take place on the third floor. "So," he informed his companions, "I heard there might be a couple of…uh, midgets here, and they're among the benefactors of this fine event, so try to restrain yourselves from being total douches. For all our sake."

"Damn." Justin sighed. "I suppose we can try."

From what Maps Cat had said during a phone call earlier that day, the attendees would be mostly human but a few "passing" preternaturals would be among them—those who resembled mortals enough to evade serious suspicion.

This, Remy knew, meant a few dwarves, possibly a gnome, a few lycanthropes, perhaps a vampire or two, and maybe a couple of shapeshifters of one kind or another. Gremlins or zombies were unlikely to attend. They tended to stick out.

They reached the third floor and were engulfed almost immediately in the crowd, which represented the majority of what New York had to offer. Voices buzzed and mercifully drowned out most of the awful night-core tune some asshole had put on whatever mix was being used as background music. Remy hoped that the next track would be something more palatable.

And he could smell the drugs.

As the four of them mingled, he took a bottle of beer out of a public-domain cooler and planned to nurse it through most of the evening. He couldn't risk getting too drunk, let alone high. But carrying an adult beverage around would act as functional party-camouflage.

Almost immediately, there was dissension in the ranks.

Craig started it. "Okay, so. Bitches, or drugs? I vote drugs."

"Nah," Justin disagreed. "Bitches."

While they argued, to the annoyance of both of them—and Remy—a couple of girls, attractive if overly-caked with makeup, seemed to have noticed Conrad and were trying to strike up a conversation.

The investigator barged in. "Hi," he said. "This is Conrad, my butler and chauffeur. He's does a good job too although, believe it or not, I do in fact know how to drive myself. It's merely so boring."

The lycanthrope responded only with a smarmy smile, which the girls laughed at in a way that suggested that Remy had already been excluded from whatever thing was going on with them. Something on the back of his neck prickled and he swallowed a sudden, moronic urge to break his beer bottle over the werewolf's head.

Instead, he wandered a few paces away to rejoin Justin and Craig. The latter seemed to have won the debate since they now headed toward a table in a dark corner where a couple of shady-looking dudes may or may not have been selling something.

"David," Craig whispered, "these guys supposedly have everything. How long has it been?"

"Uh..." he stammered, while he tried to guess whether "everything" included Snow White. "Too long, but honestly, I'm still serious about the whole booze-only thing. You can do what you want, but..." He shook his head. "I can't afford to get high anymore."

The other man stared at him, uncomprehending at first and then disappointed. "Suit yourself. Me and Justin are going to get fucked up. Find us if you feel like it." He left.

Remy stood, awkward and alone for the moment, in the center of the crowded, bustling room.

He noticed, though, that Conrad had shooed the two girls off. The man was a professional, he had to give him that. He strolled over.

"Hey," he urged and poked him in the kidney, "Wonder Boy. Have you seen Riley around? She was with us when we first arrived, but I haven't seen her for, like, five minutes. I assume she smelled something with fructose in it and is off stuffing her face or whatnot, but..."

The lycanthrope shook his head. "No, sir, I'm afraid not. I did see her drift up a side staircase to the right before we passed into the party area, but I interpreted my orders to mean that I should prioritize your safety over hers."

Remy grimaced as he adjusted his cuff links. "I mostly agree with your interpretation, but only because she has mystical arcane powers, whereas I am merely charming and talented. She can generally take care of herself. Still, let's look for her, shall we?"

They did not have to look for long. Almost as soon as they reached the staircase Conrad had mentioned, they heard footsteps and looked up toward their source.

"Riley!" Remington exclaimed, caught off guard. "You... uh, failed to mention that you'd show up in...costume."

She smiled, blushed, and shrugged her shoulders while tittering, an act which greatly flattered her beauty. "Sorry," she said. "I wanted to surprise you."

Not only had she assumed human form and size, but she had also opted to debut a new outfit—a slinky, barely decent red tube of sorts into which she had somehow squeezed herself and perhaps only with the aid of magic.

"Well," he remarked, "you have surprised me. Congratulations. That dress is so short that, with us positioned beneath you here, the question of whether or not we can see up it is almost a moot point."

The fairy blinked in confusion as she descended. "Um… thanks, I think."

She still didn't completely understand the human taboo on nudity, as he recalled. Still, at least she wore panties, and the double-folded top-front portion of the garment was thick enough that she might possibly be wearing a bra.

Conrad, he noticed, stared at her. He'd managed to keep his jaws closed, but his eyes picked up the slack and bulged with a look much like a puppy in view of a roast beef dinner being consumed on an inaccessible dinner table.

Slowly, Remy extended his hand in front of the werewolf's face and snapped his fingers. "It's not polite to stare, you know," he informed him. "Didn't they teach you that at whatever prep school you went to before Harvard? Or butler school after that, perhaps."

The other man shook his head and reasserted his composure. His cheeks reddened slightly.

"Pardon me." He folded his hands in front of himself at the waist. "I'm concerned that she might attract unwanted attention, which we might then have to deal with."

"Oh." He sighed. "I'm sure she will. That simply means she'll draw attention away from us, though. And again, she can usually take care of herself."

It occurred to him that since the fairy had flown there and probably hadn't levitated a bag while she was at it, she must have "borrowed" the dress from somewhere within the building. They'd simply have to hope the original owner didn't arrive to protest.

He reached out his hand to take hers and helped her down the last couple of steps. Once she was on the same level, he found that he could see down her dress as surely as, seconds before, he could see up it. She wasn't wearing a bra.

"All right." He breathed deeply and gathered his thoughts. "Everyone needs to remember why we're here. Snow White. Conrad, you try to find some dwarves and see what they say. Riley and I will work the humans."

The man nodded. "Whatever you say, sir."

They returned to the mass of revelers and almost at once, Remy's plan fell apart.

Four guys surrounded them and all stared at Riley. "Who's this? Party favor?" one of them asked.

Riley giggled. "I'm his date," she explained. "Out of everyone I could have chosen, I went with him."

"Exactly," Remy replied. "Look out, coming through…" He pushed through them, dragged the full-size fairy behind him, and Conrad brought up the rear.

He kept an eye on things as they gradually made the rounds. There weren't very many dwarves, so the werewolf stayed close. Most of the drugs that were passed around were standard.

He did find a girl who impressed him as being an obvious junkie, but even she kept half-ignoring his questions in favor of staring at Riley and her red dress.

When he finally pulled the fairy away from the young woman, he exhaled and pinched the bridge of his nose.

"This is getting us nowhere," he muttered. "It might be easier if I was alone...fewer distractions and what have you."

When he looked up, Riley was gone. She must have interpreted his half-assed comment to mean she should go mingle with the menfolk. Already, he could see her submerging herself in a circle of them, devouring their attention.

Conrad placed a hand on his arm. "I'm afraid she's the type who can't be depended upon," he suggested. "Once a girl who's that attractive realizes the power she has over most men, no one will ever be good enough for her for more than, say, an hour at most. Often less. Something better always seems to come along and she leaps at it, knowing full well it won't last, because she can."

"Thanks." He grunted, turned away from the direction Riley had wandered in and looked sidelong at his body-guard. "Split up but stay close enough to see me. Again, you look for dwarves and pretend to be inquiring about...I don't know, regular preternatural shit. Try to turn up a lead. I, on the other hand, have experience with recognizing human drug dealers."

Conrad obeyed, and Remy drifted back into the crowd of mostly users and the clueless. One or two might point him in the right direction, but he wasn't optimistic. He worked his way toward a room near the back of the floor and Conrad trailed about one room behind.

Finally, he noticed a guy slouched against a far wall, who had "the look." It was difficult to describe or explain and was rather something which his sixth sense picked up on, a cluster of subtle indicators born from over a decade of wanton substance abuse.

He sauntered over to the man and made an effort to remain casual. There was no point in trying to be too surreptitious, especially amongst this crowd, but he didn't want to be too blatant either. It was better for people to not specifically remember having seen him speaking to the dealer.

"Heyyyy," he said as he sidled up and instantly grasped the man's attention.

The guy was probably in his late twenties, sallow-faced and streetwise-looking, with a stocking cap pulled down over his head and a long, heavy coat. His left hand was thrust into the coat's deep front pocket, while his right hand continuously twirled a hand-rolled cigarette which probably contained more than tobacco.

"Hey, what's happening," he replied in a half-friendly, half-bored monotone.

Remy laughed for no particular reason and sloshed a mouthful of beer into his mouth. He assumed this would help his act as a dumb hedonist with a poor understanding of consequences. "Just, you know, seeing what's available. To be honest, I've tried to mostly keep clean lately but, well…"

He trailed off when he sensed the man's growing interest, then took a deep breath and resumed speaking. "It's only that the same old shit wasn't doing anything for me anymore, anyway, you know? Like, I want to feel that first-time rush again. Something completely new and different."

Now, the man straightened even more from his

formerly slumped position, and a faint gleam crept into his eyes. "I might know a way to help you out," he replied.

For a few minutes, they exchanged banal, vaguely worded comments. It seemed obvious that the guy was trying to make sure he wasn't a cop. To help convince him, he shifted his position to the guy's other side and allowed more of the light to fall on his face.

"Hey," the stranger said and pointed at him, "you're that David Remington guy, aren't you?"

He laughed, nodded, and sipped his beverage again.

"I heard about that shit in Times Square before Christmas, and someone was talking about everything else you did last summer."

Remy nodded and pretended to be amused while the man recounted some of the absolute worst of his misadventures. His stomach knotted and it took considerable effort not to hang his head in shame.

But, for the purpose of the investigation, it was good that he still had his old reputation.

Conrad looked typically impassive, but Remy could feel the strait-laced bastard's disapproval. It almost seemed like he was embarrassed on his behalf.

After bullshitting for a couple more minutes, he finally had results.

"I can introduce you to Snow White," the guy offered slyly. "I've heard good things about her. It's a once-in-a-lifetime experience if you have an open mind."

"That," he responded at once and beamed, "sounds like exactly what I'm looking for."

The dealer glanced around. "Okay, do you wanna go right now?"

"Sure," said Remy. "Wait...uh, let me see if I can collect my date."

He scanned the crowd but couldn't locate Riley. Acid roiled in his gut as he imagined her already back to her old ways, shaking down some random, hormone-addled dude for gifts and compliments.

The man tapped his arm. "Hey, I ain't waiting all night. You wanna go, we do it now. Also, what's with this guy? He your fuckin' bodyguard or something?" He meant Conrad, of course.

Remy turned back. "He is, actually. Don't worry, he's cool. But...uh, yeah, let's go."

Shit. Where the hell is she? We could use her on this. Besides, she's alone and I hope she'll be okay.

He could not, however, pass up the opportunity. The dealer offered to walk them directly to their next lead.

For starters, he guided them through the crowd, across a kitchen, and out a back door, which opened onto a staircase descending into an alley.

"Hey," the guy commented without stopping or looking back, "sorry about your girl. She'll text you if she needs you, though, right?"

Remy adjusted his tie. "Oh, of course she will."

CHAPTER NINE

Port Morris, the Bronx, New York

It turned out that their new friend's name was Serge and that he'd had a car waiting in the alley.

Remy had to admit he was relieved. Getting into a vehicle with criminals whom he did not personally know was risky, to say the least—Conrad shot him a couple of sharp glances—but he really, really didn't feel like walking all the way to the East River in the current tit-freezing weather.

The car's driver was a big, hairy bruiser who looked like he weighed around three hundred pounds and was almost certainly armed. Before they departed, the hulking man patted both Remington and Conrad down to confirm that neither carried a gun.

"Damn," the investigator drawled and still pretended to be a dumb rich kid with no appreciation of what he might be getting himself into, "you guys seem like professionals. That's good to know. It's usually the stupid amateurs who try to screw you over."

Serge chuckled. "You got that right."

They drove for ten minutes or so, seemed to zig-zag across major streets and down minor ones, and eventually arrived on a wharf in the industrial area of eastern Port Morris.

A sentry materialized out of the shadows the instant their driver killed the engine. Remy noticed that the silhouette was short and broadly built.

"It's cool," Serge said, "I know these guys. Let me do the talking, all right?"

"Sure," Remy agreed. "Oh, do me one favor, though—don't tell them my name. I mean…since I'm kinda locally famous and all…"

The man nodded. "Right, yeah." He stepped out of the car and gestured for the two passengers to stay where they were until further notice.

Through the side of the vehicle, they heard him greet the sentry to briefly explain the situation. The huge driver, meanwhile, kept an eye on them via his rearview mirror.

"Why," the sentry growled, in a definite dwarven accent, "did you bring them here? You could have dealt to them on your own."

Hmm. Either our boy Serge is about to get us machine-gunned and taken to the trash compactor, or we're about to meet one of the head honchos of this little operation and crack the case a couple of days earlier than I'd guessed.

The dealer apologized to the dwarf and explained that his customer was a rich guy with a major habit and numerous friends—the kind of person who might want to buy wholesale. They hadn't really discussed it like that, as Remy recalled, but he wasn't complaining.

Conrad turned to him. "Wholesale?"

"Absolutely," he stated and forced himself to smirk. The driver looked unamused but didn't react at all.

After a little more haggling with the sentry, Serge opened the door. Remy and Conrad got out.

The dwarf glowered at them. "Be still. Raise your hands over your head." They did as he instructed and he patted their lower bodies down. "Now, get on your knees so I can search the top."

Remy bit his tongue to keep from cracking up at that but obeyed. The dwarf resumed his search and ran his hands over their chests, arms, and shoulders.

"Good." He grunted. "Now, come."

He led them toward a big-ass shipping container next to the river, one end opened toward the water. A few short men walked in and out, carrying improbably large loads in their arms, and others milled around and appeared to be on watch.

The guards, Remy saw, were definitely armed but only two had guns. The rest carried axes and hammers.

The sentry made a few odd hand gestures and said some things to the others in one of the dwarven languages, and no one bothered them as they proceeded toward the open end.

For the sake of maintaining his act as a dumbass, Remy considered cracking a joke about short people now having their own mafia but thought better of it.

"There," the sentry indicated and shoved the human and the lycanthrope into the back of the shipping container.

Within, the workers were busily unpacking crates and moving multiple large bags of white powder onto a metal pushcart near the water's edge. The lighting was too poor for Remy to get a good look, but the product resembled cocaine. If it was Snow White, it must need to be mixed with water or something before being injected.

A relatively thin dwarf greeted them at once from the other side of a small folding table, on which a lamp rested. He was mostly bald except for a thin strip of black hair running down the center of his head, and his chin was covered by mere stubble, although he had an impressive Fu-Manchu mustache that trailed against his chest.

"You," he rasped, "you are here to buy. Wholesale? To resell?"

The investigator smiled and straightened his tie. "The notion had occurred to me. At the very least, I'd like a good-sized personal stash so I can keep coming back to it if I like it, and sell it along to someone else—cheaply—if I don't." He chortled. "No harm, no foul, right?"

"I see." The dwarf smiled in a nasty way. "Most people like it."

He laughed again and did his best to seem as careless as hell, like an overgrown frat boy to whom this was all a game. "Awesome. That's what I like to hear."

When he thought back to the druggies in the ware-house yesterday, he tried not to shudder. Somehow, he didn't imagine that they'd liked the drug once they tried it.

"To be clear," he went on, "we are talking about Snow White here, right? I haven't seen the stuff before, myself, and it almost looks like you're moving coke or some shit." He glanced around for effect.

Fu Manchu's manner grew grimmer and more officious

but not exactly hostile. "Yes, and do not question its authenticity. We are trustworthy. You will get exactly what you came here for."

"Wellllll," Remy drawled and made a show of tapping his lips with his finger, "can I get a demonstration or something? It's not like I'm questioning you but so I know how you...uh, do this stuff."

The dwarf sighed. "You must mix it with clean water." He instructed them to wait, cast a sharp look at Conrad, and walked off to find an appropriate sample.

One of the guards who carried a battle ax that looked like it weighed a good twenty or thirty pounds moved in a little closer behind them.

"You," he rumbled, his voice directed toward Remington, "must have a great deal of wealth to be able to afford someone like him as your protector."

Shit, does that mean he knows Wonder Boy is a werewolf? Or does Conrad simply give off an ex-Special-Forces or ex-Russian-Mob vibe or something?

"Oh, ha," was all he said. He grinned and rocked on his heels. "We make do. I have thought that maybe Conrad really should grow a full beard instead of going with the goatee. It's kind of half-assed, don't you think?"

The lycanthrope merely smiled pleasantly.

Up ahead, toward the back of the container, it looked like Fu Manchu had found what he was looking for and now headed back to them.

At the same time, someone else—probably a dwarf judging by the short heavy footsteps—had come in behind them. Remy glanced at a typical dwarven silhouette, likely another guard or middle-manager type. He turned his head forward.

Fu Manchu was about ten feet away when the guy from behind passed Remy on the side. Suddenly, he stopped dead in his tracks and looked at the two guests. His face was hidden by a long, slanting shadow.

"Hi," Remy quipped and waved.

The dwarf leaned forward to peer at his face. As he did so, light from a portable lamp fell across his own.

It was Surrly.

"You!" the dwarf snapped and drew back as his hands clenched.

Ohhhhh fuck. Remy moaned inwardly, although he kept the smile nailed to his face. For a moment, he wished he'd been able to smuggle a bazooka down the front of his pants and that the dwarves wouldn't have noticed.

All around him, the other crew members tensed and he could feel their angry eyes on him. A similar adrenaline vibe emanated from Conrad. This might well get ugly, and fast.

"He," Surrly went on, "is not a buyer. He's here to snoop on us. He's Taylor's assistant."

Gasps and snarls were uttered all around.

Remy pushed his cufflinks back from his wrists. "Partner," he corrected them.

Behind him, something crashed and almost exploded, and a blur of speed and motion turned the area near the mouth of the container into a whirlwind of violence. Surrly stumbled back a few more steps as another guard charged and hoisted a huge mallet, and Fu Manchu dropped his drug sample to fumble for a weapon.

The investigator grasped the folding table and flung it at the hammer-wielding guard. The lamp tumbled and cast its light sideways along the floor.

The dwarf swung his mallet and knocked the table aside, but one of the legs scraped across his face under the eye and he cringed, momentarily stunned. Fu Manchu emerged from behind a crate, now armed with a loaded hunting crossbow.

In the split second he'd bought himself, Remy hunkered down and looked behind him.

As he'd suspected, Conrad had changed into his wolf form—heedless of the fact that doing so had shredded most of his clothes—and launched himself at the bruiser with the ax. He bounded off the dwarf's body and left it mangled, bloody, and twitching slightly.

For obvious reasons, it looked like the werewolf would draw most of the aggression.

"Crap." Remy hissed a sharp intake of breath and ducked aside as splinters of wood rained like shrapnel and dwarves converged upon the werewolf. Another guard stepped behind the investigator and aimed a sawed-off shotgun at his chest.

He fell back with his hands up. They must have planned to kill Conrad and take him alive for questioning. He did not like the thought of that.

The lycanthrope, growling and spitting in primeval fury, surged past Fu Manchu and attacked the guard with the mallet who Remy had thrown the table at a moment before. His teeth sank into the dwarf's head and separated the top of his skull from the rest before the whole tangle of bodies crashed out of clear sight.

"No!" the shotgun wielder gasped, distracted by the death of his comrade.

Remy seized the initiative. With one hand, he swatted the gun aside while with the other, he grasped the thick hair on the back of the dwarf's head and drove his knee into his face.

The shotgun fired and boomed with terrifying volume, but the buckshot scattered against the wall while the dwarf's nose crunched against his patella. Then, before the guard could counterattack, he bolted for the exit.

Conrad, although farther back, was already doing likewise. He engaged the guard with the shotgun as Remy emerged into the open air.

He had to think of something, and fast. Surrly and Fu Manchu shouted behind him and outside, two of the exterior guards had begun to jog toward him.

Only a few feet in front of him and not far from the lapping, ice-tipped waters of the East River was the big rusty pushcart onto which the dwarves had piled the majority of their merchandise.

Remy dashed toward it. "Mix it with water, you say?" He almost cackled. "I bet it doesn't quite work when it's mixed with the entire fucking river, does it? I imagine it would be a little too watered down, like basic white girl coffee before they add the pumpkin spice."

He threw himself at the cart. It squeaked horribly and budged about an inch.

"Well, shit." He panted.

One of the exterior guards pounded toward him. "Get away from that, you little bastard." He rumbled a warning.

"Little?" He scoffed. "I'm at least a foot taller than you."

In a snarling tornado of fur and teeth and claws, Conrad burst out of the shipping container and intercepted the charging dwarf. Remy quickly lost sight of the details as the two struggled.

He turned back to the cart and pushed it again. It now actually started to move, although it still made way too much noise and resisted his efforts as much as possible. Not only had the wheels begun to sink into the cold mud, but at least one of them was bad and twirled haphazardly on its vertical axis.

"Of all the fucking times"—he grunted and shoved his shoulder against the cart—"for there to be a failure of some cheap-ass mechanical component. Aren't dwarves supposed to be good at fixing stuff?"

Behind him, the sounds of the struggle intensified. Conrad hadn't overcome the dwarf yet, but he seemed to be winning. However, the others had now begun to pile out of the container. If they could surround him, they might be able to kill him.

And then, although it pained him to admit it, Remy knew he would be easy prey.

He saw a flat square of wood on the ground, the fallen cover of one of the crates. Leaving the cart where it was, he dashed over, retrieved the wood, and ran to the front of the cart where he jammed it right in against the bad wheel.

"This had better work," he snapped. "It worked in college when Justin's car was stuck in the snow. And snow and mud are basically the same thing, right?"

When he returned to the front, he once again heaved

himself against the bars and directed all the force his body could muster toward the river.

The cart squealed and his body trembled with strain before the wheel jumped up onto the flat, hard surface of the board and the whole mass lurched ahead. It began to pick up momentum on its route toward the water.

"Ha, ha, ha!" Remy guffawed. He turned and shouted toward the melee. "Say goodbye to Snow White, everyone."

The volume of his voice was enough that it echoed across the waterfront, magnified by the river itself, and rose even above the din of dwarf-on-wolf combat. He wondered what any random New Yorkers might have thought if they heard him.

For a brief instant, the fighting stopped cold.

"No!" Surrly howled. His gaze locked onto the rolling cart. "Get it. The merchandise—save the merchandise!"

Conrad detached himself from the brawl and his powerful lupine body bounded over to Remy as the dwarves made a beeline for their precious drugs.

"Time to go," the investigator suggested. Without waiting to see if his companion was about to argue, he bolted down the waterfront. He didn't even bother to bob and weave but only sought to put enough distance between himself and the cartel to be well out of the effective range of a horde of guys with stumpy little legs.

Fortunately, Conrad's four feet sounded like they trailed right behind him.

Someone stepped out from a shadow ahead.

"Hey, man!" Serge protested and flailed his arms. "You can't—"

Remy shoved him aside and he sprawled into the snow, his legs kicked straight up as the escapees sprinted onward.

Over the next few seconds, the sound of Conrad's gait shifted from the loping of four feet to the pounding of two, and the dark silhouette in the corner of Remy's eye went from horizontal to vertical and identifiably human.

Behind them, in their mad, breathless flight, they heard a deep and gravelly voice shout after them.

"You'd better run. Don't think this is over."

Oh, I'm sure it isn't. I can't believe I actually retrieved that asshole's stolen diamonds. Ungrateful son of a bitch.

After a moment, they ducked through a fence and reached a street well away from the waterfront. Sirens were approaching and if a cop came past, he might guess they'd been involved in the incident.

None did, however, since they were on a back street for the moment. They very illegally cut across Bruckner Expressway and did their best to vanish into the mostly commercial district beyond.

Remy started to fall behind. He was in better shape than he'd been for years but still not quite up to running a marathon.

"Hold." He panted. "Need...breath."

Conrad slowed and gave him a moment. "Sir," he suggested, "I think it's about time we thought about calling another Uber, anyway. We seem to have gotten clear of the police, for now, not to mention the cartel."

"Good idea," he admitted and pulled his phone out. "It'll go on your tab this time, though." He looked at the lycan-thrope and for the first time, realized that he was practically nude, save for the torn remnants of his pants which hung from his waistband like a grass skirt.

"Especially," he then added, "since we'll have to deal with your wardrobe malfunction before we do much of anything else."

Absent-mindedly, he wondered how Taylor was doing.

CHAPTER TEN

Moonlight Detective Agency Offices, Bushwick, Brooklyn, New York

Taylor stood with her arms folded gingerly over her midsection, about two feet behind and to the left of her own computer chair. In the seat sat the dwarf Andrew Volz, the agency's technology specialist, whom Remington had brought on board more or less accidentally a month and a half before.

"Ha!" He laughed and continued to grin under his red facial hair as his finger dashed madly over the keyboard and clacked away. "Oh, this is rich. The lack of proper challenge is offset by the pleasure of seeing exactly what pointless, stupid nonsense the humans have come up with this time."

She almost smiled. "I often feel the same way, albeit usually not about technology. What you said applies to most human behaviors, really."

Since they'd hired him, his main duties had consisted of getting the office outfitted with state-of-art advanced gadgetry to efficiency-bolstering alterations, as well as basic troubleshooting.

Of course, he did have other skills which also came in handy for a detective agency, such as hacking.

"Now," she instructed, "scroll down and let me see all this account's transactions for the last six months. Of course, we're mainly interested in the ones going back and forth between Israel and the United States, but it will be helpful to know anything else she might be up to."

The redheaded dwarf chuckled under his breath. "No problem at all, miss."

The vampire nodded with approval. She was fairly computer-savvy, but Volz was practically a savant. During the investigation that had led them to capture Alex, he'd even managed to crack into the FBI's database and slip out without them even knowing their security had been breached.

Currently, they viewed a bank account registered to someone named Salma Tarif—supposedly an Egyptian woman who had arrived at John F Kennedy International Airport about six weeks before.

However, while they had finagled proof from the airline that she had departed from Cairo, all her foreign communications and financial transactions had gone to and from Dimona, Israel, which suggested that she'd gone to Cairo by land or sea and obtained a fake Egyptian ID.

If she was not simply Moswen Neith's alter ego, she was at very least a lackey or co-conspirator.

"Hmm," Taylor mused, her eyes and brain taking in the account information quicker and more efficiently than a human's would have been able to. "She's been a busy girl.

Look at all these mysterious transactions...personal gifts and dividends payments from bullshit front companies."

"Aye," Volz affirmed. "So it would seem. She took some precautions, but I think she left most of this business in the hands of so-called human 'experts' in her employ. If you're right about how old she is, she might not completely understand the intricacies of modern technology."

She drummed her fingers on her arm. "I am unlikely to be wrong. Moswen was imprisoned in the Negev at least two hundred years ago, and between what Alex has told me, and what I...saw when our minds locked, I suspect she might truly date all the way back to ancient Egypt."

The thought made her uncomfortable. She was centuries old herself and not easily fazed nor intimidated. Even when outnumbered by wily opponents, few could match her. But a vampire of almost prehistoric lineage was nothing to be taken lightly.

"All right," she said and returned her attention to the screen before them, "move on to the next name on the list."

There were still four more accounts they needed to hack and examine. All of them belonged to persons—or, at least, to false identities—whom she had heard of over the course of her own investigations.

Such things had kept her busy for a long time now. She was glad Remington was handling the Surrly business as well as their more mundane cases and had to admit it was good to have him around.

Volz continued to scoff and brag as he easily slashed his way through the feeble protections employed by the various banks and credit unions.

"The simplicity of human computer systems is truly fascinating," he monologued. "It's like watching a child build a sandcastle on a beach, proclaim himself an architect, and then having the opportunity to throw water on it or kick it over."

"Now, now," Taylor chastised him, "that's mean."

He laughed again. "Well, in all fairness, theirs is a species that has the distinct disadvantage of an absurdly short lifespan. How much knowledge can one really acquire, not to mention pass down to their children, in only seventy or eighty years? But even considering that handicap, they simply don't display much of a knack for engineering or programming of any kind."

Taylor had once been a human, if a very long time ago, and still had cause to present herself as one when dealing with mortals. Since she made it her business to protect the poor creatures from preternatural depredations, she found that his pompousness was beginning to annoy her.

"I would say that humans do the best they can with what little they have, relatively speaking." Her voice took on a slight edge.

"And why digital money?" the dwarf ranted and seemed to ignore her comment. "It can be deleted and has no real, actual existence. Really, it's nothing but light particles on a screen, representing a kind of promise to be exchanged for true wealth."

The vampire had to admit he had a point there. "Yes, it makes human money incredibly fragile but also quite convenient. Lugging around heavy bags of stones is a hassle."

"But I thought you were strong," Volz interjected and chuckled. "I kid. And I don't intend to sound too condescending. Sometimes, I simply think humans would have an easier time of things if they'd acknowledge us and accept our guidance. Storing wealth and value in gems, for starters, inconvenient or no. It's worked splendidly for dwarves for the last few millennia, after all."

Sighing, she glanced at the clock. Business hours were long gone. Bobby had shut the reception desk down and gone home sometime before, and Alex had recently gone to bed. Finding an affordable place for him to stay had proven problematic thus far, so they'd merely converted one of the closets into a bunk and threatened to mail him to Moswen by certified mail if he interfered with any of the office supplies overnight.

Then, she stopped. Her sense expanded outwards. Something was wrong. She didn't know what, but...

Footsteps came toward the back office from the repurposed closet, and the door burst open to reveal none other than Alex.

"Taylor!" He fixed her with a frantic gaze. His eyes bulged, his body shook, and his muscles seemed to tighten every two or three seconds.

She immediately shifted mental gears. Her usual frame of mind grew colder, harder, and sharper and a calm yet intense focus set in. "What is it, Alex?"

"It's Moswen," he exclaimed. "My brand—it's burning. Not like before when she had full control, but she's coming. I can feel it."

Taylor had no reason to disbelieve him. When they'd captured him, she had expended great effort to remove most of Moswen's influence from the brand on his chest.

He was no longer her slave and she could not track him except in the broadest of terms.

But enough of her venomous essence remained for him to notice when she was on the move.

Without hesitation, she stepped around her desk, reached under it, and retrieved her sword, pulling it free of its scabbard in a single fluid motion.

It was loosely modeled on a Japanese katana, although slightly shorter and sturdier, having been designed to function as a military-grade machete if necessary. The handle consisted of black polypropylene encasing the tang and bound with leather cord to improve the grip.

She'd had it custom-made by a reliable smith about seven years before, and it had held up well enough, despite a few slight chips in the edge from the last time she'd used it extensively. That had been a few months before during the junior vampire Gabriel's ill-advised attempt to murder her and take over New York. She'd ended up cutting his head off with it for his trouble.

As Volz hung back and braced himself for combat if need be while Alex gulped and cowered, she stepped out through the doorway and onto the main floor of the office. The front entrance thumped open in time with her first footfall.

Four—no, five—vampiric thralls streamed in. They screeched and howled with crazed and bestial anger. It was a tactic that might create fear and confusion in an inexperienced opponent.

In her case, all it did was indicate to her exactly how many of them there were a moment before she saw them and informed her of the fact that her foes would attempt an all-or-nothing bum rush.

They might not have known that she would be there.

At the front of the gang was a man, thirtyish and strong-looking, who wielded a crude machete-sword of his own with a blade that looked like it had been sprayed with silver nitrate. Silver was not fatal to vampires except in extreme quantities, but it could slow her and make her temporarily sick if it got into her bloodstream.

Taylor noticed something else in the split second before the man was on top of her—he was a willing thrall. That essentially meant he was one of those humans who had knowingly pledged service to a vampire, either out of cowardice or ambition or simple madness.

She preferred to spare the lives of those mortals who acted under pure compulsion and who served only because their minds had been ensnared and knew not what they did.

When dealing with these types, though, she had no such inclinations toward mercy.

The man, urged on by Moswen's borrowed power, moved with both speed and force, but he was neither as fast nor as strong as a true vampire. Moreover, his movements were easy to predict.

The vampire stepped under, around, and through his attack, and her sword followed even before her assailant knew what had happened.

The blade moved in perfect time with her graceful step and sliced cleanly through the left half of the thrall's neck and part of his upper chest and shoulder, despite the minor nicks along the edge. With a squawk, he stumbled before he sank to his knees. It took him a moment, in the heat of his battle-lust, to realize he'd taken a mortal blow. Blood sprayed from the wound.

Taylor caught sight of the red fountain out of the corner of her eye, and the smell washed over her, tantalizing and intense. The savage old hunger threatened to overwhelm her. She quashed it with a fast and willful thought and committed herself to the fight.

The next two advanced in tandem, a man and a woman. The latter also held a silver-coated machete, while the man was armed with a makeshift meteor hammer consisting of a chunk of pig iron welded to a chain.

The idea, in his case, was probably to break enough of her bones to briefly cripple her before she could regenerate and allow the others to move in and remove her head or heart.

With mild surprise, she watched as the pair tried to feint their way around her. A blindingly fast movement of her arm put the point of her sword through the woman's face, spitted her head on the blade, and killed her instantly.

She expected the man with the chain weapon to circle behind her and try to attack that way, but he did not. Instead, he barreled past her toward the door of the rear office.

The vampire flash-stepped toward him and pushed him from the rear to thrust his own momentum into overdrive while she stuck a foot in front of his legs. With a grunt, he sprawled forward at an angle and pounded into a stack of shelving a few feet to the side of the office door.

The last two thralls attacked in the next second. She spun to face them and turned the movement into another broad yet precise slash, having ascertained the closer one's trajectory based on sound and slight disturbances in the feel of the air.

The blade cut through the thrall's makeshift spear first, and his ribs and sternum second. He fell back from the blow's impact and his eyes bulged as the blood from his severed heart leaked into his gashed lungs.

One more thrall was still in motion and therefore still a threat. Smarter than the others, he had scampered up along the wall, lizard-like, and bolted toward the office.

They're going after Alex. They aren't here for me at all.

She was about to throw her sword at the thrall—a slightly risky proposition, although she had all but perfected the difficult technique by now—when he, pretending to ignore her, shoved a hand into his pocket. It emerged clutching a plastic baggie, which he crushed in an offhand motion that flung a cloud of dust and granules into her face.

Stunned for an instant, she tensed and froze beneath a wave of pain and nausea. Silver dust, battery acid foam, and mere sand. Her eyes reddened and her vision blurred.

Almost at once, she recovered well enough to fling herself after the man, aware of his position but unable to operate at peak performance. She was almost close enough to cleave his spine when he plunged through the door.

The third man with the meteor hammer whom she'd flung into the shelves bolted to his feet and wound his chain around her neck. In the same motion, the metal links hooked against her sword and pulled it back to trap its blunt edge against her own shoulder.

"Volz!" she cried, half-strangled. The vampire

summoned her full strength, took hold of the chain, and swung the man. They both spun through the doorway into the office.

The dwarf and Alex both attempted to fight the wall-climber. The thrall had kicked the man in the stomach and hurled him against the desk and the assassin and Volz now wrestled. Dwarves were strong, but Moswen's thralls seemed powerful enough that it was impossible to guess who would win.

Taylor suddenly bent, still grasping the chain in one hand, and threw her attacker up and over her back and onto her desk. He recovered faster than she would have liked, left his weapon, and rolled off the surface. Before she could attack, he surged at Alex.

The Australian, to his credit, ducked and slipped under the man's clumsy grasp. He headed toward her.

Annoyed, she seized him by the collar of his shirt.

"Hey!" he protested, "what are you—"

She tossed him upward at a slight angle.

He careened through the ceiling and plaster dust immediately rained on all of them while he rolled off to the side somewhere within the rafters, conveniently placing him out of the intruder's reach.

The vampire locked gazes with the now unarmed man. "You still have to go through me," she stated, "to get to him."

With a loud bellow of desperation, he thrust toward her, probably in the full knowledge that he was essentially dead and seeking only to delay her in the hope that his companion would overpower Volz and complete the mission.

He failed. Taylor met him head-on and ran her sword through his solar plexus while she struck him on the collarbone with her off-hand. She pulled back sharply and down to crack his spine while the blade dug through his torso, effectively breaking him in half backward. He crumpled without a sound.

She turned as Volz pinned the last thrall's arms behind him and drove the man's head sharply into the corner of her desk. He screamed in pain and fell, twitching and badly wounded but not quite dead.

The dwarf stepped back, panting, as she swiped her sword down through the thrall's trembling throat. His blood spattered over the desk, floor, and walls.

"Is that it?" he asked. "Are you sure there are no more?"

Taylor gestured to the main floor with a nod of her head. "Go check."

"Yes." He nodded and ran out to do as she'd instructed.

Taylor looked up. "Alex, we appear to be in the clear. You're not too badly hurt, are you?"

"Uh…" The Australian groaned. "That's kind of a fucked-up question when you think about it, considering you hurled me through the ceiling. But I don't think anything's broken. Why don't you take me out of the attic and have a look?"

She climbed onto her desk and from this elevated position, reached into the large hole in the plaster to pull him out and lower him to the floor, holding him as if he weighed no more than a puppy.

"Shit," he sputtered and brushed dust and cobwebs from his hair and clothes. "It might be a few minutes before I notice any wounds, at this rate. But I don't seem to be dead."

"Good," she said. "Not that I place that much value on your life for its own sake, but as long as you continue to function as our early warning system, you're useful to have around."

He pursed his lips. "How nice to be useful."

The vampire left him where he was and strode out toward the lobby. Volz, nervous but handling himself well enough, had closed the front doors and now checked the rear exit.

"Well..." He breathed deeply. "I do think that's the end of it for now."

Slowly, she nodded her agreement. "Another strategic feint, which even had a decent chance of depriving us of our little anti-Moswen alarm. She's close, though. I can almost sense it."

Volz raised part of his unibrow. "How close? And how soon?"

"She's not coming right now, fear not," she reassured the dwarf. She pulled a few tissues from a box on one of the desks and used them to wipe most of the blood from her sword. It would need proper cleaning shortly.

The dwarf sighed with obvious relief. "We dealt with them handily—well, you did most of it, I'll grant you that—but it wasn't quite easy, was it?"

Taylor opted to not respond to this. Instead, she remarked, "My computer may well have been damaged in the fracas. It will need to be repaired as soon as possible. When we finally meet Moswen herself, I can handle the combat side of things, but in the meantime, I'll need you to keep my tools in top condition."

He nodded. "I don't look forward to meeting this... woman in the flesh, especially not if she has three times as many servants with her at the time."

"She may," she admitted. "But the idea, I suspect, is that she intends to meet me first."

CHAPTER ELEVEN

Moonlight Detective Agency Offices, Bushwick, Brooklyn, New York

"Uh-oh," Remy said as their Uber driver pulled up.

Conrad made a low sound in his throat. "What, sir?"

He dismissed the question with a few flaps of his hand as he didn't feel like discussing it in front of the driver. The man had been kind enough, thus far, not to ask perfectly understandable questions as to why Conrad was half-naked and barely covered with rags when he'd first climbed in, and had taken them to a twenty-four-hour department store so Remy could quickly buy some replacement clothes. There was no point in pushing the man's tolerance any further.

Now, the driver parked next to the office and let them out. They thanked him and watched him drive away into the night.

The building was one of the only extant businesses within half a block. As such, it had a distinctly lonely and even eerie look about it at night when its lights stood out glaringly against the general blackness.

In the few parking spaces available to the front and side of the office were Taylor's black Tesla, as expected, along with a black SUV.

"Okay," he began and indicated the latter vehicle, "the 'uh-oh' was in reference to that right there. No one who works for us drives a goddamn SUV, and no one except Taylor and maybe Volz ought to be here at this hour. So yes, maybe it's only a customer."

The lycanthrope frowned and nodded. "Do you think we should go in?"

"Well, yeah," he retorted. "I'm merely saying be careful and stuff. Ugh, I hope it isn't the feds."

It was, unfortunately. As they pushed through the front doors, Remy was half-shocked and half-relieved to see Senior Special Agent Kendra Gilmore of the FBI standing in the middle of the floor and directing two of her usual henchmen, plus a couple of agency medics.

He sighed, ran a hand through his hair, and waited for the inevitable debriefing.

Fortunately, the agent who approached him was one he recognized, a guy named Mortensen and Gilmore's right-hand man.

"David Remington, also known as Remington Davis," the fed greeted him. "I was under the impression you worked the day shift. Who is this?" He looked at Conrad, then back at Remy, which suggested that he did not expect the lycanthrope to introduce himself.

"Oh," Remy began, "he's Conrad Warfield, my new

bodyguard. Can we come in? What the hell happened here?"

The agent seemed to have made a mental note of Conrad's name and facial features—he probably intended to do a background check on him later—but was already turning back to the scene. "An attack," was all he said.

"Wow." Remy sighed. "Really? I would never have guessed, what with the blood everywhere and these guys zipping the body bags. Sorry, it's been a long day."

Fortunately, Mortensen was already ignoring him as he returned to helping mop up the carnage.

Taylor stood beside Gilmore while the others loaded corpses onto a cart, and Remy caught the end of their conversation. The agent did most of the talking.

"...will continue to keep the NYPD off your backs, but there's not much we can do if they arrive on the scene before we do. Particularly now that the chief of police has taken a personal interest in your prior 'disturbance' here."

The vampire's eyes registered that she noticed Remy approaching, but she kept her gaze on the agent. "Yes, I understand."

"So," Gilmore went on, "next time you plan to self-defense the living hell out of Neith's drugged-up hitmen, you need to let us know ASAP. Or better yet, flee the scene and let us deal with it."

"I will try," she responded, "but the nature of 'surprise attacks,' such as this one, means that, by definition, I may not have time to call you before preventing myself and my staff from being killed."

The woman sighed. She was a tall, fortyish woman of mixed heritage, both professional and reasonable, and had thus far proven willing to bend the rules while working with Moonlight Detective Agency on the Moswen situation. Still, being technically a cop, Remy never felt entirely confident that she wouldn't turn on them once she decided that they'd bent the law a little too far.

She also was not among the initiated. The agent still believed that Moswen was a mortal gangster and that her minions were merely hopped up on drugs.

"Don't push your luck," Gilmore chided. "We're running out of time to take care of this whole mess before the NYPD, not to mention my superiors, start asking too many questions."

Her subordinates had finished gathering the bodies and now, with a curt nod, she turned away from Taylor and walked toward the door.

Remy waved to her. She inclined her head briefly in his direction but didn't bother to speak to him. Which was something of a relief, even if it suggested that she thought him far less important than Taylor.

He clapped and rubbed his hands together as the feds disappeared out the front entrance. "So, what did we miss? Pizza? Karaoke?"

The vampire appeared to be dwelling on various inner thoughts and only half acknowledged him. "Moswen's thralls," she replied in a low voice. "No one is seriously hurt."

Conrad, examining the extensive damage to the walls and desks as well as the copious bloodstains, added, "Except them, it would seem."

Remy looked askance at him. "That's what usually

happens when people try to kill Taylor. I thought you knew who she was."

"I do," he replied softly.

He ignored him and approached her. "We had a little excitement ourselves which culminated in an unpleasant but useful discovery. Or a couple of them, really."

Taylor's eyes regained their brightness and fixed on him. It seemed she'd finished whatever mental calculation she was doing. "Oh? Have a seat, then, and tell me. You look like you could use a glass of water, by the way."

"Water," he muttered, "isn't exactly what I had in mind, but I'll take what I can get."

She turned away from him and shouted toward the back office. "Alex, get Remington a glass of water."

A few vague mumbles came in response and the Australian, who looked like he'd stepped in from a day job as a graphite miner, shuffled toward the break area. The water cooler, miraculously, had not been damaged in the scuffle.

The vampire looked at Remy. "I think you've had enough adult beverages lately. It's still an improvement over the past, but don't allow it to creep back up on you. You were doing quite well with your experiment in sobriety for a while."

"Yeah," he grumbled. "I'll be fine."

Alex hurried to his side and handed him a plastic cup filled to barely below the brim. He thanked the man and drank half the water in one swig. "Conrad, how about you finish the second half?"

"Thank you, sir." The lycanthrope accepted the cup.

The investigator took a deep breath before he began his account of all he'd discovered.

"First of all," he stated with an emphatic motion of his hand, "the main, most important conclusion. Surrly has moved into the drug trade, and the shit he's dealing is so bad even I wouldn't have touched it at my worst."

Her eyes widened noticeably, and a tremor of tension went through her. She must honestly not have expected to hear that. "Go on. Start at the beginning, and don't leave out the details."

Remy continued and paused occasionally to let Conrad confirm what he'd said or add his own two cents' worth. He had, after all, played a major role in saving his ass and helping to advance the investigation.

"And so," he concluded, "we finally called another Uber —in Conrad's name this time, in case someone was looking for me, specifically—and hitched a ride all the way back here. We stopped to get him new clothes on the way since he Incredible-Hulked his old ones while transforming. Somehow, I half-expected that you were dealing with something else this whole time, although I didn't figure it would be another mook assault."

Taylor took a moment to assimilate all he'd said. She closed her eyes and moved her head slowly from side to side.

"I almost can't believe it," she said in a soft yet grim tone. "Surrly never impressed me as being the most upstanding of persons. He can be greedy, callous, and stubborn, and his 'lending firm' has its fingers in a few badly stained pots. But I quite honestly would never have guessed he'd be both this stupid and this...immoral."

Remy saw the muscles along her jaw tighten and there was a slight shift in her demeanor. He immediately recognized another of the subtle signs he'd learned to interpret since meeting her. It meant she was contemplating someone's destruction.

"I really have only two rules for the preternaturals in this city," she went on and her voice deepened. "Do not fuck with humans, and do not fuck with me. By selling new, preternatural-specific drugs to mortals, the cartel is breaking the first and barely toeing the line of the second."

He stroked his chin. "Well, they fucked with me an hour or so ago, which is almost the same thing as fucking with you, so I'd argue that they pissed all over both."

She half-nodded. "They had to expect that there would be horrible side effects of that kind and that it would garner far too much attention. Hideous mutations and unnatural deaths amongst humans are exactly what our community doesn't need."

Scratching his ear, Remy mused, "Is there any community that does need those things?"

To his surprise, Conrad made a snorting sound—probably an aborted laugh—only to immediately regain his composure.

"Be quiet, Remington," Taylor snapped. "Some of us are too busy dealing with serious issues to tiptoe around the minefield of every possible smartass remark you could think of."

He shrugged. "I'll concede it's one hell of a big minefield."

Paying him no heed, she drummed her fingers on her arm. "Dwarves have always had a problem with avarice, but this is a step too far. The cartel has completely lost its mind in the name of profit."

She paused for a few more seconds to think and then looked at him. "Now, then. You have—once again—done good work in unraveling a criminal conspiracy, but also managed—once again—to draw undue attention to yourself. After your little escapade earlier tonight, you've effectively doubled the number of people who want your heart on a plate."

Remy blinked. "I hadn't quite looked at it that way, but now that you mention it…"

"The cartel will come after you," the vampire extrapolated. "They'll probably try to claim plausible deniability of my involvement since they don't want me coming after them, so they'll content themselves with simply murdering you when they think I'm not paying attention and then say they assumed you acted outside my orders."

"Nonsense." He scoffed. "If they killed me, you'd totally kick their ass…right?"

Frowning, Taylor said, "Before we get into that, let's prioritize keeping you alive."

"Fair enough." He straightened his tie and noticed his palms were sweating again. Rather than wipe them on his pants, which had taken enough abuse for one night after running through cold mud, he plucked a couple of tissues out of a nearby box.

"With Moswen and her servants," the vampire continued, "we at least have Alex to provide us with some warning of when they're about to strike. Dwarves are not usually subtle, but Surrly's cartel has run clandestine operations for some time now. They could attack you at any unguarded moment. Considering all of this, I'd say the time has come for you to swallow your pride and take residence at my house until the worst of the danger has passed."

Remy groaned. "Not this again. It's really not fair to spring an argument on me after a day like today." He was half-tempted to simply give in to her urgings, only to avoid having to bicker with her.

His pride, however, would not allow him to do that.

"Remy," said Taylor, "you must understand that—"

"I understand," he burst out, "that after all the progress I've made toward self-sufficiency, putting myself in your care would be a step back. Yes, yes, maybe it would be the 'safer' option, but there's also the future to think about. If I do this now, how much easier will it be next time? Do you expect me to rely on you forever?"

She actually leaned back a few inches at that and must not have considered such a notion.

"No," she responded. "I do not expect—or want—you to live off my largesse. But that is not exactly what I'm offering. This isn't secondary-school emotional drama, Remington, and it isn't office politics, either. It's strategy. We are at war, and it's easier for us to win if we all stay alive."

He rubbed his eyes. "Okay, I grasp that but wait. I propose a compromise. One more day. Give me another twenty-four hours to see if I can resolve the whole dwarven cartel problem. If I can discover where they're based, we can effectively strike at them before they can retaliate."

There was a long and fairly intense silence while the vampire considered this.

"And," he added, "if that works, I can continue with my plan to beef security up at my apartment. Which ought to suffice against a couple of Moswen's thralls."

Before either of them could say more, Conrad interjected.

"No matter what," he stated with a smile, "I'll continue to protect him as per our contract."

"Thanks, Conrad," Remy conceded. "Good point. See? He will be there to help if strictly necessary. And if I can't deal with things on my own by tomorrow night, I'll accept your invitation."

"Deal," said Taylor. "Of course, I'll hold you to those terms. Don't try to renege."

He snorted. "I'm a poker player. I would never."

The vampire smiled but it faded abruptly as though something had just occurred to her. "Where is Riley?"

"Oh, hell." He sighed. "She wandered off in human form at the party. That was the last I saw of her. She's been doing that lately—flirting with every guy she sees, getting them to buy her shit, and then mysteriously disappearing to the colony. She's probably fine."

He wasn't so sure, though.

"Well," she replied, "please check on her in the morning. And take her with you, for your own safety."

Remy agreed. "I think it's time, though, that Conrad and I got going. I need to pass out."

"Very well." She looked a little tired herself. "Where do you plan to start looking for the cartel? Certainly not at

Surrly's Lending. At this point, that would either be a dead end or a trap."

He paused, already halfway to the exit. "Yeah, yeah, I won't go there. Let me think it over on the drive home and I'm sure I'll have a brilliant plan in the morning." He waved goodbye and reached for the door, Conrad a few paces behind him.

"Wait," Taylor called. "Come to think of it, Surrly did say a few things, over the years, which implied that he was not, himself, the leader of the cartel."

The investigator stopped and cocked an eyebrow. "Oh? Well, that's intriguing."

"An upper-middle manager, an underboss or *caporegime* of sorts, and his company was certainly a valuable asset," the vampire continued, "but ultimately, I always suspected he was taking orders from someone else."

CHAPTER TWELVE

Port Morris, the Bronx, New York

Starik Grayhammer stood near the edge of the wharf and watched the passage of the sun as it slid above the far horizon. Its journey was reflected over the waters of the Atlantic and the increasing light it gave off as its angle shifted mirrored the waxing of his own anger, which he pictured as a great, fiery ball that cast its illumination over everything around it.

The two groups of dwarves certainly seemed to sense this, given the way they all secretly cringed in fear. He could tell. Their stony-faced facades did not deceive him.

"How much," he asked and paused deliberately, "of my merchandise was washed away?" He did not address the question to anyone in particular.

Surly, of course, was the one who answered. He stepped forward, cleared his throat, and tried not to hang his head. "About a quarter of it, my chieftain," he stated. "No more than thirty percent at most. Perhaps as little as twenty percent. My men were able to save the majority."

The leader looked at his subordinate's head. It looked oddly small and fragile. Then again, Starik was the largest known dwarf in New York and possibly even the largest in North America. His height would have been considered "average" by human standards, and his muscular bulk gave him far more weight and mass.

"Twenty percent," he rumbled and enunciated each word in precisely the way he did when he still had control of his temper, "is not what I would call little. The Order demands detailed explanations for any unexpected loss over five percent."

His normal speaking voice had often been compared to the sound of distant thunder, and he'd always taken that as a compliment. It went well with his appearance. In addition to his size, he also had both hair and a beard that reached almost to his waist, richly black but shot through with iron-colored streaks. His eyes, beneath his heavy and jutting brow, seemed to change color from black to deep grey, depending on the light.

Surrly looked up. "I know, my chieftain. And there is an explanation. Outside interference. People who should have known better than to cross us. We had no way to know they'd be this stupid."

The pitiful remainder of his troupe—he'd somehow allowed over half of his men to get themselves killed, again —huddled in around their boss and nodded their heads dumbly. Apparently, the motley group sought safety in the notion that this was all someone else's fault.

These stragglers constituted one of the groups present. The other was Starik's hand-picked Gray Dwarves. There were six of them and they followed him almost everywhere. He had selected them for their mixture of size, strength, cunning, and loyalty. Other, lesser dwarves feared and respected them. But even the Gray Dwarves feared their chieftain.

As well they should.

Starik flexed his hands, spread the fingers, and clenched them into fists. On his right hand, four golden rings, each set with a different colored stone, reflected the morning sunlight in brilliant flashes.

"Surrly," he said. "The Vampiric Order will not accept an explanation from someone of your lowly, untrustworthy stature. That means I will have to be the one to deliver the news to them. I will have the honor of informing them that a large fraction of their profit margin has vanished into oblivion."

He paused again to feed his own anger with the lesser dwarf's barely suppressed squirms. It made him feel better about his own coming humiliation when speaking to their European benefactors. "That makes me look incompetent, Surrly. Am I incompetent?"

The lender shook his head. "No, my chieftain. Far from it. If anything, I'd say you give off such an impression of being strong and capable that the Order will have no choice but to believe you. Especially when you tell them that it was because some idiots betrayed us and screwed us over."

"That means," Starik bellowed and the implied thunder in his voice broke into a full storm, "that they will think I somehow allowed these people to fuck us over. Is that what happened? Did I allow this?"

His Gray Dwarves pretended to look at nothing, and

the other crew cringed visibly at the sound of his voice. The lender even shot a quick, terrified glance at the enormous hammer resting on his leader's back.

"No, sir," Surrly admitted. "It was my mistake. And I will take responsibility for fixing it."

Starik pretended he didn't hear this comment and strode slowly past the other dwarf to gaze at the city beyond the waterfront. His connections had yanked the leash of the human police, which simplified matters somewhat, but this was still the type of situation that should never have happened.

He liked to think of himself as a businessman, someone with class to go along with his family's ancient warrior reputation. That was why he dressed in the finest suits and saw to it that his hair and beard were always impeccably groomed. He also put a tremendous amount of effort into maintaining his composure, even when things like this happened.

Sometimes, though, he failed.

"The Order," he began, "might be more understanding if we could present them with the culprits who perpetrated this. That way, they could question them, confirm their guilt, and punish them according to their own methods and specifications, which are far crueler than anything known to dwarfdom. Or, barring that, we could at least deliver their heads."

He turned and allowed his shale-colored gaze to fix on Surrly again. "But because you permitted them to escape, we cannot do that, can we? Not yet."

"I'll find them, my chieftain." The dwarf grunted. "I

know who they are. They're not strangers, and they can't hide from me."

Starik took a step closer to him. "Who are they, then?"

The other dwarf looked up and for a moment, his fear ebbed, replaced by anger as he recalled what had happened.

"A human," he explained, "named Remington Davis. And a werewolf he had with him as hired muscle. That guy was the one who did most of the damage. Davis is a half-assed, wannabe private detective who recently started at Moonlight Detective Agency. He did one minor job for me a few weeks ago, and—"

The leader cut him off. "He's with Taylor?"

"Uh…" Surrly gulped. "Yes. He is. He may have been acting on his own, though. He seems like the kind of asshole who's always trying to prove himself and advance his career. The problem ought to go away when he's taken care of."

He gestured to the opened shipping container, where a human corpse hung upside down by its ankles.

"Also," he added, "that moron there—some bottom-feeding dealer—led this Remington character here. He thought he could negotiate a cut of a wholesale purchase while we were in the middle of unloading, for fuck's sake. I'll make sure the right people see what we did to him. That ought to get the point across."

"It's a start." Starik grunted. The sight of the dealer's body made him feel a little better.

"Still," Surrly continued and sounded frightened again, "we have to consider that Taylor might be onto us."

He turned his head to the lender.

"How?" he asked, his voice again the early rumbling of a coming crescendo of thunder. "How is it that Taylor's man would have even looked for us to begin with? How, when we only sell our product during the day? How, when—even at times when a shipment arrives at night—we ensure that she is busy elsewhere? Explain this mystery to me, Surrly."

His subordinate's shoulders slumped and he spread his hands.

"My chieftain," he began, "she'd never been hostile to us or, to my knowledge, suspicious of us. We'd worked together before. With that Egyptian bitch consolidating her power lately, I thought if anyone could protect our shipments, well, it would be Taylor. I...may have approached her with a job offer."

Grayhammer stared. "Oh. Well, that"—he reached back, took his war hammer in both hands, and swung it forward and down—"would fucking explain it, wouldn't it?"

The hammer pounded into Surrly's head, shattered it, collapsed it, and continued through it to transfer its excess force to the rest of his broad body. The blow drove so hard that a tremor went through the earth, and the other dwarves almost stumbled as the tiny fragments of the dwarf's brain and skull rained around them.

"You," Starik raged, his teeth bared and spittle flying from his mouth, "you fucking idiot! You piece of shit."

His voice took on a raw, almost hurt tone as he abandoned himself completely to rage and battered again and again at what remained of his victim. The hammer crunched and splattered and destabilized the earth while it effectively reduced the dwarf to little more than paste.

When it was over, his Gray Dwarves had all assumed

the usual expression they wore after an execution—faint amusement at seeing an inept traitor get what he deserved combined with a vague sense of relief that it hadn't been one of them instead.

He stood, half-hunched over the almost liquefied dwarven remains, and caught his breath as his composure returned to him. Finally, he straightened, cleaned the head of his hammer on the sand at his feet, and wiped the remaining chunks of Surrly off his face.

The Grayhammers had lived in the far North of the world even during the coldest epochs and had long had a reputation as fierce warriors. Among their species, some looked up to them as examples of true, pure dwarvenness, noble-savage types possessing a virility which the rest of dwarfdom had lost.

Others merely thought they were cruel and primitive berserkers who no longer had any place in the modern world.

Starik had long dreamed of proving the second group wrong but without disappointing the first. His cartel would achieve levels of success on par with the most sophisticated of modern dwarven merchants but they would still be barbaric when the situation demanded it.

After all, fear and respect were two sides of the same coin.

"Let it be known," he announced, his voice calm again even though he spoke louder than he had before, "that Surrly was right about one thing. We must find these perpetrators and deal with them."

One of the Gray Dwarves was the first to speak. "My chieftain. Which option—dead or living—is preferred?

You said the Vampiric Order liked to get them alive, but—"

"No," he interrupted. "Not this time." He looked out across the waterfront at the dead dwarf's men, who tried only half-successfully to hide their terror.

"You people," he went on, "are now all my deputies. Which of you was most familiar with Surrly's business? His front, I mean."

A dwarf with a lengthy black mustache stepped forward. "Myself, sir."

Starik nodded. "You, then, run his lending firm until further notice. The rest of you will join my dwarves on the hunt. Your late boss's stupidity has threatened to send a message that we can be fucked with. Now, we must send a very different message."

They all stood in silence and waited for his next words.

"A message that no one—absolutely no one—interferes with our business, makes us look incompetent in front of our benefactors, or insults our honor and intelligence. Not even Taylor. She allowed her pet human to shit where we eat. Now, we make an example of him."

He put his war hammer over his shoulder, allowed it to loom there behind his flowing mane of hair, and clenched and unclenched his hands. The four rings glimmered.

"Find this stupid human known as Remington Davis and his lycanthropic boyfriend along with him, and kill them both," the chieftain commanded. "The werewolf goes into the woodchipper. As for the human... We send his head to the Order and his little finger to Taylor."

When he grinned, his men almost flinched at the sight.

CHAPTER THIRTEEN

Por's Bar, Lower Manhattan, New York

Remington had lied. He hadn't actually been that tired, or so it seemed once he got back in the car. In fact, he'd felt a strange and powerful urge to detour the teensiest slide over to the lower part of the island and pay a visit to Porrillage.

After the ordeal of finding a parking space, he at least didn't have to walk far in the cold before he reached the familiar unobtrusive staircase leading down to the basement pub.

Judging by the noise—audible from the other side of the door even before he gave it a push—it was a busy night.

He cleared the threshold and stepped in. The lighting was dim, the music was low enough to faintly be heard under the chatter of voices, and someone at the pool table careened a group of balls into each other as he entered.

Remy approached the bar and planted himself on a stool.

"Por!" he exclaimed. "How's your night going, my man?"

The bartender, also the proprietor, appeared from behind a shelf carrying another patron's drink, some elaborate poofy cocktail.

"Remy," he grunted. "About like any other night. I assume you're having a rough one if you're here."

Porrillage was tall enough that he could pass for a little person, and gnomes had physiognomy that was only subtly different from humans, anyway, so he was usually safe if any of the uninitiated stumbled onto him. His clientele, though, mostly seemed to consist of either preternaturals or those humans who had dealings with them.

"Correct," he said. "It's been one hell of a long goddamn day. I'm thinking a nice scotch on the rocks. Basic, but effective. A single, since I need to drive myself, sadly."

The gnome climbed the step he'd constructed behind the bar and handed the cocktail to a woman whom Remy suspected was a dryad since she appeared to have baby tree-branches growing from her shoulders and leaves sprouting in her hair.

"One scotch on the rocks, comin' right up." Por leapt down and went to work.

Remy tapped his hands on the bar's surface and looked around while he waited for his drink. He was relieved to see that there weren't any dwarves around tonight.

It disturbed him to think that Surrly and his crew were now the proverbial bad guys. He'd always thought of dwarves as lovable, tough, jolly types who could be relied on to do the right thing. Evidently, they were as fallible as humans.

Or vampires.

Por placed a glass in front of him. "*Muchas gracias*," he quipped, and immediately went to work on the alcohol.

He'd drunk about half of it when he turned toward the dryad woman. "Do you come here often? That's a nice...uh, spring look you have going, by the way. It's kind of refreshing in January."

The woman stared at him, bug-eyed. "I am sorry," she replied in a slow, wispy accent. "I do not talk much."

Remy shrugged. "Mkay, then." He pivoted away from her.

Por passed him and seemed almost to hesitate for a second as if he expected to be met with some comment. When nothing happened, he continued to check on another customer at the far end of the bar.

On his return, he glanced at Remington and asked, "No conversation tonight? You don't feel like telling me about all your problems and how they're someone else's fault? You must be really wiped out."

"Yeah, I am," he grumbled. "Plus, you know, the usual Taylor issues."

The gnome chuckled and turned away to wipe a couple of glasses.

Remy drained the remainder of his scotch as he watched the other patrons. The alcohol mingled with his tangled emotions and the dim vibe of the bar itself.

"Hey, Por," he said and swirled the ice cubes around the otherwise empty glass. "Change of plans. I'll need another scotch. Single, again, don't worry. And I'll take an Uber home and have someone pick my car up in the morning or something. It won't be towed, right? I can't remember if that's how we did things before."

Although he studied him with a little suspicion, the gnome took his glass, suddenly produced a bottle, and refilled it. He didn't bother to add more ice since the majority from the first round was still unmelted.

The investigator accepted it and sipped the first quarter. His thoughts wandered to the disagreement he'd had with his business partner.

He saw that Por was still roughly in his field of vision, which probably meant the gnome was listening, so he went on. "Let me tell you, it's completely goddamn unfair, and it gets even more unfair the more I think about it. Who does Taylor think she is?"

The proprietor, half-coughing as he exhaled, ventured a quick response. "I'd say she thinks she's the same person that most of New York thinks she is."

"Well," he drawled, "I don't know exactly what that means, but she isn't my frickin' mother. Where does she get the authority to make major life decisions on my behalf, as if I don't have the volition to do so myself? 'Now Remington, I hereby order you to live where I tell you to live.' That's almost literally what she said. Almost."

Por seemed to be only half-listening, but he assumed it was only since he was busy. *He ought to hire more bartenders. Especially for nights like tonight.*

The gnome ducked out of sight to retrieve more ingredients. When he returned, Remy resumed his spiel.

"I haven't shared a place with anyone since I was in college. I've been my own man ever since I graduated. Someone like me belongs in a private penthouse, not someone else's guest room. At least, not on a long-term basis."

"Oh," Por replied as he returned, his eyes on another man who'd entered, "of course."

"Besides," he continued, "it's not as if she and I are that close. We haven't known each other long enough to be slee —I mean, living together. We work opposite halves of the day. And we're from different species. How do I know that one of these evenings she won't get tired of drinking the canned stuff and decide to have me for a midnight snack?"

The barman delivered the drink to his newest customer, paused for a breath, and wiped his presumably sweaty hands on his apron. "I don't think she'd do that."

Remy swished the ice in his glass. "Maybe not. But it's still...ugh, embarrassing."

"You know, pal," Por commented, "I ain't so sure that this is really about your independence or dignity or whatever you seem to think it is. Maybe it's more about..." He spun a hand in a circle and searched for the right words. "Fear of intimacy. Something like that, the kind of stuff women like to talk about when they want to take things to the next level or whatever."

Frowning, Remy turned it over in his mind while he sipped his scotch.

Meanwhile, the gnome conferred with one of his waitresses on the massive tab that the pool players were generating. Apparently, one of them had managed to knock a ball off the table itself and almost lost it in a dark corner.

So what he's saying, the investigator concluded, *is that Taylor is probably doing this as some kind of coded message about the two of us getting closer or some shit.*

He crunched an ice cube between his teeth. *I know I'm one hell of an eligible bachelor, what with the good looks, charming personality, towering intelligence...oh, and bravery in the face of danger, multifarious useful talents, and whatnot. But she's presuming waaaay too much about our relationship.*

As Porrillage turned back to the bar, Remy set his empty glass down and slapped a hand on the wooden surface.

"Por, you're right," he proclaimed, his jaw set in determination. "The time has come to make it perfectly clear to Taylor that she and I are only friends, and the way to do that is by sleeping in my own bed, at my own place, for as long as reasonably possible."

The gnome's eyes rolled skyward for a moment before he responded. "That's...uh, not exactly what I meant, but I wish you all the luck in the whole wide world, my friend." With a grunt, he shuffled away to dispense a few mugs of frothy golden beer.

The investigator stood, almost knocked his stool over with the motion, and left one of his business cards on the bar. By now, Por probably had a large collection of them, but it was easy to lose such things and there was no reason to make things difficult with such an excellent bartender.

"Bill me. You know I'm good for it." He turned and trudged past the taciturn dryad and a handful of other customers toward the door.

Outside, the air had grown even colder in the brief period he'd spent having his nightcap. Winter had arrived late, but he wouldn't particularly complain when it packed up and left for the year.

He knew he'd made the right decision. Taylor would walk all over him if he didn't stand up for himself, even if she did try to make it a question of his safety. As though he hadn't already thought of that.

Besides, based on what he'd seen so far, Moswen Neith was the type whose battle strategy consisted of trying something, waiting, re-planning, and then trying something else a while later. It was what she'd done by sending Alex to kill or capture him and going dormant after that.

Then, she'd sent a few minions against both himself and Taylor recently, which meant that they were—probably—now at the end of her next feint.

There was no way she'd try something again so soon.

"None whatsoever," he drawled aloud, mostly to himself, as he stumbled to where he'd parked. A couple of Elven women glanced curiously at him as he passed before they descended the stairs to the pub.

For a moment, while he fumbled for his keys in his pocket, he had the vague but powerful sensation that someone was watching him.

That car across the street, the dark one? No. There isn't even anyone in it. Ugh, this whole business has my nerves about as frayed as a natural brunette after too many excursions into blondeness in too short a time. No wonder I'm drinking again lately.

David Remington's Penthouse, Midtown Manhattan, New York

Having lied to Taylor about wanting to go straight home, Remington had also lied to Por about taking an Uber home.

He'd made it in one piece. While he knew his capabilities well enough to judge that he'd probably be okay to drive himself, it still came as a relief to pull in at his building with neither body damage nor a DUI. Either would have been even more inconvenient and embarrassing than having to pick his car up from Por's Bar in the morning.

Therefore, he told himself, *let's never do that again. It's not worth it.*

Dawn wasn't too far off. Enrique, the usual third-shift concierge, didn't seem to be on duty when he approached. Usually, the man would see his car on the camera and come out to welcome him home.

"Whatever," he mumbled as he trudged through the residual crust of snow. "It's not like I'm incapable of opening a door by myself. I'm not that drunk. Not by a long shot."

He stepped over the threshold and into the lobby. Enrique wasn't there and neither was anyone else. The concierge must have been taking a crap or something. And at this hour, it wasn't very likely that anyone else would be around, anyway.

Behind him, a car pulled into the adjacent lot—probably someone turning around. The one-way streets in this part of town seemed to have that effect on motorists of below-average skill.

Once inside the elevator, his thoughts turned once more to how he would handle the Taylor situation. First of all, the simple fact that he'd made it safely home proved that he was right—obviously. He allowed himself a smirk.

Of course, he did have to follow-up on his promise to fortify his apartment. At the first convenient opportunity, he'd need to draw up a detailed plan of how he'd add security systems, what his own emergency procedure would be for getting out or calling for help, and maybe design a couple of really cool booby-traps or something.

"That'll teach her." He chuckled as the elevator pinged and opened for him at the penthouse.

Remy stepped out into the hall and walked to his door, placed his hand on it, and frowned when it swung open immediately. He must have forgotten to lock up before he'd left in the morning. Hangovers did that to a man.

With a shrug, he stepped into the place he called home.

The lights were still on, too. He'd tried to save a little money by turning everything off when he wasn't using it, but a single day's worth of wasted power wasn't likely to run his bills up terribly much.

He took his coat off, already almost fantasizing about his nice warm bed while keeping his tired gaze on the floor. Without looking, he hung his coat and began to kick his shoes off.

A muddy boot print leading toward the kitchen drew his focus and he looked up.

His gaze settled on the unmistakable face of a dwarf—a short one even by dwarven standards, with wild blond eyebrows and hair and beard and a mustache of the same color. He wore bulky clothes with enough angles under them to suggest a hidden suit of armor and a double-bladed ax rested against his back.

Incongruously, a sandwich hung out of his mouth, made of bread, meat, and cheese he'd taken from Remington's fridge.

The investigator sputtered and his hands clenched

involuntarily. "Who the hell gave your ass permission to come in here and eat my food?" he demanded.

The intruder spat the sandwich out and reached for his weapon.

Heavy footsteps sounded from the living area and another short, dark, thick form strode in, holding one of the bottles of Swedish vodka Remy had been saving for emergencies. It was two-thirds empty.

"Is it him? He's here!" the second dwarf burst out, asking and answering his own question at once. He tossed the liquor onto a sofa and suddenly produced a heavy wooden crossbow laden with wooden studs and loaded with a nasty barbed bolt.

In an instant, pandemonium erupted. Remy's brain took a second to catch up with what was going on, since— as he was now forced to admit—he was too drunk for this shit.

The blond dwarf swung his ax. The investigator threw himself to the side but the room spun faster and more wildly than he would have liked. It seemed the whole planet had been knocked off its axis to tumble into the depths of space.

"Shit!" he exclaimed when one of his legs tumbled a potted fern. A loud snapping sound heralded the second dwarf's crossbow bolt that rocketed over his head to embed in the wall.

He continued his roll, already almost as afraid of throwing up when he came to a stop as he was of being axed or skewered.

His attackers' pounding feet moved closer, and as he came to rest against a loveseat with his hips and legs somehow twisted over his chest, his face was pointed toward the still-open doorway.

Something else—fast, dark, and hairy—careened into the apartment.

"What?" The crossbowman's voice growled with fury. "Kill it!"

Judging by the dwarf's slurred cadence, Remy had the awful suspicion that he'd already drained another entire bottle before he'd drunk the first two-thirds of the second.

"Conrad!" Remy shouted and rolled to his side so he could boost himself to his feet. Nausea threatened to overwhelm him. "That's you, right? The other guy has a crossbow."

The werewolf and the blond assassin tangled within the kitchen. The dwarf must have been unusually strong since he'd forced Conrad back into one of the shelves to upend the new spice rack and cover the counter with spilled cumin and rosemary.

The second dwarf had finished reloading his bow. He seemed to hesitate for an instant, unsure who to shoot first.

Remy scooped up the fallen fern pot and heaved it at the assassin. He staggered forward himself with the momentum and decided he was barely sober enough to pull off some kind of airborne dropkick. His martial arts instructors recommended against flashy, overcommitted shit like that, but it could catch the dwarf off-guard, not to mention that regular takedowns might not work against such a heavy, stolid creature.

The projectile shattered in his adversary's face and he stumbled back a step with a grunt so the crossbow's business end wavered toward the ceiling. By then, the investigator had already leapt into the air.

"Haaaaa!" he cried as he launched himself and tried to bring his legs up in time to drive them into the dwarf's face or chest.

Instead, one of his feet snagged on the edge of a sofa and he again somersaulted helplessly, this time toward its cushions. It would have been a soft impact if his stomach hadn't landed directly on the discarded vodka bottle.

"Fuck!" he exclaimed in pain, twirled off the couch to the floor, and landed on his knees before he finally vomited.

Behind him, Conrad seemed to have incapacitated the blond dwarf and had pounced over the half-wall to engage the crossbowman. Snarls, pounding, and curses filled the air.

"Okay," Remy gasped and crawled madly away from the brawl, "I'm not in peak condition here. It's time to let Wonder Boy handle it." It took him a second to realize he'd brushed a knee through his own puke, which almost made him gag again.

He honestly paid very little attention to where he was going. His only goal was to escape being trampled by the struggle between dwarf and lycanthrope.

In the midst of his mad scamper, his eyes focused on what was directly ahead of him. His landline phone rested on an end table. When he'd first acquired this penthouse, his parents had prevailed upon him to install a landline as a backup measure, even if the damn things were obsolete.

"Uh, yes!" he snapped and hurried toward it. Then it occurred to him that he wasn't sure who to call. The mortal police? That, of course, was a bad idea—they'd ask way too many questions.

Taylor? She could handle these dwarves, but even she couldn't get there fast enough. And she'd have words to say about the whole situation that Remington did not want to hear.

He looked over his shoulder. Conrad had clawed the face and chest of the crossbowman, but the dwarf had pinned him against the sofa and now punched him repeatedly in the head. His heavy fist had begun to take a toll.

From the corner of his eye, he saw the other attacker drag himself gradually toward the door out of the apartment. Conrad's jaws had savaged his leg and it was bleeding badly, even with a crude tourniquet tied around it.

Remy thought he could hear someone shouting and cursing elsewhere in the building. Then, he almost jumped in place. His phone rang.

"Goddammit," he muttered, finished his crawl toward it, and grabbed the receiver off the hook. "Hi, how are ya?"

"David," a man's voice said. "Could you please keep the noise down? Here we were these last few months, thinking the dark age of all your stupid loud parties was over, and now this. We're trying to get some sleep here and we don't want to have to call the cops."

He sighed. It was Mr. Blankfein, his neighbor on the floor below.

"Oh...uh...ha ha, yes," he stammered as wolf-snorts and inhumanly low grunts sounded behind him and furniture scraped the floor. "Sorry about that, Murray. Don't you worry, though. I'll have these cockamamie party animals under control in no time."

A chair spun, dangerously airborne. He ducked and it passed over his head to crash into the wall, shatter to splinters, and leave a hideous gouge in the plaster.

"Uh," he resumed into the phone and cut off the nascent tirade of profanity that Blankfein was about to launch into, "like I said, in no time. We're having some technical difficulties—you know, chair problems. Let me take care of that."

He hung up.

Remy spun toward the action as Conrad lurched at the dwarf again and finally yanked the crossbow away from him, ripped it to pieces with his foreclaws and fangs, and kicked the dwarf in the stomach with one of his hind paws at the same time.

The assailant toppled back and landed next to his partner, both of them mere feet from the open door leading to both the hallway and the elevator.

The investigator remained where he was, frozen while he waited to see what they did. So did Conrad, who hunched and growled at them with bloody drool dripping from one of his curling wolfen lips.

The crossbowman muttered a curse in his own language and seized his partner under the arms, dragged the man out into the hall, and slammed the door behind them. The sounds of their shuffling progress dwindled and finally faded altogether.

After a short moment of silence, Remy blew out his breath and allowed himself to fall limply against the wall.

He drew his hand across his brow to disperse the worst of the sweat.

"Well, that was fun," he drawled. He turned toward the werewolf. "Conrad...uh, thanks again. I could have handled them if I was sober, though. You know how it is."

His rescuer was already half-transformed into his human shape. The dark hair receded and revealed him to be naked as he hurried toward the kitchen. He must have stripped again before he changed so as to not have to buy another outfit in one night.

"Sir," the lycanthrope said, "please excuse me for a moment while I get dressed."

"Sure," he flung in response. "I can't say I'm overly interested in seeing your bare ass cheeks, no offense." He looked in the opposite direction. "Why did you let them live, though? You probably could have killed the bastards. Then, we wouldn't have to worry about them showing up again later."

From behind the kitchen's half-wall where the other man now crouched, Conrad's voice wafted up. "I didn't think it would be a good idea to kill anyone in your home, sir. That presents certain problems."

Remy sighed. "I suppose you're right. Couldn't you have maybe, like, eaten them, though?"

"The size of a lycanthrope's stomach," his bodyguard explained by way of reply, "is still limited by the same laws of nature that govern a human's. Also, dwarf bones are extremely thick, which makes them difficult to crunch through and digest."

"Fair enough." He put a hand on the wall and returned to

a full standing position. Having thrown up a minute or two before, he felt marginally better. "Ugh, couldn't we have gone to war with a cartel made up of...I don't know, leprechauns or something? Dwarves are proving to be a pain in the ass."

He scanned the wreck of his apartment and shook his head slowly. Inebriation cocooned him against being too upset about it—yet—but it still sucked. His home hadn't been this badly trashed since his final party before he'd started working with Taylor.

"So, then," he announced as Conrad finished re-clothing himself, "obviously, my apartment is compromised. I don't know how the sons of bitches found out where I live, but they did. I'm not in any condition to go someplace else tonight, though, so I think I'll have to simply crash here."

The werewolf walked toward him and stepped carefully over the various blood patches and pieces of debris. "I don't think that's such a good idea—"

Remy flapped a hand dismissively. "It'll take them a while to come back with heavier artillery. Plus, they'll probably assume we're tattling to Taylor already, which ought to give them pause. I'll decide what to do in the morning."

Conrad grimaced uncomfortably and adjusted his shirt at the neck.

As he turned and headed toward his bed, the investigator said over his shoulder, "Please keep an eye on things, if you could. I trust your 'werewolf-sense' to alert me to further danger. You do have something like that, right?"

For once, the other man did not respond right away.

"Oh," he added, before he stumbled into his bedroom,

"feel free to help yourself to that sandwich the first dwarf spat out. It should still be on the kitchen floor somewhere. The ingredients were all still good as of a couple of days ago."

His bodyguard coughed. "Ah, thank you, sir."

"No problem." He closed the door with his foot and allowed himself to plummet forward, face first, into his covers. It took him all of about fifteen seconds to fall asleep.

CHAPTER FOURTEEN

Moonlight Detective Agency Offices, Bushwick, Brooklyn,
New York

As a way to thank Conrad for providing rescue services, Remy had bought him a cup of coffee and decided to let him do all the driving. It was the least he could do.

"Your doorman," the lycanthrope explained as they made their way toward Bushwick, "had been incapacitated with a sleep spell combined with a low-level memory wipe. Normally, dwarves can't cast enchantments of that kind themselves, but they have enough connection to the preternatural that they can still manage to make a magic scroll work if someone else imbues it with power."

He was too groggy to exactly be aghast but he was still a little shocked that someone with Conrad's education would disrespect Enrique in this fashion.

"How dare you call him a doorman," he said. "The preferred term is concierge."

"Oh." The man gasped and instantly blushed. "I'm

terribly sorry, sir. I didn't take the time to look into how your residence handled—"

"Yeah, yeah," he interrupted him and waved a hand lazily. "But don't let it happen again. In any event, at least he's okay, right?"

The werewolf nodded. "He should be. The whole idea of using spells like that is to leave uninitiated humans none the wiser when there's preternatural activity going on."

"Right." He rubbed his eyes. Unfortunately, he'd only had a single cup of average-strength coffee after getting up. More and stronger would have been better, but he didn't want to have to pee every twenty minutes for the first three hours of work.

They were now only a mile or so from the office. Conrad seemed content to drive in silence. He probably regarded it as more professional that way.

Remy spoke up again soon, though. "So..." He sighed. "I appreciate you saving my life and all, but what I could really use right now is your...uh, confidence. Let's keep what happened at my condo between you and me, right? There's no need for Taylor to know that I've already been ambushed by homicidal dwarves."

His companion frowned. "Well, sir, if we look at the big picture, she did hire me to look after your safety, and you see—"

"I know that," he protested, "but we also agreed on some rules, most of which boil down to 'I'm in charge and you have to do whatever I say.' So, right now, I'm saying don't tell her."

Conrad swallowed whatever further commentary he might have had. Still, the vibes he gave off told the whole story. He disapproved, probably out of legitimate concern for his charge's well-being.

Remy reminded himself that the man did seem to be a damn good bodyguard and explained further.

"I only…I worry that she'll try to lock me in a box, so to speak. You know? 'This is for your own good, Remington,' like she's my grandmother babysitting me while the parents are out of town. Of course, it's only because she cares, but it's so…patronizing."

The other man replied almost at once. "Pardon me, sir, but you may be mistaken," he commented. "It's really not like Taylor to care much about anyone else."

Remy blinked, temporarily stunned. That was definitely not what he had expected to hear.

"What the hell?" he retorted. "I could tell that the two of you were acquainted, but that's awfully familiar for a butler type. Exactly how well do you know her, anyway?"

Conrad blushed again but seemingly overcame it quickly. His demeanor had grown harder and grimmer than usual. He cleared his throat before he answered the question.

"She and I dated—for a brief period—several decades ago. A little before your time. Or perhaps right around when you were born. I can't recall. Sadly, things did not work out in the long run."

He almost sputtered as he wracked his brain for a way to respond to this. "Taylor used to go on dates? The idea of her having a boyfriend is beyond fucked up, frankly. She's a complete ice queen. You weren't simply her BDSM slave, were you?"

Even as he said this, he remembered his conversation

with Por at the bar last night and his own notion that Taylor was trying to...expand upon their relationship. Something in his gut roiled uncomfortably. Maybe he needed breakfast.

"Yes, ha," the lycanthrope replied and pretended to be amused by his reaction. "The part about her...uh, dating, I mean, not the 'slave' part. We had a...relatively normal relationship, I suppose."

He paused and his hands grasped the wheel more tightly so the knuckles stood out against his skin with the tension.

"However," he went on, "we never reached the point at which she invited me to move in with her. I wasn't about to beg and, well, she certainly never asked."

Conrad turned his head to him and fixed him with a subtle look of concentration as the office appeared a little farther ahead of them. "For you to have received that kind of offer, sir, you must be something special in her eyes."

Remy took a deep breath while his mind considered that statement.

Jesus. It's too damn early for me to deal with this kind of crap. I have a job to do here, a business in need of success, and the last thing I need is a ton of emotional drama. Especially if it involves Taylor of all people.

He tried, therefore, to shove any thoughts or feelings pertaining to the matter far, far away from his consciousness. Some of them, however, lodged between the squiggly parts of his brain and refused to leave him alone.

Specifically, the notion of Taylor and Conrad being... intimate. The fact that he did not want to even consider it made it almost impossible to completely blot out the image.

No. Seriously, no. We are not dwelling on that. It's not even the allure of the forbidden because there's nothing alluring about it. It's plain wrong, goddammit.

"Sir," the lycanthrope interrupted, "are you okay? We're here, but I'm sure we can spare half an hour if you'd like to get something to eat, perhaps."

"Uh," he mumbled and snapped back to reality, "no thanks, I'll be fine. I'll have Bobby or the intern get me another cup of coffee, and maybe...I dunno, have a mint off the reception desk or something."

His companion shrugged. "If you say so." He parked the car toward the rear of the lot and they both emerged into the frosty mid-morning air before they pushed through the door into their place of employment.

Bobby was already set up in the lobby and waved to them as they entered. "Hi, guys, good morning and all. I sent Alex off to get donuts. Do you want any coffee in the meantime?" She wore a tight red sweater that did not reveal much but nevertheless earned its bones by accentuating both the size and shape of her bust.

Remy shrugged himself out of his coat and draped it over his arm. "Definitely, absolutely, and thanks. Donuts don't sound too bad either. Ugh, I had to miss an MMA class so I'm going to have to find some way to burn off the extra calories as soon as possible, though."

He held a hand up to Conrad to indicate that the man should wait in the lobby, while he went to his office to hang his coat and turn his computer on.

"At least Taylor won't be in for a few hours yet," he

muttered, "so I'll have more time to wake up and decide what to tell her. On the other hand, it might be nice to get it over with, so perhaps she'll make one of her surprise early appearances."

After entering the boot-up password, he left his computer to load and wandered into the lobby, where their receptionist had already returned with a tray set with three steaming paper cups.

"Ah." He sighed and smiled for the first time that day. "Thank you, Bobby. Somehow, the caffeine tastes better when someone else makes it." He snatched a cup and drank half of it in one long gulp.

Conrad took one, too. "Actually, sir, caffeine is virtually tasteless, except in large and concentrated quantities. Such as if you were to get it in its pure, powdered form, which is available at some health-food stores, although significant doses can be toxic."

"Thanks, Conrad," Remy quipped. "I'm learning a ton of useful info here."

The werewolf gave a mostly fake chortle at this and turned his attention to his coffee, the better to save himself from having to respond.

As they drank, waiting for Alex to get back with his fried and sugared bread, Remy watched Bobby lean back behind her desk and raise an issue of The New England Inquirer in front of her face.

"Huh," he remarked. "I must be moving down in the world. The front-page story isn't about me for once."

She peered at him over the paper. "Oh, ha-ha, right," she agreed. "There've been a few that weren't about you, but yeah, now that I think of it, those have mostly been the recent issues. You were an extremely popular subject for them last fall."

"Oh," he began and allowed himself to be flattered for the moment, "I know, I know."

The receptionist returned to her reading and, bored, he examined the front page in more detail.

Existence of hard-drive backups for human brain proved by politicians' behavior, the headline shouted. He leaned closer and squinted at the text of the story proper.

Bobby looked at him again. "I already read that one, Mr Remington, so if you're curious, I can tell you what it's about." She smiled.

"Sure," he said. He didn't have anything better to do for the moment.

She set the paper down and turned the cover toward him. "So, there's this city councilman and a couple of his aides...and, like, an alderman and a couple of sheriff's deputies, and this lady who runs the sanitation department, and they've all acted really weirdly lately."

"Oh? Interesting..." he commented as he nodded and glanced at the clock.

"Yeah," she went on. "The reporter—that Jenny Ocren lady, actually—noticed that all these politicians have acted the same way, though. They are always seen wandering around outside late at night and trying to sleep during the day and stuff. The councilman passed out at a meeting, even."

Now, both men listened intently.

"And..." Bobby's eyes widened. "They keep having mysterious chest pain. Like they're having a heart attack, only it comes and goes too fast for it to be cardiac arrest—

they're in agony one second and perfectly fine the next. The sanitation chick said she was talking to her doctor about it, but they haven't heard anything yet."

"Well," Conrad quipped, "that is rather curious."

The receptionist nodded. "There's more, too. People are reporting that they've all been eating a ton of red meat. Even one of the deputies, who's a vegan. Isn't that weird?"

"I've heard weirder," Remy observed, "but yes." What he did not say, however, was that all the symptoms she'd mentioned had a curiously vampiric feel to them.

"It's so scary," she continued. "Like, the article goes on to talk about this super-obscure experiment done in Russia in the eighties before the Soviet Union broke up, where they tried to make the human brain compatible with a computer."

The investigator somehow doubted this had much to do with vampires, but if she had no goddamn idea what she was talking about, that was just as well.

"Like"—she raised a hand as if gesturing to something that wasn't there—"this Russian scientist was trying to make a kind of floppy disk for the whole human neural network, or at least the important stuff, that could be plugged in and out of one of their super-computers. You know, the ones they used to open a portal to another time-line over Tunguska. The fabric of the continuum was really weak there after the 1908 Tunguska Event."

"Uh..." Remy coughed. "Yeah. You don't think it could be indicative of...uh, anything else?"

"Nah," she countered. She rambled on for a couple of minutes about how the bizarre experiment in question led some of the patients to report symptoms similar to the ones described in the article.

For good measure, she also mentioned a couple of Ms Ocren's previous articles, in which the woman claimed to have "inside sources" in the US government who claimed they had stolen the Soviet intel at the end of the Cold War and had tried to develop the technology ever since.

"This proves that it's true," Bobby urged and slapped the page emphatically. "They've reported on it here and every-thing, with all this in-depth research and evidence, but I'd bet any money that no one will ever actually talk about it. This stuff is right in front of our faces."

Remy nodded blankly. What was right in front of his face, of course, was the prospect that Moswen had acquired a few thralls in the local government. That scared him more than a few rumors in a no-account paper about a Russian urban legend older than he was.

"Bobby," he asked, "could I cut that article out to have a look at it? I think Taylor might find it interesting also."

"Oh, sure," the receptionist said. She produced a pair of scissors from her desk drawer and carved the entire front page off. "I'm done with the other side, too, don't you worry."

"Thanks."

He turned to Conrad. "Hold on a sec. I'll be right back."

The man nodded and simply sipped his coffee.

With the clipping in hand, the investigator walked through the space toward Taylor's office. She wasn't there yet, but he could easily leave the article on her desk so she could immediately evaluate it after she arrived.

When he rounded the corner, he almost bumped into Volz.

"Watch your step," the dwarf rumbled. "I'm reinforcing a few wires here, as you can see. There's also the matter of my feet. I can guarantee you wouldn't want to step on those, even a human of your relative boldness."

Something about the dwarf's mischievous smile, almost hidden under his mustache, improved Remy's mood, at least a little.

"Right," he agreed. "You guys seem to more than make up in mass what you lack in height."

Then, something occurred to him. The dwarf was the only preternatural in the office right now. Things seemed a little empty.

He stepped carefully over both feet and wires but on the other side, paused to ask Volz another question. "Have you seen or heard from Riley, by any chance? We...uh, misplaced her at a drug party—these things happen—and she never found us afterward."

The dwarf furrowed his brow. "Hmm, no, I'm afraid she never showed up last night, nor has she been in this morning. Usually, it seems that after a mission with you, she returns to the office and falls asleep at that ridiculous upended coffee mug you gave her to use as a 'desk.' Or occasionally, she'll even help me with my work."

Another pang of worry struck Remington. Volz was right. The fairy was not acting like herself lately at all. And hearing the dwarf say as much confirmed that it wasn't only his suspicions. Now, it was obvious to everyone.

"I see," he replied. "That's...odd. She can handle herself,

mostly, but she was in human form last we saw her, and she…well, loses most of her powers when she does that."

He put his hands in his pockets to keep from suddenly needing to adjust his tie or wipe the sweat from his hands. "I only hope she had the good sense to transform before anything dangerous might have happened."

Volz nodded. "Likely she did. The fae are wily when it comes to their own self-preservation, I've found."

Remy had noticed the same thing. But Riley was atypical for a fairy, and even by her own standards, she hadn't displayed much interest in self-preservation.

He sighed. "Well, I need her. For work, I mean. So it looks like it's back on the hunt."

After a quick glance at the piece of paper in his hand, he decided not to bother with Taylor's office. She might have locked it, anyway.

"Say, Volz," he inquired instead. "Could you see to it that Taylor gets this article when she comes in? You're good at remembering stuff, and it's definitely something that I think she'd want to have a good, long look at. Hell, you might as well."

The dwarf took the clipping and glanced at it. "Oh, ye gods—the Inquirer. This ought to be amusing. But yes, I will ensure that she receives it."

"Thanks. It may be only a gossip sheet, but broken clocks and twice a day…uh, however that expression goes. Taylor will know what to make of it."

He spun on his heel and headed to the lobby to collect his werewolf. Alex came through the front door as he arrived, carrying a large flat box.

"I got us some donuts," he announced.

Remy stepped forward and opened the box while it was still in the intern's arms and plucked out a vanilla crème-filled one.

"Thanks, Alex." He closed the box and made a shooing motion for the man to take it to the lobby table. "For someone who tried to kill me a couple of times, you're not so bad, after all."

The intern sighed. "Don't mention it, mate."

Conrad stepped forward. "What now?"

"Reinforcements," he stated. "You're good to have around and all, but to round things out, what we really need is…"

He trailed off. Rather than saying "fairy" in front of Bobby, he made little wing-flapping motions with his hands.

"Ah," the lycanthrope responded, "say no more."

CHAPTER FIFTEEN

Park Avenue Shopping District, Manhattan, New York

"Confession time." Remy almost groaned. "I do not have a plan to locate Riley beyond driving or stumbling around and hoping we see her. Granted, that exact method has usually worked in the past since she always seems to stick to a few streets, I think. Let's hope she hasn't expanded her repertoire or whatever."

"Hmm," Conrad responded and stroked his goatee. "It's possible I might smell her or hear her voice before you could. That does give us one advantage."

He almost made a comment about buying a supersonic whistle and using it to punish the bodyguard for bad behavior but reined himself in at the last split-second. Right now, the main thing was to find their friend and make sure she was okay.

And if she wasn't there in the shopping district, the only other place that suggested itself was Melrose. After the ugliness in the shipping container, he had no desire to go there again anytime soon.

They'd begun the search at the most obvious locale—Fluttershire, in Fort Washington Park—and it had proven to be a bust. Mainly because Riley hadn't even been there, but they'd also caught the colony's guards in an even worse mood than usual.

"Who," the blue one had insisted, shrill with anger, "exactly who is this foul lycanthrope, and why have you brought him to our sanctuary? Haven't you already brought enough outside influences into our domain?"

Conrad had attempted to introduce himself. "Hello," he'd said tentatively, "my name is Conrad Warfield, and I'm only here to protect both Remington and Riley, once we locate her. I'm under contract with Taylor, and I can assure you that—"

"Silence!" the orange one had interjected. "We know all too well why you're here. The meat of the fae is as the sweetest morsel to the tongue of the dog."

The werewolf had almost visibly bristled at that. "Wolf, if you don't mind the correction."

After more pointless squabbling—during which a couple of other fairies had emerged to fling baseless accusations that Remy planned to marry Riley off to the werewolf without paying the required dowry—he had thrown his hands up in disgust, turned, and marched away.

Conrad was all too happy to trail behind him and tried not to look or sound as flustered as he obviously was.

"They're certainly...contentious," he'd griped after a moment.

"You know," he had observed and felt as though an epiphany were upon him, "they're actually more dog-like than you are in that most of their behavior is an act designed to convince people to give them a treat."

The lycanthrope, struck by this insight, hadn't replied immediately.

"Almost every time," Remy continued, "they act as though they don't remember who I am. It's as if I've never done anything for them and can't ever be trusted to make up for it but every time, they suddenly love me as soon as I give them some or other honey-based product or sugary nonsense. In this case, we weren't here to actually procure services from them—only a little recon and info-gathering —so, screw 'em. They can wait until I need to renew Riley's weekly contract. Then, I'll buy them...I don't know, a bag of butterscotch candies or some crap."

"Fair enough, sir." His companion had shrugged. He wondered how much interaction he'd had with the Fair Folk, even in his preternaturally long lifetime.

They'd piled back into the werewolf's car, having ignored a couple of dog-walkers whose pets became oddly agitated when Conrad passed, and headed to the second most obvious place on Remy's mental list—Park Avenue. Riley's usual haunt when she picked up her "dates."

The avenue itself was less crowded than usual, presumably due to the cold and the waning of the post-Christmas shopping season. It was still New York City, though, so the level of traffic—both human and vehicular—could hardly be called sparse.

Remy snapped his fingers. "One advantage we have is that she shouldn't be too difficult to see. Her fashion sense isn't exactly restrained. You saw her at the party, so keep an eye out for a five-foot-three, twenty-something platinum blonde who looks like she stepped out of a seventies sci-fi flick or something."

"Will do, sir," Conrad assured him.

Sadly, no one seemed to meet that description. A few blonde girls and a handful of garishly dressed people were there, but no one with quite the right combination.

"Okay." The investigator exhaled. "It's time to proceed to Plan B. We get out, browse on foot, and poke our heads into any store that seems like it sells the kind of bullshit that lovesick rich guys are happy to buy for hot girls who blatantly use them for materialistic purposes."

They parked on a side street and, to work faster, each took a different side of the road and looked into shops that seemed appropriate before they emerged to signal the other.

In all cases, the answer was no.

After completing the first street, Remy motioned Conrad to traverse the crosswalk and regroup.

"This will still take too long," he explained to the lycanthrope. "She could be half a mile ahead of us and working her way forward as all we do is trail behind her."

The other man waited, probably in case his boss was about to suggest something else.

His head slumped between his shoulders. "She's obviously okay—of course nothing bad could have happened to her—but this is still discouraging. We might end up having to stake out the damn colony and wait for her there. Which would require bringing a portable space heater and a generator."

And that was only for dealing with the park, not the colony itself.

"And a metric ton of honey, to keep the little dickheads off our backs while we sit around." He brought the palm of his hand to his eyes and left it there.

"Sir," Conrad interjected, "you said she comes here often. We've only searched for a short while. If we walk around for a little longer, I might be able to pick her scent up. I remember it."

He straightened slowly. "It's worth a shot. Needing a tracker to track down a tracker... God, that sounds like some terrible movie tagline."

The werewolf was already on the task and marched down the sidewalk to the north with Remy following closely. It annoyed him to think that anyone who looked at them might think Conrad was the one in charge.

Fortunately, though, they were only on the streets for about another five minutes.

His bodyguard stopped in his tracks and made a readily audible sniffing sound. He noticed it at once and shouldered around a briefcase-toting yuppie to stand directly next to him.

"What is it?" he asked.

The werewolf nodded directly ahead. "That way. On this side of the street." He hurried on and his legs worked so fast, his companion almost had to jog to keep up.

A moment later, he stopped again, this time in front of a clothing store that looked like it mostly sold swimwear. There were a few scantily clad mannequins in the front window, and the picture on the sign even featured a Chibi cartoon woman wearing a microscopic bikini.

Uh-oh, Remy lamented. *I have a feeling I know where this is going.*

Conrad gestured to the shop. "She's in there. Or, at least, she was very recently. I'm almost positive."

"Good," he said, stepped in front of him, and pushed the door open.

Within, they immediately noticed a small group of women hanging back near the checkout desk, talking in hushed voices. Despite the low volume, there was an obvious tone of annoyance.

"I cannot believe them. Not like I should be shocked," one of the women remarked.

Remy took a few steps further in. The store stretched deeper inward than he would have guessed, and although its layout was relatively uncluttered, there were still a couple of shelves blocking his view of exactly what was going on in the back.

It involved a large crowd of people, though. That much was obvious.

Conrad sidled up. "She's here, sir. I can hear her voice. Her...uh, big voice, I mean."

He frowned. "That doesn't surprise me. Let's go make like a politician and tour the disaster scene."

They walked forth and ignored the sharp, disapproving stares of the women near the counter. He saw that the gaggle of persons at the other end seemed to consist entirely of men and also heard a few clicks that he identified as coming from a pro camera.

Once they were past the shelves, they found themselves in an open area in the rear where a couple more mannequins stood on a small stage. Various men were clustered around it and at its center, between the two mannequins, stood Riley.

The breath leaked out of his lungs at the first glimpse of her. She was, as suspected, in human form. It appeared she was auditioning to become a swimwear model—if she didn't have the job already. She certainly looked good enough to be a shoo-in.

Her current bikini was an example of the barely-there style, consisting of two pieces of fabric that, on their own, could easily have been mistaken for accessories—backpack straps or hairbands, maybe—rather than clothes.

The top was basically only a few strings attached to two small, round patches of cloth which cupped her breasts tightly but did nothing to inhibit their size or shape. The bottom, meanwhile, consisted of perhaps even less material, with a back thong that scarcely bothered to widen in front. She wore nothing else.

One of the men in the surrounding crowd, who wore a long and droopy stocking cap and had horn-rimmed glasses, sighed and shook his head. "Beautiful. Simply beautiful. The proportions and grace...such a well-designed swimsuit."

A few others held their phones up to take pictures or videos, probably intending to break them out later when they had more privacy. Still others eschewed mementos in favor of simply crowding around the stage and trying to catch Riley's individual attention with an endless stream of breathless compliments and supportive hand gestures.

The fairy did very little but soak up their attention. She moved slowly in circles and adjusted her posture slightly, occasionally striking a more dramatic pose when the professional cameraman off to the side suggested it.

The pro was an older gentleman wearing a derby hat

and armed with a fine and pricey camera mounted on a black polymer tripod. It was difficult to tell if this was a formal event with the man having been specifically hired to take pictures or if the whole event was more of a happy accident.

Conrad whistled softly. "I must say, to be frank," he whispered, "her humanoid form is aesthetically pleasing. Knowing her...ah, kind, much of it is glamour—a type of magic, not regular glamor—so it's debatable if what we see is entirely real, but it certainly..." He hesitated. "Looks nice."

"Gosh," Remy replied and didn't even try to hide the biting edge to his voice, "that's way too many words to simply say 'I'd bang her if I thought I could get away with it.'"

"Sir!" his bodyguard protested. "That isn't what I said and it isn't what I meant. Women are special creatures and must be cherished and respected. We can appreciate their appearances, but we must remember that—"

"Yeah, yeah." He cut him off. "You probably have a dungeon in your basement, don't you? Dog collars and so forth. And not for yourself. Don't try to deny it, Conrad. I know all about you and what you get up to behind closed doors. It's scandalous and disgraceful. Even thinking about it makes me sick."

The werewolf's mouth opened and closed a few times in befuddlement as he wracked his brain for a way to respond to this.

Remy used the peace and quiet to study Riley. More to the point, to observe her facial expressions, her body language, and the look in her eyes. He had an unpleasant hunch.

It was immediately clear that she was even more enraptured with the men's attention than they were with the sight of her lovely face and body. She drank it in with a needy hunger—almost a ravenous desperation—that disturbed him.

It wasn't only jealousy, although he had to admit that played a part. It was the fact that something in her whole demeanor was familiar.

He placed it after a second or two. Her face looked much the same way his own did shortly after he'd gotten high—while he was still cruising but right about the time he began to get scared, deep down, that the fun might end and necessitate another trip out to get more.

And then even more.

Once his mind made the connection, he almost jumped and tackled her. After a deep breath, he merely took a few steps forward instead.

Riley noticed the two of them. Her smile dimmed and her eyes widened, and she glanced around a little frantically, possibly looking for an escape route.

Remy decided it was time to act. "There you are. What in tarnation are y'all doing with my sister?" he demanded in a fake hick accent. The photographer and a few other men stared at him, slack-jawed.

"Remy!" the fairy exclaimed. "Why are you—"

He cut her off. "Now, you stop this nonsense right now, young lady." He caught her by the wrist and dragged her off the stage. "Ma's gonna have a few words with you for this one. Hush up and come back to the farm right now, where folks still appreciate what the Lord says about modesty and idle hands. Them cows ain't gonna milk themselves."

Conrad followed, flabbergasted, as he pulled her through the store. A few of the men who'd watched her shouted, "Hey!" and made empty threats or tried to demand an explanation for what was going on. The body-guard glared at them and gave them enough hesitation for the three to escape the store without things getting ugly.

As they hurried toward the car, he shrugged out of his jacket and draped it over her shoulders. None of them spoke. When they arrived, the lycanthrope slid into the driver's seat but Remy sat in the back and pulled Riley in with him. Conrad did not ask questions and pulled out into traffic as soon as it was safe.

The investigator stared straight ahead. He inhaled deeply.

All right, he told himself, *we're having that special talk right now, regardless of Wonder Boy being here.*

"Conrad," he said, "please stay out of this conversation. This is between Riley and me."

The werewolf nodded. "Okay, sir, I understand."

Remy looked to the side. The fae had already trans-formed into her true shape and now, her tiny body sat naked, her legs drawn up to her chest and arms resting on her knees. That she was sulking and pouting was obvious even at her current size.

"Riley," he began, "we need to talk."

"No," she replied, "you need to leave me alone."

What is she, my rebellious teenage daughter now? he wondered and tried not to get angry.

"Bullshit," he responded, although he managed to keep his tone fairly mild. "I'm looking out for you. You obviously have a problem with...uh..."

He found, to his sudden embarrassment, that he couldn't find the right words. That, unfortunately, was the result of the fact that he didn't want to admit his own problems to her, especially not with Conrad around.

She spoke before he could. "I was only having fun. And I made other people happy, too."

Remy shook his head. "You don't understand. Have you heard of..." He hesitated again, swallowed, and continued. "Addiction? Do you know what it is?"

Riley looked quickly at him and returned her attention to her own kneecaps. "You mentioned it before, and a couple of other people did, too. It's what happens when a human poisons himself and decides he likes it."

He vaguely recalled having said something like that once and wished he'd been clearer.

"Is that," she asked, "why you're acting like this?"

"No," he replied quickly. "Well, not on my own part. Listen, addiction is anything—and I mean anything—that seems like it's so much fun that you start to feel like you can't live without it. It gets inside you...like in *The Evil Dead* where the invisible demonic spirits from the Necronomicon possess everyone and cause their faces to become hideous and corpse-like, and then they start stabbing each other in the ankle with pencils."

The fairy stared at him with eyes that almost bugged out of her head. "What? I thought the Necronomicon was only a human myth. That's awful. Are you okay?"

"No—shit. Shit! No," he stammered. "Never mind.

Forget I said that. I'm fine." He raised a hand to his face and pinched the bridge of his nose.

Conrad cleared his throat but Remy resumed speaking before he could contribute.

"Listen, Riley. You need to stop spending so much time around all these...men, because it...uh, it wastes too much of your time."

Well, that sounded lame, he admonished himself. *I think I need to spend time meditating on this issue or something. I've never really talked about my own addictive problems to anyone much so I should have known I'd fumble the hell out of it while trying to intervene with someone else.*

"Time?" she inquired. "What does that have to do with—"

"I need you," he said. "As a fairy, I mean. As a helper and a friend. We still have a job to do, and your powers would definitely come in handy. Plus, you're still under contract, as per the next few days' worth of honey-roasted peanuts."

She uttered a tiny sigh, wistful and pained. "Fine."

And by keeping her close to heel, I'll be able to watch over her for any further symptoms and make sure she can't get away to indulge them.

"So," she asked, "what are we doing?"

He hadn't thought that far ahead, but as he began to panic in his haste to think of something, an idea popped into his head. A rather good and clever one, in his opinion.

"Tracking some dwarves." He adjusted his tie and smoothed his hair. "Two thugs from the cartel attacked my apartment last night. There should be numerous traces of them. If we can find out where they went, we might be able to find the rest of their Snow White and put an end to this little operation before it can cause any more damage."

Additionally, although he did not say it aloud, they had to finish the job before tomorrow. Otherwise, the terms of his bargain with Taylor would come due and it was back to boarding school with his new headmistress. He shuddered at the notion.

"All right." The fairy's voice was distant. She was resigned to her duty but her heart was still in that goddamn swimwear store.

Conrad raised his hand. "Uh...sir, I'm not sure it's a good idea to plunge into potential combat, especially since we already did that once and they're likely to expect another incident. We might end up in over our heads."

"Fear not," Remy consoled him. "We won't launch a commando raid, exactly, merely do a little reconnaissance." He coughed. "Besides, if it looks like things become too dangerous, we can always call in the big guns. Meaning Taylor."

CHAPTER SIXTEEN

West Harbor Motel, West Harbor, New York

The one disadvantage of Riley's magical tracking abilities was the simple fact that every trail had to start somewhere. In this case, the most obvious start was at Remy's apartment.

The three of them drove back to his home, therefore, so the fairy could pick up the scent of one of the dwarves who'd ambushed him the night before. The blond one who'd bled all over Remy's kitchen floor was possibly the better target.

"Eeew," Riley protested when Conrad graciously followed orders to fish one of the blood-soaked paper towels out of the trash can. "His blood doesn't smell good. Too much meat and alcohol."

"Well," Remy quipped, "when we find him, you can advise him to start consuming vast quantities of pineapple juice instead. I've heard it improves the odor and flavor of bodily fluids."

The fairy had seemed to consider this as she struggled to tolerate the pungent aroma. "Okay. That's a good idea."

Indeed, it somehow cheered her up enough that she barely complained as they trekked all over New York, retracing the steps of the height-challenged assassin.

She had been invisible to the concierge as they passed through the lobby, so Nikki only saw Remy and Conrad again. Fortunately, she didn't press him on who Conrad was. He simply hoped people wouldn't gossip too hard. Yet.

Neither man was much surprised when, at first, the trail led them north into the Bronx and toward the Port Morris shoreline. At about the same time, Riley detected a second trail going back the way it had come.

Remy held a hand up. "Okay, stop. We can tell that the little prick went back to that same shipping container and then left. We don't need to sniff our way all the way to the edge of the river. Wonder Boy, turn us around. Riley, we're now following the second trail, the one that goes the other way."

His companions had not argued. They then worked their way back into Manhattan and a tedious drive all over the island followed. Their progress slowed as traffic thickened. Rush hour hadn't been far away.

Finally, after a couple of minor detours to sandwich shops and liquor stores, missed turns, and places where the scent faded, they arrived at the end of the trail at West Harbor.

"Man," Remy complained as Conrad drove them closer to their final destination, "what is it with assholes and hotels? Those two werewolves and the vampire who plotted the coup against Taylor took over a big fancy one, and Alex holed up in a shitty one. Now, we have the dwarven mafia in a mid-grade one. I bet the next horde of pricks to show up in town will use a student hostel as their headquarters."

They were still a few hundred yards down the road from the imaginatively named West Harbor Motel, but there was no doubt that it was the right place.

Five or six short, stout forms milled around out front, and it looked like there were a few more at the side, as well. There were no regular cars in the lot. Instead, three large trucks and vans were parked there.

From what he could recall, the shorter dwarves had trouble operating human vehicles. As a result, they preferred to travel in groups with the taller, longer-legged ones playing bus driver.

A few construction signs and barricades were posted around—fakes, he guessed—to discourage too much traffic from creeping past.

"Keep going," he instructed Conrad, "and keep your heads down. Don't make eye contact with them."

"Yes, sir," the werewolf replied, "I know. I've done this kind of thing before."

"Right, of course you have. Now, turn left up here."

The deviation away from the motel saved them from getting close enough for the dwarves to examine them. Once they were confident that they weren't being followed, Conrad found a parking space a good half-mile from the water in a generic commercial area where they would not attract attention.

Remy got out first. "Okay, usual drill. Riley, magic the car so it's protected while we're away and do the same for us when we get close to the motel, only make us...uh, less noisy. You can do that, right?"

"Yes," the fairy confirmed, "more or less. But don't do anything too loud."

The men nodded and both set off toward the motel and the harbor beyond. She floated over their heads all the while.

Halfway there, she initiated the spell when no one was too close and seemed to encase them in a bubble of silvery light, which then faded and gave the sounds around them a faintly muffled quality.

A low concrete wall, perhaps three feet high, and a line of trees partially blocked the motel from the sight of the rest of the city unless a motorist came right up to it, as they had a few minutes before. Ducking low, they scampered forward and hid at the wall's base.

Riley followed, now between them at about knee height.

"Okay," said Remy, "we spend a short while waiting, watching, and listening. See, Conrad? Merely stealth and reconnaissance. Nothing too crazy."

"That sounds excellent, sir." The werewolf didn't seem entirely confident that this would be a nonviolent operation, though, since he unbuttoned the top half of his coat and rolled his sleeves away from his wrists.

Over the next ten minutes, they counted at least twenty dwarves. A few came in and out of the front office as well as some of the individual rooms in addition to those already gathered outside.

Remy couldn't hear much, but Conrad whispered to him that they mostly simply talked about beer. Interspersed with this, though, were comments that were more useful. A few mentioned how someone named Wurdegast obviously screwed up. They sounded grim on the subject. Others asked in complaining tones when "he" would address them.

"Interesting," the investigator whispered. "I say we creep closer and try to look in through the windows or maybe see what's around the back."

His bodyguard frowned. "That will be dangerous."

"Everything is dangerous," he pointed out. "Do you know how many traffic fatalities there are in this city per year? I don't, but it's probably a considerable number. Riley, create a distraction. Nothing too dramatic, merely something that will draw most of them that way—to the right—for a minute or two."

"Okay," the fairy agreed. "Right now?"

"In a minute." He turned to the lycanthrope. "Conrad, when the dwarves rush to investigate, we haul ass to the left and get between the sign and the tree over there along the side of the building."

"Yes, sir."

Nodding, he gave Riley the go-ahead. She began to move her arms to cast the spell and it occurred to him that maybe he should have been more specific, rather than leave the nature of the distraction up to her own judgment.

Marching footsteps off to the right was accompanied by the swelling music of a full brass band that played a rousing tune he vaguely recalled from his school days. Somewhere within the din was the unmistakable sound of someone blowing a kazoo.

He gawked at the fairy.

"I like parades," she stated and smiled.

"Okay," he responded, a little bemused. "Whatever."

The dwarves snapped to attention and most of them hurried away in the direction of the racket as they looked around and conferred with each other.

"Who forgot to check Google Maps?" One of them grunted. "They usually say when there's going to be a fucking parade."

To Remy's annoyance, Conrad was the one who gestured for them to move out about a second before he could himself. Nonetheless, he followed the werewolf and moved as fast as he could while keeping low to the ground. A few dwarves had remained out front, but they weren't looking in their direction.

The trio ducked behind the sign and a large pine tree loomed behind them. From there, they had a better view through a side window from which the curtains had been removed and could almost see into the back lot.

On the other side of the motel, the phantom sounds dwindled and faded as though the parade had come close but turned a corner and moved away from them. Muttering, irritated dwarves returned slowly to their posts.

The investigator peered through the window. Another five or six occupants in that room alone added to an already significant total.

"Sir," said Conrad, "between the visual scan, the sounds and smells I pick up, and an estimate of the motel's occupancy, I would estimate there is a bare minimum of forty dwarves here. Maybe more like fifty or sixty."

He groaned. "Sadly, I think you're right."

The cartel must have rented the place the normal,

legal way and used one of their magical sleep scrolls to knock the staff out and thereby ensure total privacy for their gathering. Or perhaps they owned the place, to begin with, and had closed it to the general public for the day.

More importantly, if the cartel was this large and powerful, he wondered if even Taylor could fight them all. Their prospects against these pricks and Moswen at the same time did not seem good.

Remy glanced at both his companions. "All right, let's sneak around back. It seems like there's someone there."

"Yes," Conrad confirmed, "there is a conversation between at least two, although I haven't been able to make out the words due to interference."

Another distraction would be suspicious so they simply waited for a lapse in the nearby dwarves' attention before they darted to a lamppost whose base was surrounded by bushes. Fortunately, there was no snow on the ground to crunch underfoot since most had been plowed or shoveled and the temperature had risen to a few degrees above freezing besides.

They reached the post at the same time that a general chatter went up amongst the dwarves, whose boots suddenly pounded the earth.

"Shit!" Remy cursed and almost winded himself as he dove behind a bush. He noticed the tension in Conrad as well.

The dwarves did not run toward them, however. Instead, they all converged on the back lot itself, having apparently been summoned by a verbal message passed through their ranks.

Remy peeked through an opening in the shrub and shook his head in disbelief.

In the center of the lot stood a hulking figure so large that he at first doubted it was even a dwarf. A fine charcoal-hued suit covered the broad, ungainly form and a huge black carrying-case rested at his feet.

Aside from the height, though, he could be nothing else but a dwarf. The stocky build and heavy facial features, not to mention the salt-and-pepper hair and beard, were dead giveaways.

His huge hands were wrapped around the throat of none other than the blond home invader Remy had seen last night.

"You fool!" the massive dwarf raged, his voice thunderous. The corded muscles in his arms stood out as he squeezed. "One drunken human wastrel and he spilled your blood. How dare you even show your face here again? At least your comrade took the honorable way out. Coward."

All the other dwarves present, save a few cursory sentries out front, had gathered in a ring to watch the execution. With horror, they watched as the would-be assassin's face turned an ugly purple and his eyes bulged. Meanwhile, the apparent leader towered over him and all the others.

"You had your chance, Wurdegast. Runt. Imbecile!" The giant's whole body trembled and finally, something crunched within his victim's neck. He spat blood and his injured leg, already buckling, went limp. The leader released him and his corpse sagged into a heap.

Remy tried not to cringe at the bestial wrath on the

enormous face. The guy was pissed. As he retracted his hands, the pale winter sunlight reflected on four colorful rings arrayed on his fingers.

"The rest of you," he boomed, "listen closely. I need not remind you that failure of this magnitude"—he gestured at the late Wurdegast—"will not be tolerated. Therefore, focus on your responsibilities. We have most of our shipment. It must be prepared for distribution and nothing must interfere."

It occurred to the investigator that Surrly was nowhere to be seen. And somehow, he suspected that this man's authority trumped the lender's anyway.

"Back to work, all of you," he commanded. "I must place a call to our benefactors."

With nods and grunts, the dwarves dispersed. A couple shot nervous glances at their dead comrade, but Remy suspected that most simply reassured themselves that they were not so incompetent as to share his fate.

The two watchers ducked low again and tried not to even breathe as a couple of dwarves passed the bushes. Thankfully, they kept walking, speaking in their own language now, and moved on.

When it was clear, Remy looked through the gap in the bushes again. The towering, well-dressed boss had taken a cell phone out and reclined in a large, steel-reinforced beach chair.

He pointed at the dwarf. "We need to get closer. I want to know what he's talking about."

"I can hear him," Conrad whispered sharply and made a chopping motion with his hand to indicate that he ought to shut up.

Bristling, he said no more. He was willing to make some sacrifices for the sake of the objective, after all, although he didn't like it.

Relative silence set in. The dwarf spoke in a much lower tone now, although Remy could still make out a few words—"Europe" and "profits," notably. Still, he waited, itching with impatience, for his bodyguard's report.

After two or three minutes, the leader ended the call and slipped his phone into his pocket. He relaxed in the chair to soak up the minimal rays. Cold obviously didn't bother him much.

Conrad turned to the investigator. "Bad news, sir. He was talking to..." He seemed almost nervous for a second. "To someone from the Vampiric Order in Europe. That means this is serious business. He assured them that even with the recent losses—probably the drugs you pushed into the river—they could expect record profits now that they were expanding their customer base to include humans."

Riley looked surprised, to the point that she might even have forgotten about her nascent modeling career.

"And," the lycanthrope added, "he seems to have referred to himself as 'Grayhammer.' I believe I've heard the name. It's an old, powerful dwarven family."

Remy rubbed his chin and weighed the new information.

"So," he remarked, "this whole drug operation goes beyond the cartel. However, I don't think the cartel goes beyond that guy." He pointed a thumb at the colossus in the chair.

Conrad nodded. "I'll agree with that."

Encouraged, he continued. "He's clearly the one who makes the big decisions and keeps the others in line, probably through fear. Without him around, they might collapse into infighting, at which point, Taylor could divide and conquer them into oblivion."

The fairy was silent and the werewolf narrowed his eyes. "Sir, what are you proposing?"

"That we should probably kill him," he responded cheerfully. "Now, I mean. While he's alone."

The other man looked at something beyond the clouds. "Ah...I would advise against that. To begin with, he's enormous."

Remy shrugged. "Yeah, he's big, okay. By the standards of their physiognomy, he is practically a giant. But still, it's only one dwarf. One. Conrad"—he extended a finger—"I've seen you fight three or four of the bastards at once and end up without even a scratch. We faced that entire shipping container a couple of nights ago, and..." He sighed. "Admittedly, you essentially handled those two last night all by yourself."

Conrad's eyes grew a bit distant and he seemed to be thinking it over.

"I can handle a few of them, yes," he conceded, "although, in fact, I did take several wounds. I simply regenerated them fairly quickly. Massive trauma can kill us even without silver being involved, but mild to moderately severe injuries are generally survivable."

The investigator waved his hand in a circle. "Yes, right. Survival is the goal." He turned to the fairy.

"Riley, point number two," he went on and added a second outstretched finger to the first. "You have magic.

Considerable magic, in fact. I've seen you deflect bullets, put men to sleep with a wave of your hand, absorb most of the impact of car crashes, make large objects invisible, and probably a couple of other things I can't remember offhand. That all counts significantly, trust me. It's…uh, the other reason I keep you around besides, you know, that I like you."

"Aww," the fairy chirped and her face brightened, "thank you."

"And finally," he concluded and extended finger number three, "I have, in fact, worked hard at my martial arts training, even if I had to miss a class this week due to the investigation."

Noticing Conrad's vague look of disapproval, he immediately followed his third point with a sub-point.

"Last night doesn't count, by the way, because I was impaired. Today, I'm sober again, which always helps with the whole 'being good at things' thing. I totally know what I'm doing now that my reflexes are working the way they're supposed to."

A look of resignation settled over his bodyguard's overly handsome, goateed face.

"You do make several valid points, sir. But if we can't eliminate him right away, there's an excellent chance that the other dwarves will hear the racket and converge on us. We can't fight four dozen of them at once. Perhaps if we were up in a tower with a heavy machine gun and a couple of rocket-propelled grenades, but we don't have any of those things, not to mention using them would attract police attention very quickly."

Remy nodded impatiently. "Yes, I know. It's not like I

plan to walk up to the bastard with you guys as my 'posse' and make a succession of weird circular arm motions while I insult his mother's sexual proclivities for five minutes before we fight. Quite simply, we'll assassinate this fucker."

Saying that, part of him liked how kickass it sounded. At the same time, another part recalled his past experiences with lethal violence and the nightmares it had given him. What he proposed was ruthless as well as dangerous.

But then again, the cartel had already tried to murder them.

Conrad closed his eyes and rubbed his temples. "So be it...sir."

CHAPTER SEVENTEEN

West Harbor Motel, West Harbor, New York

Remy crouched behind an empty crate the dwarves had left near the perimeter of the back lot. He glanced up first and then to his left.

Above him, Riley had camouflaged herself against the clouds and was now perched in a tree almost directly above the cartel leader's head. It would be easy to rain sleep or paralysis spells on him.

To his left, Conrad had snuck around to the edge of the harbor itself and began to strip his clothes off in preparation to enter wolf-mode. A quick sprint would bring him within killing distance of the dwarf from behind.

Remington hesitated a moment. Grayhammer gave no indication that he'd noticed them, but even in relaxation, there was a kind of savage alertness to him that was not encouraging.

He also had no idea what was in the massive black case next to the beach chair.

One dwarf, he reminded himself. *Only one. Riley and*

Conrad will have him out of the game in a matter of seconds. I simply have to distract him for a heartbeat or two.

The boss's eyes began to drift half-closed. He adjusted his position in the chair and a shaft of light glinted across the rings on his hand. All four were made of gold and each was set with a different type of stone—amber, opal, pearl, and jade, from the looks of it. The preternatural drug business must have been highly lucrative.

And now, it seemed, the dwarf paid no attention to his surroundings at all.

Remy raised a thumbs-up toward Riley. He darted out from behind the crate.

"Whoops!" he said loudly enough to be obvious to anyone in the back lot but hopefully not loud enough for the dwarves out front to hear. "I seem to be lost."

To his shock, the dwarf—whose size made him look like he'd be slow—had somehow already sprung to his feet and now stood half-crouched in a battle stance. His dark eyes blazed.

"Who—"

Riley cast the spells.

One after the other, two waves of magic surged from her elevated position. The first encased the back lot in another soundproof cocoon. The second targeted Grayhammer himself.

The huge dwarf looked up as a shaft of silver light struck him like a moonbeam falling from a suddenly cloudless night sky. He growled but almost immediately, his face broke into a hideous smile.

What the hell?

On the plus side, Conrad had shapeshifted and was already halfway across the beach.

The four rings on Grayhammer's hand flared with different colors of light and for a moment, it seemed the blazing glow of them struggled against the silvery emanations cast by the fairy. All the lights winked out at once, although the stones in the rings continued to pulsate.

"Remy!" Riley screamed somewhere above. "It didn't—"

Grayhammer cut her off with a roar of laughter. "Magic? Is that all you have?"

Remy's bowels suddenly felt a little squishy.

"No," he replied as Conrad attacked.

The dwarf pivoted with startling speed and, to Remy's horror, caught the wolf in midair and heaved him at the human.

"Oh, crap!" The investigator yelped, dropped, and rolled to the side. A dark, furry mass careened past him and the hairs brushed his back. Seconds later, the lycanthrope impacted with the frosty ground beyond him.

As Remy jumped to his feet, he tried to take everything in at once. Conrad was already recovering but they'd lost the element of surprise. Riley's spell had done nothing. She drifted down from the tree now and waved her arms, hopefully preparing something else that equally hopefully might work.

Worse, Grayhammer had opened the black case and removed its contents. His name instantly made complete sense.

The weapon wasn't much smaller than he was. A steel bar at least four feet long and as thick as the business end of a baseball bat formed the majority of it, although an iron ball was attached to the lower end as a counterweight. The head was a huge hammer, one side larger than the other and pentagonal in shape, and was inscribed with strange runes.

It might have merely been his keyed-up nerves, but Remy could have sworn the thing gave off a faint, low hum.

"You," Grayhammer rasped, "must be those fucks from Port Morris. Taylor's impotent pets. She's grown truly desperate if this is the best she can do."

Conrad, back on all fours, crept forward with his massive, fang-filled jaws clenched and drool running from them. The buzz-saw noise that issued from his throat was unnerving even to his friend. He was glad the werewolf was on his side.

Riley cast her next spell. This time, a spiraling wave of silver speckled with the various hues of the rainbow, coiled around the hulking dwarf.

Again, his rings flashed, countered it, and engulfed it. Grayhammer didn't even look at her and had apparently already dismissed her from consideration.

"Well," Remy muttered, "it looks like we're on our own, Wonder Boy."

Trusting Conrad to do the same, he charged.

The werewolf was right at his side. It occurred to him that he had no idea what to do if he reached the dwarf before his teammate. The werewolf could probably bite the bastard's head off.

He, on the other hand, didn't think any of the take-downs he'd learned would work against a man who was built like a dump truck and probably weighed close to four hundred pounds.

Despite his very real misgivings, he tried not to panic. He could always poke Grayhammer in the eyes or something.

Conrad drew ahead of him and surged at the dwarf's face. Their enemy fell back a half-step, and Remy believed for a moment that this might truly still work.

In fact, up close, their adversary wasn't that big. Maybe five-seven or so—a little shorter than him although still damned tall for a dwarf.

The cartel boss's titanic left hand closed around the werewolf's throat and his right hand brought the hammer down on his back.

The air cracked with a flash of eerie grey light. Conrad yelped horribly and hurtled back eight or ten feet while he writhed in pain. A ribbon of blood followed him and a faint, evil-looking shimmer played about the wound.

Grayhammer laughed again, although the sound was more angry than triumphant. On some level, the dwarf was furious that they'd even considered attacking him.

"Now," he rumbled, "you've seen what I can do to a lycanthrope." His gaze fixed on Remy, and he raised his war hammer. "Picture what this will do to a human. Cower!"

He almost heeded the suggestion. Instead, he turned and bolted, thankful that he'd taken a piss at a gas station shortly before they found the motel.

As he passed the crumpled form of Conrad, though, he clamped down on his panic. The werewolf was badly wounded but not dead. The hammer had caved in his front right shoulder and torn the surrounding flesh. Worse, it looked as though his preternatural healing factor struggled against whatever dark magic flowed through the dwarf's weapon.

A canine whimper transformed itself into something resembling speech. "Remy..."

He stopped and turned. The earth vibrated a little as Grayhammer pounded toward them.

Riley appeared behind him and levitated the beach chair he'd sat in to hurl it at him. He stopped, stunned for a barely a second, and spun to face the tiny creature.

"Come closer," the dwarf boomed. "By all means, you little bitch. You can't harm me. Come and find out the reason why."

Riley, instead, rocketed away in the opposite direction and was lost from sight.

While their adversary was momentarily distracted, Remy kicked a crate in front of Conrad to form a slight impediment to any attempt by the dwarf to finish him off.

That done, he ran around to the side. The water of the harbor was in sight.

Okay, he brainstormed, *Conrad can regenerate, right? Werewolves are hard to kill. He merely needs a little time. Actually, he needs a distraction.*

"Hey!" Remy bellowed, "you, uh..." He tried frantically to think of something to say that would piss the dwarf off even more and draw his attention. "You're not only a regular moron, but you're also an oxymoron! Get it? You're basically a giant midget. That doesn't even make sense."

The dwarf's thick head snapped toward him and his

long dark mane flapped in the cold breeze. "Shut up. Wretch. Motherfucker!"

Like an enraged bull, he launched toward the human and his thick legs sent vibrations through the earth with each step.

Grayhammer's fine motor reflexes were startlingly fast, but when covering any amount of ground, he was still a tad slow. That and his short temper seemed like they might be his only weaknesses.

So, Remy thought, his brain abuzz with fear and adrenaline, *I need to get out of his way before he's within arm's reach.*

He jumped to the side but unfortunately, should have waited for a half-second longer.

The dwarf had enough time to veer to his right and pivot as he swung his terrifying weapon. It passed within an inch of the investigator's neck, and cold prickles shivered down his spine as though his flesh had sensed the magic in the hammer and recoiled from it. A slight nausea also rose in his gut.

The enraged attacker growled madly at having barely missed on a killing blow as his target tumbled around the base of the tree. He was glad his MMA instructors had started by teaching him how to fall and roll.

Unfortunately, Grayhammer was already making his second attack. His weapon pounded into the tree, which groaned horribly as the wood splintered. Remy crawled— faster than he thought was possible to move on his hands and knees—to the side to avoid the falling tree but also away from the dwarf.

"Ha!" He scoffed as the trunk collapsed. "Not only did you miss me but your unwarranted attack on that big, hard piece of wood makes me wonder if you're not envious of it. Didn't you actually use the word 'impotent' a minute or two ago?"

With a roar like a bear, the dwarf swung into another assault.

"Shit," Remy muttered and ran.

Each insult or act of defiance seemed to send the huge dwarf deeper into unhinged rage. Their only hope, he knew, was to trick him into doing something stupid.

As he bolted away from his foe, he saw a truck near the far corner of the rear lot with its back hanging open. It would not, he surmised, be hard to force the truck into neutral and let it roll into the water. Especially not with a nice heavy dwarf locked in its rear compartment.

"So yeah," he called over his shoulder, "you're fairly fat and slow. I can tell that all that weight isn't actually muscle."

"Hold still." Grayhammer snarled. "Hold still and find out."

The investigator sprinted right to the edge of the truck's open back. "Hold still? That sounds like something a child molester would say. Or...uh, a really ugly and stupid dwarf."

He was running out of good insult ideas by this point, but the cartel boss was so livid that it didn't seem to matter. The dwarf roared once more and continued the charge.

This time, he told himself, *don't jump too soon.*

Remy flung himself to the ground barely in time. The dark, heavy form of the dwarf hurtled past him and thudded somewhere within the vehicle.

"Hell yes!" he cheered and moved hastily to heave the back door shut. He threw the bolt across it as soon as it closed. "Now, hopefully, this thing won't need too much of a push once it's in neutral."

The back door exploded and the leader's hammer protruded from the darkness while debris rained around it.

When his brain seemed to freeze, he smacked himself in the face. "Okay, I give up. We need Taylor to deal with this guy."

Grayhammer was already out and after him.

He did the only thing he could think of—he sprinted wildly toward the chalky, cold waters of the harbor and reminded himself that he was a fairly good swimmer. The dwarf, on the other hand, looked like he'd sink, especially with that weapon in hand. It would have been better if the harbor was frozen. That way, he might have jogged across it while his enemy broke through and slept with the fishes. But he'd take what he could get.

"Conrad!" he yelled as he ran. "Get out of here! Riley! Everyone! Abort the mission. Retreat!"

Out of the corner of his eye, he thought saw the werewolf creep away toward the bushes. He had no idea where Riley was.

Behind him, Grayhammer was gaining. He was a slower runner than his quarry but he also seemed to have unlimited stamina, whereas Remy was nearing the end of his, even with adrenaline still urging him forward.

The beach had almost come to an end. Rather than take his chances wading out and perhaps being slowed, he increased his speed for a final burst and jumped out into the harbor itself.

White foam sprayed all around him, and not far behind, Grayhammer yelled in wordless rage.

"Merciful God in heaven above," Remy shrieked. After the initial impact with the water—which was almost refreshing after the sweaty exertion of battle—he suddenly regretted his decision in a big way.

It felt as though the water was a gang of sadistic doctors who'd flayed him with scalpels and squirted liquid nitrogen directly into his bloodstream.

"Not good." He gasped, hurled himself forward, and tried to swim as far as he could before he had to return to shore. "Not good. Hoo, boy."

Still, his brain reminded him, at least it was better than being meat-tenderized to death by the least-dwarfish dwarf in New York and his hammer of doom.

He glanced over his shoulder and the agony of the icy water abated for a second as he was swamped with relief. Other dwarves had converged on the back lot, but the cartel's leader had hung back from pursuing him. He stood a good two yards from the water's edge, glared at him, and brushed defensively at his suit.

The son of a bitch didn't want to ruin his clothes, he realized. *For someone who looks like a refugee from an old barbarian comic, he's more of a stereotypical effete rich guy than I am.*

The stabbing pain and stiffness in his muscles informed him, though, that it was probably better to be effete and stereotypical than dead.

CHAPTER EIGHTEEN

David Remington's Penthouse, Midtown Manhattan,
New York

"I—wonder," Remy began and still had difficulty controlling the wavering of his voice and the chattering of his teeth, "if—continuing to fight—that huge fucker..." He paused as another spasm of shudders went through him. "Might have been—less dangerous—than going for a— swim at this time of year."

Conrad, who'd been driving faster than usual, glanced at him. "Perhaps, sir. You're looking better now, but I was afraid we might have to take you to the emergency room. Hypothermia is no joke."

He wasn't about to argue with that.

The reality was that he'd only been able to swim a short distance before he felt his limbs begin to seize up and he'd barely managed to struggle into the shallows where he could stand. He'd worried that he was still too close to the dwarves at that point but a couple of cars drove past and they did not pursue him.

Conrad, already mostly healed and having started his car, found him only a moment later.

"Sir—get out of those clothes!" he'd exclaimed.

Under any other circumstances, Remy would never, ever have heeded that particular suggestion. But when a man is halfway to death via an overdose of ice water, it changes his perspective on certain matters.

At least it had turned out that Conrad had a large blanket in the back of his car. He'd wrapped the naked investigator in it, helped him into the car, and cranked the heat up to a ridiculous degree.

By now, it had begun to work. The werewolf looked ahead at the road and sweated visibly from the temperature within the vehicle. "If you'd been out there even one more minute…"

"Yeah," Remy acknowledged. "I know. Death and—so forth, probably. Also, now that I'm—better, could you—drive slower? Don't want—a cop to pull us over—and have to—explain why I'm—naked and wrapped in your —blanket."

The man eased back on the gas. "All right, but keep a close eye on yourself. As for the police, if they did pull us over, I'd simply tell them something very close to the truth —that you fell into the harbor and we were trying to get you to the hospital. Medical emergencies are usually justified and any fool can see that you're half-frozen."

He managed a jerky nod. "Fair—enough. And—thanks" He paused for a moment, then inquired, "You're taking me —back to my condo—right?"

"Ah, yes," said Conrad. "That should work, provided your condition keeps improving."

"Yeah, yeah." He sighed. "It—will." He looked out the window. "Where's Riley? Did you—see her?"

The werewolf grimaced and responded with, "Yes, briefly. She was flying off toward Midtown. I haven't seen her since."

Remy, to his own surprise, kicked the lower part of the dashboard in front of him. The slight pain in his toes at least meant his extremities weren't totally numb.

"Goddammit," he mumbled. "She's probably off to— feed the hunger again. Stupid..."

Even thinking about that, not to mention the stress of having to deal with her problems himself, made him want to do the same thing. Images of mirrors and razors and lovely white powder floated through his brain. They slow-scrolled along with memories of combining liquor with all manner of strangely colored pills and nice clean needles.

No, he commanded himself. *Totally no. That would be approximately the worst thing you could do right now.*

"Well," Conrad suggested, "she might simply have gone home. To the colony."

"Maybe," he conceded, although he wasn't optimistic. "We'll look for her—later. First, take me—home so I can get fresh—clothes and have a cup of—hot cocoa, or something."

The rest of the drive passed without incident, and he began to feel relatively normal again. Conrad's car pulled in at the building where he lived.

"So," Remy asked, "I don't suppose my clothes are dried out by now, are they?"

"Very unlikely, sir, I'm sorry to say." His companion glanced over his shoulder at the damp pile resting on a couple of plastic bags on the floor of the back seat. "I'll bring them in, though, so you can hang them out."

The investigator put his shoes on, at least, and got out of the car. He stood awkwardly with his improvised shawl as the only thing between himself and an indecent exposure charge, while Conrad gathered the clothes. The werewolf opened the entrance door and ushered him through. He took a deep breath as he stepped in.

The current concierge on duty, Nikki, was behind the desk, attending to a four-person nuclear family who seemed to be asking about housekeeping services while they were in South Florida.

All five of them, including the two children, stopped talking to turn and stare at the two men who'd come in.

"Hello," Conrad quipped. "Pardon."

Remy trudged in silence for about two seconds.

"I fell in the harbor," he snapped. "Hypothermia is no joke, okay? He has my wet, half-frozen clothes right there, which proves what I said is true." He pointed to the bundle in his companion's arms.

As they reached the elevator, Nikki asked, "Are you okay, Mr. Remington?"

"Peachy," he called. "Thanks."

The door dinged and opened and they stepped in. He sighed with relief as the elevator ascended. For a few brief, sweet, precious moments, he almost felt like today might not turn out to have been a complete disaster, after all.

Then, they walked into his penthouse.

"Christ on a cracker!" He exploded. "What the flying fuck? Did I somehow miss it this morning? I didn't think I was that hungover."

The werewolf shook his head sadly. "No, sir, things were definitely not this bad when we left. Someone has been here since then and worked the place over."

If the fight against the two dwarven assassins last night had left the apartment looking like a couple of cherry bombs had gone off, it now appeared as though someone had detonated a respectable payload of C4.

Every piece of furniture had been overturned and all but one of his plants and art objects had been either shattered in place or hurled to the floor. Cabinets and cupboards stood with doors hanging open—or, in some cases, torn off their hinges—and their contents were strewn at random. The entire kitchen was covered with food debris and spilled garbage. The intruders had even ripped up part of the carpet.

Remy hung his head and almost struck himself in the chest with his chin. "Oh... Conrad, could you make me hot cocoa, or a cup of coffee, or something? If they didn't toss it all out the window or into the toilet or something, anyway."

"Of course, sir." The lycanthrope hastened to the kitchen and placed the bundle of damp clothes down on a relatively clear space of the counter. He noticed that the smarmy bastard seemed legitimately sympathetic to his plight right now.

No one liked to see their home destroyed.

He turned a chair over, placed it upright, and slumped into it. Right next to his feet lay a miniature copy of a Greek nude in imitation marble made by the infamous art-faker Osman, who'd also conned the Guggenheim into purchasing his Egyptian Black Cat model.

The small Greek statue wasn't actually worth much but it was nice to look at. It added a touch of class to the living room, in his opinion. Now, it lay in four pieces, broken at the knees, neck, and one of the elbows. Parts of the edges had disintegrated amidst the general chaos, so it would be virtually impossible to repair without obvious fault lines.

Additionally, the paintings and other *objets d'art*—the things that were worth real money—had also been reduced to rat-scraps and they'd broken his big flat-screen TV.

"Well." He breathed deeply. "That's it. All the rich-guy stuff I once owned is ruined and gone." Everything from his trust-fund days would soon collect grime and bird shit in a landfill.

Conrad stepped out a moment later, holding a mug filled with steaming brown liquid.

"Here you go, sir. I couldn't find any hot cocoa mix at all, but there was some undamaged instant coffee and I added sugar to it. I hope that's all right."

Remy normally preferred his coffee sugarless but today, he'd make an exception. He thanked the man, took the cup, and sipped it gratefully, still huddled naked under his blanket-wrapping like a homeless guy who'd been stripped, beaten, thrown into a drunken frat boy's trunk, and dumped out in the wilderness for shits and giggles.

His bodyguard drew up a mostly intact stool and sat beside him. "I'm inclined to suspect that this wasn't the work of the dwarves," he admitted.

"No." He finished his coffee but kept the warm mug between his hands. "It must have been Moswen's thralls. She probably worked them into a frenzy, the idea being to kill me as gruesomely as possible. When they didn't find me, they took their rage out on...well, everything I own, basically, aside from my cars and those wet clothes."

He suddenly froze and his stomach clenched. "Uh... wait. Could you check on my cars? Especially the Lincoln. I'll look for a viable outfit in the meantime."

The lycanthrope nodded and retrieved Remington's keys from his pants, then headed toward the elevator to head to the garage.

Remy stood. He bit his tongue and tried not to look too hard at anything as he slogged through the devastation toward his bedroom.

At least we now have no choice but to get Taylor directly involved in this crap. Of course, she'll find a way to make everything my fault, but once she draws the sword, we'll be able to settle the score with that fucking cartel.

He thought back to the big, ugly dwarf who'd driven him into West Harbor's deadly, frigid water. Imagining that prick's head on a plate made him feel slightly better.

Slightly.

Moonlight Detective Agency Offices, Bushwick, Brooklyn, New York

Before they'd departed the condo, it had occurred to Remington that Conrad had already gone above and beyond the terms of his contract. He'd helped him all night, even though he'd technically only been hired for daytime protection duties.

Therefore, he had decided to give him the evening off.

"Are you sure about that, sir?" the man had asked. He thought he could detect a hint of relief in his voice—he did look a little tired—but otherwise, it was merely his usual mixture of honest concern and slight condescension.

"Yes," he had stated firmly. "I have to admit, you've done an excellent job of keeping me from joining the preternatural realm as a ghost or whatever. I'll go directly to the office, though, and the sun has already set, so Taylor will be right along. No offense, but she's still top o' the food chain when it comes to kicking ass, as far as I can tell."

Conrad had only nodded and said, "As you wish. I'll be available for duty again first thing tomorrow morning."

Since, mercifully, the enraged thralls hadn't dared destroy his cars out in public, he at least still had his wheels. Thus, his bodyguard said his goodbyes and drove himself home while Remy took the Lincoln out to Bushwick.

It was well past dark when he pulled in at the office. Regular business hours would be over by now and Taylor ought to be on duty but he didn't see her car in the lot. Perhaps she had other business to deal with before she arrived.

He parked his Lincoln, stepped out into the cold, and locked the doors. Quickly, he ran his hands over his suit. Amidst the carnage of his possessions, he'd managed to find an outfit that was in acceptable condition, albeit a tad grimy and wrinkled for his tastes.

"At this rate," he mumbled, "I'll probably have to start doing laundry twice a week. Which will increase the power and water bills and make it that much harder to buy new clothes."

He sighed, wondering if this was how normal, non-rich people lived most of the time.

As he opened the front door and stepped through, he almost literally ran into Bobby, who had glanced over her shoulder as she approached from the opposite direction. A ring of keys dangled in her hand.

"Oh, Mr. Remington." She giggled, a little startled. "Ha, sorry. I was about to lock up and head home…if that's okay?"

He took her aside toward the reception desk. "It should be but hold on a minute. Have you seen or heard from Taylor yet? It's late for her to still not be here."

"Um…" the woman responded and raised a finger to her full red lips, "you know, she never showed up, or called, or left any messages. I thought about calling her myself, but I assumed she, you know, took the day off. It seems like Ms Steele is always here most nights, so she probably needed a rest, the poor lady."

"I see." His gut tightened again. It was probably nothing, but given the multitude of threats arrayed against them, he could not help fearing the worst. "Yes, everyone needs the occasional break. You may go, Bobby, and have a nice evening and so forth."

"Thanks!" she smiled. "So yeah, I guess we'll have to wait until tomorrow to see what she says about that article. Volz was going to show it to her, but he already left, too. Anyway, goodnight, Mr. Remington."

She turned, waved, and left.

Remy heaved a sigh and stared at nothing as he stood in the dimmed lights of the empty office.

"Well," he said to himself, "as long as I'm here, I might as well…do something." It took him about twenty seconds to decide what.

He walked over to the office phone, opting to use it instead of his personal cell, only to realize that he'd forgotten the numbers for both Taylor's mobile and her house. Muttering profanity under his breath, he pulled his phone from his pocket and looked them up.

Somehow, it did not shock him when Taylor failed to answer her mobile, even after two separate calls during which he allowed it to ring a good twelve times.

He sent her a text message instead, saying simply, *Contact me ASAP, plz.* Before he pressed the "Send" button, he added the word *bunkmates* on the extremely unlikely chance that she might worry about someone else having acquired his phone. Since they'd recently talked about him moving in with her, that ought to act as a clue that it was really him.

When he tried her house phone, it also rang a dozen times without an answer.

"Come on, Presley, pick up," he urged. "The old chap isn't going deaf, is he? That would be sad for someone who's technically a canine, I think."

He hung up, waited two or three minutes, and tried again. The result was the same.

"Damn." He ran a hand through his hair and debated turning on the office's coffee maker, even though it was a little late for that.

They're not in trouble, he reassured himself. *Taylor and Presley are in far less danger than I am, probably. They know what's coming and they have experience with this kind of thing. In fact, they're probably planning something or carrying out some big scary maneuver against the enemy right now.*

But what?

It's not like I would have expected them to tell me about it or anything.

He slumped into Bobby's chair and absentmindedly turned the swiveling seat from left to right as he pondered his next move.

It seemed that they'd all hit an impasse. So much important shit was going down, but there wasn't much he could really do at the moment. He hated the thought of having to simply sit there and wait for it to happen. It went against the grain to let someone else be the main player, while he merely reacted.

His right hand clenched into a fist.

"Of course," he mumbled, "if Taylor had told me what the hell her strategy was, I might be able to help. Instead, she sent me off to start a war with the dwarven cartel and locked me out of the loop with regards to Moswen."

And now, he'd been left on his own by everyone. It almost made him wonder if he was once again being used as bait.

"Maybe that's her whole ploy. She wants me to get the attention of Moswen and her underlings, then have me move in with her so that they can try to eliminate both of us at once and she springs the trap. Or something like that."

If she couldn't even bother to inform him of what part he was to play in their overall battle plans, he sure as hell wouldn't shack up at her place. She had proven that she couldn't be trusted to treat him like an adult.

He recalled, though, that they'd made a deal. While he could argue the specifics and try to get a few provisos inserted, he couldn't outright renege. Thinking about that would only make him angry enough to start flipping desks, so he forced his mind toward other subjects.

"Presley," he said aloud. "The genial old Limey ought to be able to tell me something about what's going on."

And he ought to check on them, anyway. He had almost made up his mind to drive to Harrison and try to wring information out of the butler when, to his surprise, the phone rang.

"Whoa," he exclaimed. The chair made a loud creak as he straightened it and bolted to his feet. He snatched the receiver off the hook. "Hello? Moonlight Detective—"

"Hi," a man's gruff voice replied. "I'm Officer Macchio, with Best-Kept Security at the Mall of Manhattan, Park Avenue. Are you…uh, Remington Davis?"

Oh, crap. Now what?

"Yes, I am. How can I help you, Officer?"

"Good," Macchio went on. "We didn't think anyone would be there at this hour and were gonna leave a message. See, we picked up this girl, name of Riley, making a scene and—don't take this the wrong way or nothing—acting like she's off her meds, you know what I mean?"

Unfortunately, he did.

"So," the security guard continued, "we found this business card on her and thought we'd reach out to you guys before we turned her over to the cops. She doesn't have no ID on her, so that complicates things. It seems like a mental health case, though. We didn't want to send her to jail if, you know, someone could pick her up and get her some help."

Remy sighed. This was bad but not a fiasco. "Yes, thanks. You did the right thing. If you can hold her for another...uh, forty minutes or so, I'll be right over to collect her."

"No problem."

Macchio hung up, and he quickly looked up directions to the mall in question. It didn't sound like Riley had done anything too flagrantly stupid or illegal but he still didn't want to delay.

At least I have something to do again.

CHAPTER NINETEEN

Abandoned Subway Tunnel, Lower Manhattan, New York

Taylor clutched her left arm to the deep, oozing gash on her right side. It went from her navel to her hip and had missed her spine by inches. Her right arm had also been broken, although the tingling itch meant it should be about half-finished repairing itself by now.

The tunnel was blacker than a tomb, sealed off beneath the earth as it was, and all the lights had been left to die when this part of the subway system was cast aside.

Fortunately, her eyes gave off a faint rosy nimbus as they sometimes did and cast the terrain and obstacles of the environment before her in varying shades of deep-crimson, scarlet, brick-red, and vermilion. She was used to it and able to operate equally as well in pitch darkness as she could in dim candle-glow or the bright glare of electrical modern lighting.

She staggered a few steps farther ahead. Her destination was not too far now so she ought to be there in five or six minutes. She'd staunched the bleeding some minutes before and the gash was about a quarter of the way healed.

It had been a long time since she'd been so badly wounded—and in an attack that took her by surprise, no less. She made great efforts to never, ever be surprised if it could possibly be helped.

The essence of evil, the smell and vibe of the threat, had been diffused throughout much of the city, eluding her attempts to track it to its source. And then, all at once, she had come face to face with it.

A whirlwind of violence had engulfed them both. The result was a storm of contesting energies and wills, as much a duel of claw and fang as it was of sheer physical power.

And yet, she'd survived. The whole encounter had taught her much of what she needed to know.

The chain of events leading up to this point had begun only a few hours before. Taylor cast her thoughts back to the inciting moment and reviewed all that had happened, the better to ensure that she gleaned as much information as possible.

Presley had woken her about two hours before nightfall —something he only did for emergencies or other matters of extreme import.

"Miss Steele," he'd said calmly as she drifted up from her stone coffin enclosure, "Alex has called us and he insisted on speaking to you alone. He says it's urgent."

She wasn't pleased by having her rest interrupted, but the butler had shielded her from what little sunlight penetrated into the mansion's interior as she took the call.

Alex had sounded on the verge of panic. There could really be only one reason why.

"She's on the move," he'd told her. "I can feel it. The burning—not to the point of when she tried to kill me, but my chest hasn't stung like this since you removed the brand."

"Alex, take a deep breath," the vampire had replied. "Moswen cannot harm you via the brand beyond the echoes you might be feeling. Now, tell me everything."

He'd seemed reassured and complied.

She'd hurried him through the predictable narrative of chest pains and sweaty feelings of unease—which he had peppered with not so subtle, snarky comments about his unfair duties around the office—and he'd quickly reached the point.

Images and words had flashed in his mind along with the burning sensations, things that almost resembled intentions. He had glimpsed what Moswen planned to do. Namely, she was herself on the move and her thralls were again fanning out.

"Remy," Alex had told her. "She's going to move against Remy. I kept seeing his face and a building. I think it's the one where he lives. I don't know what she plans to do with him, but I can feel her anger."

"Is she going there herself?" Taylor had asked. "If not, where will she be? It's possible she'll only send thralls to harass or distract him while she moves against me."

The man wasn't sure. There was something else he'd glimpsed, though, something that was of value. A brief flash of a sealed-off tunnel and a couple of nearby street signs. Moswen's malevolent attention seemed to be moving there as well, treating it as an avenue by which she could seek her prey.

Both fear and excitement had risen in her upon hearing that. She knew the derelict old subway system well.

She had instructed Alex to come to her house so that she could have Presley put him somewhere safe. Then, she'd prepared to go out on the hunt.

It was possible that Moswen tried to lure her into a trap and that she had deliberately sent these images to Alex, knowing he'd report them to her, to draw her attention and lay an ambush.

But somehow, she hadn't thought that this was the case. Her adversary was cunning but based on what she knew, she lacked the subtlety for multi-layered plots. It was the primeval, old-world aristocratic arrogance and entitlement of hers, the belief in her own superiority and in the primacy of brute force.

Accordingly, Taylor had driven to the tunnels, although she entered them by a smaller, less-obvious route about a quarter-mile from the sealed entrance Alex had glimpsed.

She'd worn her comfortable, multi-purpose black suit and brought only her sword and a discreet, short-barreled semi-automatic pistol. The handgun was fitted with a silencer to slightly control the sonic chaos that would result from firing it in an enclosed underground space.

Before taking the plunge, she'd thought about Remy. If Moswen's forces were after him again, she'd not make the mistake of only sending two low-level thralls. This time, her human friend could expect a full assault.

It almost irked her to admit that she thought of David as a friend—not that she would have admitted it to his face.

His original purpose at Moonlight Detective Agency had been a mixture of odd jobs, deniability, expanded daytime operations, and, of course, to act as bait for Moswen. That was all.

But somewhere along the way...

Yes, she'd realized, there was no denying it. He was her partner. And she didn't want him to end up dead as a result of all this.

He was so stubborn and cocky. If he'd only taken her up on her offer and moved in to where she could see to his protection, she'd only be risking herself in the struggle against her vampiric rival. But with his insistence on maintaining his precious independence, he was perpetually one minor slip-up away from death.

Preoccupied with these ruminations and noticing no particular aura or scent as she snuck into the black and musty tunnels, she'd been caught off guard when Moswen herself had attacked.

Taylor had realized her blunder with half a second to spare. She hated herself for having been caught that badly off-guard but it was enough time to save her life.

The ensuing struggle was as confusing and uncertain as any fight she'd been in with her struggling for her very existence against a foe more powerful than any she'd seen in a long while. She still didn't know exactly what had happened.

Not all the blood that was shed on the walls and floor of the tunnels was her own, though. Moswen had paid for her efforts.

She knew that the Egyptian still lived, but unless she was grossly mistaken, she had given as good as she got.

Both vampires were now fleeing, weakened and in pain, to recuperate, knowing they would meet again.

If the newcomer had brought her small army of thralls with her, the results might have been devastating. The fact that she hadn't simply meant that her servants were elsewhere, quite possibly pursuing Remington, Alex, or even Presley.

The situation had produced one fortunate coincidence, however. She had one ace in the hole for which Moswen had not been prepared.

The Egyptian vampire was still new to New York. This was not her home turf. For all her power and wily experience, she was still oblivious to certain things which Taylor was able to take for granted, having lived in this city for many, many decades.

For example, she had a safe house in these very tunnels.

They were the perfect place for it—almost totally abandoned and ignored by humans, private and secure, and located in the heart of Manhattan. In addition, they were not too far from any place in the city where she might have business but closer than her own home if she absolutely needed somewhere to lie low and recover.

This was one of those times. Her regenerative abilities did not operate at their peak due to Alex's warning having interrupted her rest. The sheer amount of damage she'd taken meant that she would need time before she could fight at anything above a mortal level.

There was also the disturbing possibility that Moswen's attacks were somehow augmented by dark magic or even poison. They might well be enhanced by something that made them more damaging, more insidious, and slower to heal than if they were purely natural displays of force.

In any event, she needed to lie down in friendly earth and sheltering darkness. When she rose again, she could continue the struggle.

Her steps, limping and staggered, slowed as she reached the secret door to her hidden spare crypt. Slowly, she knelt and peeled away a section of metal to reveal the hole that led to her little home away from home.

Taking care not to aggravate her injuries, she lowered herself into the opening, replaced the makeshift trapdoor, and descended into a hollowed space tall enough to stand in and with only enough room for her to lie on her back. A couple of emergency supplies in boxes rested beside her feet.

Her feet touched the ground and she winced. The worst of the pain was under control but it would take significant mental effort to sleep.

Taylor had little choice, though. Mending herself was a necessity.

She only hoped that Moswen's thralls had not managed to intercept her partner and that Remington could stop himself from doing anything too stupid until she returned to the domain of the living.

CHAPTER TWENTY

Mall of Manhattan, New York City

As Remington understood it, in much of the United States, malls were situated at the center of vast parking lots the size of entire neighborhoods unto themselves. In Manhattan, however, space was at a premium, which made him wonder why they had bothered to put a mall there, to begin with.

He hurried on foot through two levels of the over-crowded parking garage and ignored a few snooty-faced old ladies as well as derelicts and stalwart street vendors who hadn't yet been noticed and ejected by security.

Of course, the real horror show was still to come.

"Terrible, awful places," he murmured to himself as he strode across the asphalt, slick with the gray residue of melted snow. "Malls might as well have been invented by some pretentious Master of Fine Arts student for the specific purpose of criticizing American consumerism or something. And parking garages are simply terrible in general. What kind of maniac would combine the two?"

Crossing the street brought him to the mall itself. It was a broad, blocky, unimaginative structure, about as sprawling as any building could be in a place as densely populated as Manhattan. It had extended itself upward rather than outward, with two stories rather than one, as in the suburbs.

He pushed through the front doors and instantly found himself in a tall, wide corridor, blindingly lit and filled with noise and color. There weren't too many people around, though. The post-holiday shopping season was over.

"Okay," he murmured to himself, "exactly where is the security office? Do they have one of those—oh, good." He saw a map and glided over to it.

After locating the *You Are Here* arrow, he was pleased to see that the guards' office was around the corner, discreetly sandwiched between the food court and the main central hall.

A moment later, he was there. Interestingly, the office had a reception window with a slot, like a convenience store or twenty-four-hour gas station kiosk.

"Hi," he said to the sleepy-eyed young man behind the glass, "I'm Remington Davis. I'm here to pick up Riley? The girl Officer Macchio called about."

The young guard looked confused for a moment, then nodded. "Oh, right. Just a sec." He pressed a button and repeated the message through an intercom.

A moment later, a side door opened and a large Italian American gentleman in a white uniform shirt and black slacks came out.

"Macchio?" Remy ventured.

"The same," said the man. "You must be Remington Davis. Come inside, please."

Remy followed him into a bare-bones back room filled with communications devices, emergency medical gear, and a couple of security camera monitors, although it looked like the guy up front was watching the majority of the cams on his desk.

There was also an extra chair in the corner, where a petite form slumped, a blanket over her shoulders.

Macchio stood back as Remy examined the girl. She did not look at either of them and barely even seemed conscious.

"She caused a helluva scene," the guard explained. "Okay, she wasn't exactly violent or destructive, but definitely…uh, you know, irregular. I could tell something was wrong. First, we had complaints from two stores one on top of the other, then we started getting complaints from customers, as well."

The investigator frowned and kept his expression grave but otherwise unexpressive. "What was she doing, exactly?" He had a hunch, of course.

The man hitched his belt up under his considerable belly. "Based on what all the different aggrieved parties told me, she hopped from store to store, trying to…ah, get the attention of the male patrons and convince them to buy stuff for her. Of course, things started to escalate…"

"Go on," he urged and glanced at Riley. She did not react to their conversation and her pale yellow hair had mostly fallen over her face.

"Well…" The guard sighed. "It seems like it was business as usual at first—you know how some women are, I'm sure

—but then she put herself in front of guys and cut them off in the aisles, while she tried on revealing outfits in an unexpectedly impromptu fashion."

Oh, crap. Please tell me she's not looking at an indecent exposure charge.

"She moved constantly from store to store, repeated the routine, asked for comments and compliments on how things looked on her, and one of the complaints we had from the first store clerk said it seemed like she was having a manic episode. You know, bipolar stuff."

Remy nodded but held off on saying anything.

"So then she starts flirting with married guys, and of course, one of 'em's wife asks 'what the hell is wrong with you' and hits her with her purse. She runs out of the store, still wearing the tankini she'd put on without paying for it, and grabs men out of the crowd and tries to get their attention. That was when we showed up and took her in."

The investigator put a hand to his face, pinched his nose, and closed his eyes briefly. Common sense told him it would be a good gesture to show the officer that he wasn't about to argue with their conduct. Plus, it was a perfectly honest summary of the way he actually felt right now.

"The manager at that store—the one she ran out of—wanted to press charges for shoplifting, but I talked him into holding off on that on the grounds that we might have a...uh, you know, a mental health case here. I didn't say so to him, but it also seemed like a substance abuse case."

He paused and his eyes hardened. "I ain't gonna leap to any conclusions since it mainly seems like she only needs help. I gave the tankini back to the proprietor, searched her, called the number on the business card, and assumed you can deal with it. But as you can imagine, I have a job to do here—keeping order in the mall—so this kind of thing can't happen again."

"I understand," Remy responded. "Let me...try to talk to her."

He bent over and, with one hand, brushed the girl's hair aside. "Riley, are you okay? It's me, Remy."

Her face, wan and haggard, tilted upward, and her eyes focused on him. The pupils dilated when she finally recognized him.

"Oh," she whispered. "Hello."

Everything about her, at this moment, screamed bender.

He shook his head at the pitiful sight. There was no condescension in the gesture, though, no holier-than-thou judgment which he cast down upon her from on high.

In fact, he almost felt sick to his stomach, considering how many people had probably seen him in the exact same state and shook their heads with much harsher disapproval.

"Riley," he went on, "everything's okay, but you need to come with me. All right?"

She nodded.

"Mkay, then," he said to Macchio and straightened. "I'll take her home and have a talk with her. Perhaps I can get her some aid. Thank you for not turning her over to the cops and letting her end up in jail. I don't see any reason why it would need to come to that."

"Yeah," said the guard. "My sister had what I guess you could call similar problems once. I'm glad I could be of help, but make sure she don't become a repeat offender here or I might not be the one on duty." He half-smiled. "Hey, have a nice evening, okay?"

Remy nodded. "We'll certainly try. Same to you, sir."

He took Riley by the arm, raised her gently but firmly to her feet, and guided her out of the security office. Outside, a couple passing by about twenty yards away noticed her and crossed hurriedly to the other side of the aisle and reversed direction for good measure.

A rude comment almost escaped but he managed to ignore them, and the other patrons, fortunately, ignored him and the girl. He thought about offering to buy her ice cream or something to perk her up, but she still looked so tired and discombobulated that it might be more trouble than it was worth.

No, I'd best get her to the car and see what condition her mind is in right now once we can talk freely. Sugar could come later.

They exited the mall and the semi-darkness of the city night and chill of winter were almost refreshing after the hot, stuffy air of the office. He noticed a bench to their left. Very few people walked past so it seemed like as good a place as any to start.

"Sit," he told the fairy. She obeyed and slumped onto the seat and he lowered himself next to her.

"Riley," he began warmly but in a tone he knew she'd pay attention to, "are you feeling all right? If you can think straight right now, we need to talk. For your own sake, I mean."

"Oh, ah..." She half-moaned. "Yes. I think I almost fell

asleep there with that man. I'm a little better now. Only...bored."

"Well," he said at once, "there are reasons for that. Pay attention to me, okay? I care about you and I want to help you here."

She shrugged and stared at an icy patch on the pavement. "Okay."

"Right. You see...like I tried to say previously, sometimes things that are fun or that feel good can actually be... well, terrible. That's because they trick you into thinking you need them all the time. Does that make sense?"

"Some," she replied. "But they're only things. How can they play tricks if they're not even alive?"

He should have expected something like this and now tried to wrack his brain for examples that did not involve horror film references that would only confuse the hell out of her. "Uh, well, it's not so much that the thing is playing the trick, it's more like...part of your brain is lying to you. Maybe you don't believe that's possible, but it is. I know from experience."

She looked up and made eye contact. "What do you mean?"

"I suppose things are slightly different for me than they are for..." He glanced around to make sure no one was too close. "Your species but really, we're not that different. Our minds enjoy pleasurable things, obviously. Like booze and drugs, or sugar, or getting attention. We don't usually have these things all the time, so we assume that we should take them whenever they're available."

She peered at him now with genuine curiosity.

"So, when we get too much of the pleasurable thing, it's like our brain can't handle the idea of going back to not having it all the time. Even though we were doing fine beforehand—when we only had it once in a while—we start to feel like we'll die or something without a constant supply."

He hung his own head, and his cheeks and neck tingled. "That's how I used to be with drugs. It's like I needed them to escape and feel normal. I couldn't accomplish anything and I kept making a fool of myself because I couldn't talk myself into being normal and healthy again. And I'm sorry to say it, but you're having the same problem right now. With men and with the feeling you get from having them look at you and buy things for you and say nice things about you. Do you understand?"

She was silent for almost a full minute. "I think so. But I do need attention. And it's not like I'm helpless. You make it sound like I don't have any power over myself. I can stop coming here whenever I feel like it."

Oh, hell, have I ever heard that before, not least from myself.

"Riley," he retorted crisply, "you haven't stopped, even if you think you can. Please, trust me on this. You'll have to keep chasing after more and more. It will never be as good as it was the first time, so without even realizing what you're doing, you'll look endlessly for ways to make it better and better, when in fact, everything keeps getting worse. Are you happy right now? Do you feel good about what happened in there?"

The fairy stared into his eyes and some kind of understanding passed between them. After a moment, she looked away. "No." She sniffed. "But I need people to like me."

Remy nodded with a sharp, almost fierce motion of his

head. "Everyone does, to some extent. I needed to feel like I wasn't a loser. Drugs were how I tried to escape from that. But what I really needed was to do something about my life, to start accomplishing things. That's the healthy alternative."

Riley tilted her head to the side and her eyes widened again.

He sighed. "Along the same lines, what I think would be healthy for you is if, instead of coming out to these places and talking to all these guys, you focused on the attention you can already get from people you know and who care about you. Such as, well, me."

Trying not to blush and feeling a little like an awkward teenager again, he put his hand on hers and held it. She smiled at him.

"So," he concluded, "if you'll let me help you with this, I will. I pulled myself out of the same hole and I can help you out of yours."

"Okay," she said, and it seemed that some of her old sweetness and warmth was already back.

His phone chose that exact moment to buzz in his pocket.

"Oh, for fuck's sake," he grumbled, turned slightly away from her, and pulled the device free. According to his screen, the caller was none other than Alex, definitely one of the last people Remy wanted to get a call from.

He swiped the green button and raised the phone to his ear. "Remington. Hello?"

"Listen up, mate," Alex said immediately. It sounded like he was scared or otherwise agitated but tried—and failed—not to be too obvious about it. "And listen carefully, because this is important. I'm not fucking around here."

"Yeah," he acknowledged, "I'm listening carefully. Go on."

The Australian cleared his throat and inhaled before he spoke. "I'm goddamn sure you're in danger. From her, I mean. Remember back when I came after you on her orders? That was only me alone—one thrall. Of course, I was better than the other ones she seems to have picked up, but even so. She's sending a whole arse-load of minions after you this time. Believe me, it's true. My brand is burning me again and I can feel what she's planning to do. It was the same way last time I talked to Taylor. I keep seeing things from her mind. Flashes of images, stuff she's plotting—"

"Okay," he interrupted and tensed when he realized the magnitude of what Alex was saying. "I get the picture. Details, please?"

"A whole fucking convention," the intern replied. "I'd say at least fifty people under her control. I think she's sending them to a few different places, but I definitely have the impression that a good chunk of them will come directly for you."

Remy took a deep breath and rubbed his eyes. "Well, that sucks. Thanks for the heads-up, Alex. Where the hell are you right now, anyway?"

"I can't say. Somewhere secure. You need to find Taylor, though, mate. She might be your only hope at this point."

The investigator nodded, mostly to himself. "Will do." He ended the call and re-pocketed his phone.

Glancing over at his companion, he saw that her face

was still morose but in a different way and now, her jaw was set in what almost looked like determination. Her eyes hadn't narrowed but something within them had hardened.

"I heard most of that," she said in a soft voice. "They're coming after us again, aren't they? I wish we didn't have to keep fighting them but…well, it makes me think how there are more important things to focus on than…" She trailed off and gestured toward the mall.

"They are indeed coming for us." He adjusted his tie and steeled himself. "And, no offense, but this time, I think we need even more backup."

CHAPTER TWENTY-ONE

Brooklyn Heights, Brooklyn, New York

Senior Special Agent Kendra Gilmore stood with carefully schooled calm. She breathed gently but deeply while her mind worked to assess the situation and tease out every possible thing that could go wrong.

They had already eliminated most of the worst-case scenarios. And, critically, they'd narrowed it down to only this one building, with measures already in place to prevent any suspects from escaping.

The biggest problem that still remained was one simple fact—they had no goddamn idea exactly what they might encounter in there.

She turned to her right-hand man. "Mortensen," she began, "do we have the okay from Officer McLarty? I at least have the impression that he can be relied upon."

Currently, she only had access to the five core members of her team. Any more than that would have attracted more scrutiny than she was willing to tolerate right now. They were the best, but for an operation like this, it meant that they had to bring along the NYPD for backup and support.

In her experience, New York's finest were generally quite good but there were always a few potential bad apples. The FBI was also not yet ready to share all the details of the situation with the city authorities. There were simply too many complications.

Mortensen checked his personal device and nodded to his boss. "Yes, ma'am. They're only waiting on us." A compact sub-machine gun, one of the newer and more accurate models, hung on a strap from his shoulder. It was loaded and the man might well need it.

Agent Villareal caught her eye. "Do you think that other guy…I forget his name, K-something, is actually gonna pull through for us?"

She frowned. "Honestly, I don't know. But the idea is for it to never come to that, anyway. He'll be our last resort."

The apartment structure before them—one of the smaller of Brooklyn Heights' old brownstones—would have been nice once, charming and possibly even upscale since it seemed like the kind of place that would have attracted the hipster-yuppie types. But it was currently abandoned and had fallen into disrepair.

Sweeping the building would be tough. But, on the plus side, there were only two directions that anyone within might be able to escape to—the sides. The rear of the edifice lay against a high dividing wall that effectively cut off any attempt at escape on foot.

The only way to clear the wall would be to leap out of a third- or fourth-story window. The jumper would plunge into a concrete-lined drainage ditch that was halfway filled with ice-encrusted water.

Therefore, Officers McLarty and Konstantinos and the two extra cops they'd each brought with them, only had to watch the front, left, and right. And based on the layout, Kendra considered the right the most likely point of egress. Hence, McLarty was there.

Konstantinos had seemed irritable and half-distracted, in addition to the fact that he was getting old and counted the days till retirement, no doubt. He'd been given the left side, where the suspects would have to crawl out of a bay window lined with broken glass. Or break through another, still-intact window.

Kendra double-checked her pistol. It was a 9-millimeter, seventeen-round semi-automatic, unflashy but reliable. Villareal carried one too, as did Agent Mgaywa. The fifth member of the team, Agent Gennaro, carried a pump-action police shotgun.

Between that and Mortensen's SMG, they ought to have sufficient extra firepower for anything short of a small army or someone in heavy body armor. Neither of which, based on the intel, was even remotely likely.

McLarty had also promised that they could have a SWAT team with assault rifles there inside five minutes if necessary. She had thanked him but inwardly, could only think that far too much could happen in five minutes.

"Okay," she stated, "we're going in. Villareal, you take the door, Mortensen on point..." She quickly reviewed the rest of the procedure with them, and they ran one last visual check on the building via the camera drone they had hovering around the upper floors' windows.

Villareal flung the door open, and Mortensen aimed his gun and went through with Mgaywa behind him. Soon, the rest of them filed in. The lobby was clear.

Working tightly as a unit, almost a well-honed machine, they proceeded through the first floor, everyone knew their role and executed it properly. She was proud of her team. They'd been together on at least two dozen sweeps like this before and they all trusted one another. There were no weak links.

Still, with the rising tide of drug-related violence, she sometimes wondered if it was all truly worth the risk.

Technically, this was simply a missing-persons case. The likely perpetrator had crossed the New Jersey state line, which allowed the FBI to get involved. Then, something about it had caught Agent Gilmore's particular attention—rumors that a new street drug might be involved.

One of the individuals was a young man of about twenty-six named Lawrence Hull, a career petty criminal although he'd been out of trouble for the last year or so. The other was a girl of nineteen named Mari Singh. It officially assumed that Mari had eloped with Lawrence romantically and may have been in danger of getting hooked on drugs, sold into prostitution, or simply held in what would probably be an unhealthy or abusive relationship.

Kendra suspected more than that was going on, though. She already knew for a fact that there were recent occurrences in New York City far beyond what most people could imagine.

The sweep completed, they congregated around the stairwell leading up, still alert.

Mortensen nodded to her. "First floor's clear. Not a single living soul." He grimaced. "Or a dead one. Nothing at all except a few dusty footprints, which might be two weeks old by now. It's hard to tell."

The building was eerily silent. She chin-gestured to the staircase. "Three floors to go yet."

She would much rather have started on the top floor and worked their way down to flush any suspects out to be caught at ground level. The NYPD had waffled and hemmed and hawed about loaning her a helicopter, not to mention that the noise those things made could have potentially sent the suspects fleeing even before they could begin their operation.

They ascended and promptly moved through the second floor. The results there were the same. This time, however, as they finished and moved toward the stairs, she thought she could hear something up above them—barely, but definitely something.

The third floor started out equally uneventful although again, the suggestion of a strange noise lay beneath the surface of what her ears could detect. It might have been the building itself creaking as they infiltrated it or her imagination and her nerves. That had happened before but she and her team were not in the business of leaving things to chance.

"Clear," Gennaro said of his sector.

Kendra, in another room, though, had found a mostly empty syringe. A slight residue, white and faintly luminous, coated its interior. She left it where it was, for now, intending to come back and put it in a sample bag on their way out.

It was far too dangerous to even try to carry with her when combat might still be a possibility. She'd seen that stupid mistake committed before.

There was now only one apartment remaining on the third floor. She posted Mortensen at the stairwell on the off chance that someone might try to get past them and escape to a higher or lower story, while the other four congregated near the door.

When she was about to give the order, they heard something within. This time, there was no doubt that it was a voice. It was loud enough that the person making the sound could not possibly have even tried to be stealthy, yet it had a strangely muffled quality to it.

Weirdly, it almost sounded like someone trying to speak but unable to form human words.

Sharp glances passed between the operatives before Gennaro, armed as he was with the big scary shotgun, kicked the door down.

Something burst out and tackled him and the two sprawled in an ungainly heap.

"Shit!" Villareal exclaimed.

All of them sprang into action, their guns up, and barely resisted the urge to simply spray bullets in the general direction of the chaos. Three or four other forms, all gleaming with a strange whiteness, barreled out of the apartment.

Before Kendra could seize control of the situation, one of them was practically on top of her.

She fell back two steps but kept herself firmly balanced as she tried to get a bead on the fast-moving shape. The druggie who attacked her was dressed in rags.

His flesh seemed oddly bulging and chalky-looking and his veins gave off a slight radiance the color of fresh snow.

A wall loomed behind her back, and she squeezed off a single shot before the mutated attacker's fist came toward her face.

She ducked and rolled and knew the bullet had struck true because blood already ran down the junkie's chest. But a single 9-millimeter round was clearly not enough.

The man's foot lashed out, brushed her side, and jarred her off-course. Suddenly, he loomed over her, his face twisted with animalistic fury and hands contorted into claws.

A shotgun boomed and the junkie screamed and staggered aside, blood flowing from a huge hole above his hip. Gennaro stood with his weapon smoking.

Kendra bolted toher feet and gestured at the rest of the battle. "Help them."

The two of them plunged into the melee.

There were at least six or seven in total and besides the one Gennaro had eliminated, two more had fallen. But the mutants were relentless, and all five of the team were slowly driven back toward the stairwell.

The instant she had a clear shot, Kendra unloaded half her magazine into the chest and head of one of them. The woman rattled and convulsed as she fell back through the doorway of an empty room.

Beside her, another one launched from a wall and landed beside Mortensen. His SMG raised in the same moment but somehow, the mutant was quicker. The clawing, whitened hands snatched the gun and hurled it savagely against the wall. It discharged a single shot, which ricocheted down the hallway.

The two combatants engaged at the same time. Mortensen stepped in and aimed the heel of his palm toward the attacker's chin while he moved his feet to trip the enemy as soon as the blow was struck. Simultaneously, the mutant simply lunged.

The agent fell with the other on top of him and the crazed druggie seized his head to batter it against the floor.

"No!" Kendra cried, surged forward, and brought her knee toward the mutant's face. Her patella drove into the attacker's cheek and jaw and he toppled and mewled in pain. His jaw hung half-broken and teeth spilled from his mouth. He rolled over backward and somehow, vaulted to his feet, his eyes burning with primitive anger, ready to return the favor.

She raised her pistol and fired two rounds into the mutant's upper face. His forehead caved in and he toppled with a wet thud and twitched.

Gennaro's shotgun had intimidated two of them into temporarily backing away. In the ensuing pause, Mgaywa and Villareal both fired on another one and dropped him where he stood.

One of the two backing away snarled and swept in at Gennaro from an angle. He punched him in the side hard enough to make him yelp and hurled him into the wall.

Mortensen, by now, had retrieved his weapon, made sure it wasn't jammed, and raised it. He opened fire on full auto to shred his fellow agent's attacker with a dozen rounds before he stepped in to help corral the rest of them.

More shots were fired and suddenly, when it seemed

the last two of the augmented derelicts would fall, one of them seized a long piece of the splintered door and careened into the midst of the agents. He howled and swung the wooden blade around his head to force Kendra away from the others.

The second one grasped her by the throat and thumped her against the wall.

A strangled cry escaped her as the air was thrust violently from her lungs. Already, she could feel her throat and windpipe burn with pain. Her vision began to go out of focus and she'd dropped her pistol, but her left hand fell to her belt and drew her knife.

She forced herself to remain calm—even though the mutant opened his mouth to bite her throat—took a split second to think, then aim, then strike.

The blade sank hilt-deep into the man's armpit. His arm fell away from her throat and he stumbled back and shrieked in pain. She yanked the blade free and stabbed again, then a third time into the torso.

As her attacker thrashed into the hallway, Mortensen and Mgaywa both circled and opened fire. Their guns crackled and the mutant fell almost instantly.

Finally, it was quiet. All their ears rang.

"Jesus," Villareal gasped.

Kendra coughed, massaged her throat, and fought the pain back as the ability to breathe returned to her. She blinked through the tears and examined her surroundings. No member of her team was dead. Gennaro was limping, though. The strike he'd taken had internal bleeding written all over it.

"Get—" She gasped. "Medics—Gennaro. We need to—finish, fourth floor—"

Two of the cops waiting outside had already entered the building to aid them after the racket of the firefight, and they escorted the injured agent out to get him into urgent care. They also noted the bodies of the mutated junkies. A major cleanup operation was forthcoming.

Mgaywa took Gennaro's shotgun. Everyone else reloaded.

"Ma'am," Mortensen inquired, "are you okay?"

"Yes," she replied. Her voice had returned somewhat to normal by now although it was a little husky and painful to talk. "Come on."

The fourth floor was empty and for that, they all gave thanks to whatever powers they might have believed in. One fight with these...people had been more than enough.

Soon, the flashing lights of even more official vehicles glowed outside on the street as body bags and cameras and first-aid kits were brought in. And, of course, someone located the discarded syringes and bagged them for analysis.

Leaned against a wall for a moment's breath, Kendra wiped some of the blood and sweat from her face.

This was not the first time they'd seen this. Only two days before, they'd tangled with another ill-fated junkie who shot himself up with this awful shit, and he'd been almost as violent and deranged as these. With five against one, they'd assumed they could take him alive, but he had jumped out a window and broken his skull and spine on the pavement below.

She only thanked God that it hadn't happened some-place crowded.

But things were getting worse already. This was the first time they'd been outnumbered. And either the potency or the quantity of the drug was greater today than anything they'd encountered previously.

Snow White was in the early stages of becoming an epidemic. It had spread upstate, into New Jersey, and prob-ably into Connecticut as well.

Kendra Gilmore had seen some horrible things in her time, but this essentially took the cake. She could almost understand why some people had begun—unwisely—to whisper that the drug was supernatural in origin. Almost.

More likely, it contained an obscure bioluminescent agent that caused the odd glow or maybe even a radioac-tive isotope. Some poor bastards would put anything in their bodies if they thought it'd get them high.

Snow White's bizarre nature reminded her of what she'd heard previously about how agents of Moswen Neith's crime syndicate had, it seemed, augmented their physical abilities with the use of experimental drugs stolen from the Israeli government.

They didn't have the evidence yet but she would not be surprised in the slightest if a link between the two turned up.

"She'll pay for this," she said through gritted teeth. A paramedic glanced at her but continued his examination of Mortensen.

Agent Gilmore, for her part, pulled her phone out and relocated to a side room, where she could have a little more privacy to talk to one of her contacts.

Taylor, however, did not answer the call.

"Where is she?" Kendra wondered. "She hasn't replied to anything lately." She looked out the window at the lights twinkling all over New York's myriad buildings and wondered how many other drug houses were convening groups of addicts to commit mass suicide.

The agent turned away. For all Taylor's reputation as someone who looked out for this city, she'd made herself awfully scarce while the whole town seemed to be falling to shit.

CHAPTER TWENTY-TWO

A Hidden Location

Her servants, so gratifyingly numerous now, milled around and cringed and chattered amongst themselves in barely contained dread. They could feel the power of her pain and anger. For the moment, she ignored them.

Moswen walked as normally as she could. Taylor had torn a large strip of muscle from her left calf, which made it difficult. There were also deep, gouged bites in her neck and ragged slashes along her chest, back, and arms.

The smaller, younger vampire may not have possessed Moswen's great strength, old-world wisdom, or intimidating bearing of regality, but she had fought with the ferocious tenacity of a cornered animal.

She would never have admitted it out loud, of course, but she had underestimated her opponent. Stupid beasts could sometimes make dangerous foes. Taylor was an animal, one which Moswen was now, more than ever, determined to hunt and kill.

One of her thralls, a female collected from a homeless

shelter by two other thralls, crept forward, fearful for herself but also legitimately concerned. "Mistress, are you all right?" she asked and her hands trembled over her chest.

Without looking at her, the vampire slapped the back of her hand gently against the woman's face. She fell back, whined from the force of the blow, and tumbled over her own feet, the side of her face an angry red.

"Do not speak to me," she said, "without being spoken to."

She continued toward the velvet-covered couch which her servants had brought for her and reclined slowly on it. Her wounds had healed enough to where, at least, she would not bleed all over the cushions. Although the thralls could steal another couch with clean cushions if need be.

Centuries of experience kept her from giving in completely to her fury. There was no legitimate reason why Taylor should still be alive. Not only was she a lesser vampire in general, but Moswen had the advantage of surprise. At least, in the immediate sense. Taylor had been prepared for something, and she had clearly taken measures to ready herself for combat.

Still, the Egyptian realized, she ought to have had servants with her rather than assume that victory would come easily, even in a duel. She'd not make that same mistake again.

She felt her wounds healing, her ancient body mending its tissues and replenishing its limitless vitality, as she gazed around the dark halls of her domain. Soon, she would have a proper golden palace again. As she had long ago in the land along the Nile.

Once her current problems ceased to exist.

If there was to be a name to her pain, it was Alexander Thomas, her wretched, treasonous former slave. She had graciously spared his miserable life in exchange for his servitude and total loyalty. In return, he had entered into the employ of her nemesis at the first available opportunity.

Now, the residues of Moswen's dominance persisted and allowed him to warn Taylor when his erstwhile mistress was on the move or otherwise contemplating some major action. It was intolerable.

She could, perhaps, have mitigated the effects of this by controlling the volume and intensity of her thoughts and feelings. But why should she? She was born to rule, a superior being. That she should be afraid of a human and his new sapling of a vampire mistress was absurd and insulting.

No. Instead, she would simply remove the problem. Soon.

It was only a matter of time until she caught up with Alex once more. And when she did, he would have considerable time in which to realize how much wiser it would have been to accept death as the punishment for failure. Killing him via the brand's power would only have cost him a minute or two of agony. He would learn to yearn for that once he discovered all the punishments for betrayal.

Simply sensing her mood and her needs and requiring no verbal command, two of Moswen's thralls brought her an urn filled with fresh blood they had collected from people of no great importance. The thralls themselves were people of some importance. One was a moderately successful local businessman and the other an up-and-coming athlete.

The vampire accepted the urn without comment. The thralls bowed and withdrew.

Feeding quickened the healing process. She drank with a long, slow draught that gulped deeply of the crimson fluid but gave no sign of desperation. Her slaves could see her anger and even her pain but she would never allow them to see her fear or dejection or abasement. Always, she must project an image of power to her inferiors.

As the blood electrified her senses and brought with it a deep feeling of satisfaction, she turned her thoughts again to the fight she'd departed.

Taylor had fled. Put to the test, she had turned and run. Moswen herself had meanwhile recognized the wisdom in regathering herself to plan for the next phase of the battle.

Her fangs seemed to extend and her eyes burned with hatred as she pictured her enemy and the bloodied and pathetic condition she must now be in. She wanted to continue the fight, to hunt her adversary and complete the task of destroying her utterly. The upstart deserved nothing less.

But cowards were good at nothing if not fleeing and hiding. Taylor's degree of speed and stealth were respectable enough. She had escaped and now, Moswen did not know where she might be.

She expanded her mind and reached out to all her thralls, seeking to see what they saw and know what they knew. There was a chance that one of them might have something that could lead her to her foe.

Her servants were many, spread throughout society,

and well-positioned to provide information on every aspect of New York's corner of the strange civilization that dominated this continent.

Merchants, teachers, doctors, artisans, and politicians had joined her ranks along with vagrants, drunkards, prostitutes, and thugs. She had, by now, acquired at least one thrall in every major institution she could find—not only in the city but throughout New York State. Each new one she took increased the bank of her knowledge that much more.

All were now aware of her call and her attention. Silently, she heard the voices of those who were not physically present.

Yes, mistress? a woman called Farwell, a bank vice president, asked.

Yes, mistress? responded a man called Hull, a thief and sometime trader of illicit goods.

Yes, mistress? Ramirez was a tough woman and the proprietor of a store that dealt in technological innovations.

Yes, mistress? Wen, a city councilman, replied quickly.

Yes, mistress? Sheandra, a locally popular singer, had been a valuable find.

Yes, mistress? A man called Aronski, a sergeant in the New York National Guard, was particularly useful.

And there were so many others.

The thralls who stood now in the chamber had all gathered around her couch and she could hear their voices with her ears as well as her mind.

Yes, mistress? they asked in unison.

She paused, drank in their total attention and fearful

reverence, and assumed the full dignity of her station before she addressed them.

"We must move against Taylor's allies and pets," she proclaimed. "Taylor herself is not within our immediate reach. But she is weakened and vulnerable. She will emerge from hiding only to find that she has no friends left, no one still alive who can help her. Then, she will be next."

Meek nods went around the group, and those who were not there in body broadcast their submission to her will.

"Find this man Remington," she went on. "Wherever he may be. Kill anyone who is protecting him but bring him back alive. I want him to spearhead the attack against his pitiful keeper in my name. She will feel the sting of betrayal before I rip her heart out."

West Harbor Motel, West Harbor, New York

"Weak?" Starik raged, his voice loud and ragged. "Does this look weak to you?"

His foot descended onto Mordhem's head, cracked the skull, and collapsed most of the face.

"Does this? Does this?" he continued and trampled the hapless victim again and again. Mordhem's arms flailed, his hands grasped, his legs kicked, and his torso bucked. His head, though, simply fell apart into wet pieces under the force and pressure of Grayhammer's boot heel and the weight of his massive body behind it.

The other cartel dwarves—all of them—watched in stoic yet discomfited silence. In a few more seconds, it was mostly over, Mordhem being well past dead. Their leader had begun to calm enough to regain his self-control.

His nostril's flared as he sucked air in and released it between clenched teeth. As he imposed his iron will on his fury, his hands opened and shut, from fists to widespread fingers, and back again. He straightened his posture and looked up and out at his subordinates.

"Does anyone else," he inquired, in a low, raspy voice, "worry that we will be seen as weak merely because one human was able to escape from us?"

Most of them did not and showed that their opinions were correct by shaking their heads, commenting, "No, no, of course not," waving their hands in magnanimous gestures of support, or simply muttering in ways that sounded right.

There was not a single dissenter among them. That made Starik feel slightly better.

He had pegged Mordhem some months previously as the type who might, under the right circumstances, make a play to supplant him as the leader.

The type who thought himself cunning because he could insert snarky comments into the discussion at inopportune times. He thought himself tough because he could easily beat up feeble creatures like gremlins, humans, and elves. The type who, in short, was a potential troublemaker.

And so he had not been surprised when he had stepped up to challenge him and suggested with his impertinent remarks that Grayhammer had somehow failed them by refusing to eliminate Remington and his allies.

But Starik was in no mood to tolerate such idiocy.

Mordhem was not a large dwarf and he'd succumbed easily. Now, he'd served the cartel better as an example than he ever would have as a leader.

He cast his gaze over his assembled troops. "All of you know well," he proclaimed, "that if I allow an enemy to escape, it is only to save us from discovery or to allow him to lead us to other enemies, that we might destroy all of them at once."

Again, nods and murmurs of unanimous assent followed. His bodyguard of Gray Dwarves, seeded amongst the rabble, were the loudest and most enthusiastic in affirming his statement.

"Now," he continued, "that is exactly what shall happen. We know much about these vermin. Surrly, inept fool that he was, gleaned a great deal of information about this Remington character, as well as about his employer, the great and mighty Taylor Steele."

He flexed his hands and the moonlight glinted on his four rings.

"Already, we have driven the human from his home. He'll not return there. No, instead, he will seek safety with his mistress. And as it so happens, we know that Taylor has commandeered the use of a neglected subway system beneath Manhattan. If she is not holed up at her estate, she is likely to be there."

Starik had convened the entirety of the cartel's enforcers. That meant fifty dwarves besides himself, now that Mordhem was no longer available.

"Every one of us," he insisted, "shall participate in this fight. Taylor and Remington have insulted us, far beyond what may be forgiven."

Even thinking about it made him want to hoist his war hammer and knock down half the motel while he imagined that each shattered piece of wood or plaster was one of the bones of his enemies. Instead, he resumed his speech.

"As all of you have had your honor impugned—almost as much as I—so too shall each one of you contribute to our revenge. We hereby declare war and shall crush, hack, trample, spit on, render unto nothing more than shit every living creature in Taylor's employ."

He fantasized briefly about how the dwarves of the future would think back to this. Perhaps they would tell stories about how the mighty Grayhammer led his men to retribution and victory against the vampire who had supposedly controlled New York.

"There must be no mercy, no hesitation, no restraint in the obliteration we shall wreak upon—"

His phone rang. Very few had the number, and it took a tremendous effort for him to not simply fling the ridiculous device into the harbor. No, as a respected leader, he had a responsibility to respond to important calls.

He raised his huge hand to excuse himself, slipped the phone out of his pocket, and turned away from the gathering.

It was his contact with the Vampiric Order, of course.

"Yes. Grayhammer," he said crisply.

The voice on the other end, slow and bearing the characteristic accent of those undead who reigned over the Balkans, did not even bother to start with formal pleasantries.

"We have heard, Grayhammer," the man almost sneered, "that you are declaring a vendetta against Taylor

Steele. May we ask why you have not consulted with us on this matter before reaching your decision?"

Starik's jaw clenched. "It is no concern of yours," he stated.

"On the contrary," the voice retorted, "it is of utmost concern. Taylor is a fixture of New York City. She is something you are to work around, not against. We thought you knew this. You are to cease this feud immediately and make peace with her."

"What?" He almost crushed the phone. A crack appeared in the screen.

"Do not pretend that you are deaf, Grayhammer. You heard me clearly. Already, the strife between your cartel and her organization has affected our profits. Human law enforcement is becoming involved. Open war between the two of you would be a financial disaster. You are to negotiate terms as soon as possible. Is this clear?"

He grunted.

The vampire continued for another minute, essentially restating what he'd already said, and peppered it with a few thinly veiled insults of the kind vampires loved to bestow upon what they regarded as lesser beings.

"Your instructions are unambiguous," said the representative in conclusion. "I need not remind you that, if you should disobey us, we—"

Starik threw the phone onto the pavement amidst the ruins of Mordhem's head and gave it the same treatment. His foot stamped four times, then five, and ground the stupid little device into nothing more than plastic dust and shards of cheap metal.

His head snapped up, and his eyes were almost crazed when they locked with the collective gaze of his troops.

"You are all to forget," he ordered them, "that any such call as this ever took place. It never happened. We move forward. Understand?"

"Yes!" his Gray Dwarves bellowed as one. "Hail, Grayhammer!"

"Hail!" the others echoed.

Their leader allowed himself a savage grin amidst the churning storm of his anger. Then, to better prepare for the slaughter to come, he reached into a small, secret compartment within the case where he stored his hammer. From it, he withdrew a syringe filled with glowing white liquid.

"My lieutenants," he announced, "I leave the details in your hands. As your leader, my first responsibility is to fight bravely at the very front of the battle."

He inserted the needle into his arm, knowing that soon, he would have difficulty thinking of anything except killing.

"Tonight..." He snarled as the ivory liquid entered his bloodstream. "New York becomes ours!"

No one disagreed.

CHAPTER TWENTY-THREE

Taylor's House, Harrison, Westchester County, New York

Remy pulled the Lincoln up to the broad part of the driveway before the estate's garage. The gate had been closed and he'd opened it normally. Nothing else seemed amiss thus far.

But, of course, there had been no response from Taylor or Presley any of the four times he'd already tried to get hold of them.

"Well," said Riley from where she reclined in her true form on the dashboard, "I don't smell anything strange. Maybe a human nearby or one was here recently, but that's all. No dwarves and nothing evil. Moswen and her servants have a special stink to them."

He frowned as he withdrew the keys from the ignition. "That sounds about right. Well, it's good to hear, but I'll rely on my eyes as the final authority." He climbed out of the car and the fairy drifted out after him before he shut the door and locked it.

When they approached the house, the butler did not

open the front entrance for them. He opened it himself, instead, with his key. Riley hovered over his shoulder, ready to deploy defensive magic if necessary.

The door swung inward into silence. He stepped through.

"Hello? Presley? Taylor?" It was dark now, so the vampire might reasonably be present.

He thought he heard a footstep somewhere farther down the hall. Somewhat wary, he strode through the foyer, turned right, and braced himself for potential combat as he turned into the sitting room.

The old butler stood there, holding a can of furniture polish in one hand and a dirty rag in the other, his face set in its usual morose, almost bored calm expression.

"Mr. Remington," he said calmly. "It's so nice to see you. Is anything amiss?"

Remy exhaled and adjusted the cuffs of his sleeves. "That's supposed to be my line, Jeeves. So I'll be rude here and respond to a question with a question. Is anything amiss? You tell me."

"Not to my knowledge," said Presley. "So far, at any rate."

"Well," he interjected, "we have reason to suspect that bad shit is afoot. You know, serious business. Where's Taylor?"

The old werewolf's mouth tightened somewhat. "Miss Steele is not present." Noticing the way he started forward and prepared to open his mouth, he quickly continued.

"And before you ask, sir, I'm afraid I don't know where she is since she did not say. May I ask exactly what you believe is going on?"

Relief and frustration mingled. He was glad nothing was blatantly wrong, but there were still too many unanswered questions for his liking. Too many hazy gray areas that might turn out to be disasters waiting to happen.

"Well," he began, "Alex called me and told me that his Moswen-sense was tingling and that we'd better expect some kind of major attack. And, to properly ice the cake, we...uh, failed to remove the dwarven cartel's leader as a threat, so it's highly likely that he'll be back for revenge post-haste."

Riley raised a finger. "Oh, and Conrad went home for the night," she added.

The old man set his cleaning equipment on an end table and ushered them out toward the foyer, talking as he walked.

"Yes," he remarked, "we received a similar call from Alex ourselves. Well, neither he nor Taylor told me the details, but I surmised that it dealt with some activity of Moswen's. And I was aware that the dwarves were displeased with us, but this still sounds like a most disturbing development."

"To put it mildly," Remy concurred. Despite his agitation and his desire to do something, he forced himself to sit in his usual chair. "Taylor might be in danger, not to mention we are definitely in danger, so a reunion with her would be advantageous to all of us. She seriously didn't say where she was going?"

Presley sat across from the younger man and spread his hands in a gesture rather like a shrug. "She does this occasionally, sir. Usually when she's engaged in some kind of espionage and wishes to leave no loose ends. Before departing, she told me cryptically to watch the house, to take no calls, and to receive no visitors for a few days until she returned. I did as requested—minus the exception of allowing you to enter, of course."

Remy's hands went to his tie. "I see. Where's Alex?"

"At an undisclosed location, albeit nearby. I can fetch him if need be, but for his own safety, it would be best not to." The butler grew more attentive to the situation although he still tried to hold back from sharing Remington's concern.

"Well, Presley," he snapped, "Moswen, whom Taylor has been locked in this little Cold War with for a while now, is now on the verge of heating things up for a full invasion. And the cartel head, this Grayhammer guy—the biggest fucking dwarf I've ever seen, and who happens to be immune to Riley's magic—is also gearing up to wipe us out."

Presley nodded, alert but neutral.

"If," he went on, "we don't rejoin Taylor, all these sons of bitches will soon be able to divide and conquer us. Or one faction will kill us while the other overwhelms Taylor. If we're especially unlucky, they might even ally with each other and attack us with a pincer movement. We need to do something, even if she said not to."

The butler raised a hand to his chin and his eyes went distant for a moment. Finally, he stood and seemed much younger and fitter than he had mere seconds before.

"You're right, Mr. Remington," he admitted. "At the very least, we should be aware of Ms Steele's whereabouts and condition."

"Yes!" Riley interjected. "I couldn't do anything to that

dwarf. He had four rings on his hand that were enchanted with very old, powerful magic and a hammer that was bewitched with something even worse."

The butler nodded. "I know of a place deep in the city where Ms. Steele sometimes goes when she needs to lie low for a time. I'd wager there's a good chance she has gone there. Let us make ready to depart and I will personally escort you."

Remy stood and smiled. "Now, we're talking. I always knew you had it in you. When was the last time you went out on the town, anyway?"

"Oh," said Presley, "the last time I had to drive you out of trouble, I believe."

Abandoned Subway Tunnel, Lower Manhattan, New York

"So, Wonder Boy," Remy inquired and smacked Conrad nice and hard on the shoulder, "it's good to be back in the field, isn't it? You had what, a few hours to relax? I hope you got some sleep. We all appreciate having you here as backup muscle, though, really."

The man half-smiled in a way that looked slightly forced. "Thank you, sir. I...ah, was able to rest a little. Technically, I am working beyond what I was contracted for, but we can always discuss overtime pay with Taylor later. After we find her."

"True that," he replied, although he almost winced. He'd have to find out if Taylor was paying the werewolf out of her own pocket or from the agency's budget. It seemed important since, after all, the company was what put money in his pocket.

Still, Conrad had more than earned his fee.

Presley turned his head in his direction. "Do please keep your voice down. Conrad and I can hear well enough to know when someone is coming in time, but it would be better to converse at a lower volume."

"Oh, right." He drew his hands back to his chest and pretended to look abashed. "So sorry."

They walked on between the rails of the old subway. The only illumination came from a faint orb of soft silver light that Riley had conjured and kept afloat ahead of them. It was entirely for the human's benefit since she and the lycanthropes had no trouble making their way in the dark.

Once Remy had prevailed upon Presley to join them, they had all agreed that it would be wise to pick up Conrad on their way to Taylor's safe house.

"It helps," he had pointed out and coughed under his breath, "to have you along, Jeeves, since that way he knows it's really serious. And not only, you know, me being an asshole or something."

The old man had offered no objection to this logic. "Mm, yes, quite right, sir. He has worked very hard lately to keep you from death."

Once they'd procured an electrified baton for Remy to use as a sidearm, they had driven to the younger werewolf's residence to cajole him into accompanying them. It would be, hopefully, one last extra job before things calmed again.

To his relief, Conrad's townhouse turned out to be on the Upper East Side, virtually on the way to Lower Manhattan. He'd been afraid that the Ivy League bastard might live way the hell out in the Hamptons on Long

Island or some such place. They didn't have that kind of time.

The lycanthrope had answered the door in a blue bathrobe and looked like he was about ten minutes away from going to bed. Presley had taken him aside and after only five minutes of quiet discussion, he'd dressed and followed them in his own car.

From there, they'd proceeded to the edge of China-town, parked a block away from the semi-hidden entrance to a system of abandoned subway tunnels, and slipped in when no one seemed to be looking.

At first, he had been tense and kept his hand on the shock-baton dangling from his belt. He expected an ambush at any moment. Or, worse, to stumble across Taylor's corpse.

Presley had noticed. "Patience, sir. We have a good half-mile to go yet, at least, and one or two twists and turns to navigate. I can detect her scent in this direction, which obviously suggests that she was well enough to continue."

"Okay, then." He had shrugged and breathed deeply. "If you say so."

For a few more moments, they'd proceeded in silence. Now, already, the quiet had grown uncomfortable. The tunnels weren't overly narrow—they'd been designed to accommodate a train, after all—yet the stuffy air and oppressive blackness all around them instilled a sense of claustrophobia beyond anything he was used to.

The only question is whether I should continue to harass Conrad or, instead, should I ask Riley how she's doing and go from there? I doubt I'll get much verbiage from either of them, but anything would be better than all this quiet.

He was about to speak when Presley beat him to the punch. It took a second to realize that the old butler was addressing Conrad.

"Mr. Warfield," he began, "if I may ask, what is your assessment of the freelancer lifestyle? I must say I'm curious how well it agrees with you at your present age."

Conrad chuckled before he answered. "And I must say it agrees with me quite well. I'm not that young anymore, of course, but it's still nice to not be completely tied down yet. I feel that my skills are well-established and that I've cultivated a decent professional reputation at the same time. Finding work has not been too difficult."

"I see." The old man nodded gently as he continued to lead them through the rusty, sepulchral depths. "That is pleasant to hear, although if I may be so bold, I might suggest you consider a different course of action soon."

"Oh?" The other man was politely respectful to his elder but sounded a tad skeptical.

"You see," Presley elaborated, "while the education we receive from the academy is perfectly well-suited to free-lancing, in truth, it is geared toward long-term, gainful employment because centuries of experience have taught us that this is the most beneficial outcome."

Remy found his curiosity piqued. "The academy? Is that a euphemism for what we call 'higher education,' or is it some kind of werewolf thing?"

Conrad glanced at him. "It's a werewolf thing, sir."

"Ah." He wasn't much surprised.

The butler resumed his spiel. "Once a young man has had the opportunity to travel and gain experience, there comes a time when he's no longer quite so young and what his soul really needs is meaning and connection. For us, the best way to achieve this is to put roots down with a master or mistress as I have done with Ms Steele."

"Well," said Conrad, "Taylor is all yours. Perhaps I'll consider it, though, if I meet someone else."

Remy realized that he still knew next to nothing about Conrad's juicy former affair with Taylor. Part of him didn't want to know, but he couldn't help at least wondering if traces of their old feelings still remained.

It could affect our work, he told himself, confident that this was the sole and only reason for his interest. *And the way things are going lately, I might not have another chance to ask.*

"So," Remy interrupted, "about Taylor. You guys were in an...intimate relationship, right? That's what you told me the other day. It came as something of a surprise. How would you say that affects your current...uh, course of action?"

He was legitimately curious about this, but if asking the question in front of Presley and Riley embarrassed Conrad, he didn't actually have to answer it.

"Oh," the man replied, "ah, yes..."

He realized that he'd caught the lycanthrope off-guard. However, neither Presley nor Riley seemed to react much. It occurred to him that the butler probably already knew about this, given how long he and Taylor had been acquainted.

Riley, meanwhile, merely looked tired. She was likely saving her strength for whatever lay ahead and couldn't be bothered with drama right now.

The werewolf found his voice and came up with a

proper response to go with it. "Well, what happened between us was never anything too serious, to be perfectly frank, and...ah, it's over now, anyway. I suppose we might qualify as 'old friends' but my business with her, and by extension with you, is strictly professional at this point."

Presley nodded. "That is the impression I had. It is useful to be able to remain professional, young sir. Never lose that quality if you can help it."

Remy suspected that Conrad was mostly telling the truth but he couldn't be certain. Again, the image of the two of them together physically threatened to manifest in his brain, and he shut it down quickly.

"Well," he went on, "Taylor never struck me as the romantic type, so I was a little surprised to hear about that. You didn't break her heart and make her like she is now, did you? Isn't there an old Pat Benatar song about that sort of thing?"

"No," the man stated. "Again, it was some time ago. And there truly wasn't much to it, sir. A brief fling, is all. Those kinds of things happen. Whatever minimal feelings that either of us might have had have dissipated since then. If I'd thought there were still emotions involved, I would not have agreed to this job."

Remy cocked an eyebrow. "Okay, then. I believe you, actually." He did, too. For all his overly well-mannered way of speaking, he did not seem the type to outright lie about things.

"Thank you," was the lycanthrope's only response.

"Yes," Presley added, "the ability to remain objective is absolutely paramount if an academy graduate expects a truly successful career."

The investigator began to examine the details of the subway's floor as his attention waned. A dull conversation between two werewolves about institutions and concepts he'd never heard of could only hold his interest for so long.

His gaze wandered to Riley. Although she had kept pace with them and maintained her orb of light, something about her was noticeably droopy.

Her wings flapped in a halfhearted, slow manner, and it seemed she constantly sagged in midair and had to correct her trajectory to keep from sinking toward the floor. Her arms dangled and her head hung.

Like Conrad—and, for that matter, Remy—she'd had almost no time to rest since the day's earlier search and the fight with Grayhammer, not to mention her subsequent bender.

And since he'd taken her away from the mall, no one had paid much attention to her.

"Riley," he said.

"Yes?" She perked up a little.

"I wanted to say thank you for helping us out, even when you could probably use a break," he continued. "I mean that. Also, you look tired. Why don't you ride on my shoulder for a while instead of flying? It won't be a problem."

She smiled, less brightly but with more warmth than usual. "Okay." Her tiny form fluttered and landed above his right arm, then leaned against his neck. "You're very comfortable, you know."

He smiled. "I do know, thank you very much."

Five minutes passed, during which their conversations trailed off and ceased altogether. They passed through an intersection in the tunnels and cut across a platform to another tunnel. It ran parallel at first, then curved gradually away in another direction.

Trepidation began to rise slowly in all four of them—an urge to know exactly what had happened and to move on with the next step in the process.

Suddenly, both lycanthropes stopped in their tracks.

"Whoa," Remy exclaimed when he almost walked into Conrad's back.

The young werewolf ignored him. The older, meanwhile, had dropped to his knees. The investigator stepped around Conrad and squinted at the floor as Riley brought her light-ball around to illuminate it.

His mouth fell open. They'd stumbled into what looked like the aftermath of a low-level terrorist attack.

A section of the metal rail had been ripped up from the floor and was twisted halfway into the air. Dust, pebbles, and general debris lay in heaps. It wasn't difficult to see where it had come from as long gashes and spiderweb cracks scarred the walls.

There was blood everywhere. Even he could smell that it hadn't been spilled long before.

"Whose blood is this?" he asked.

The werewolves were already sniffing around. The butler stood. "Some of it is Taylor's," he stated. "Not all but some. She may be badly injured. We are not far from her sanctuary. We must hurry."

Remy had no objections to that. Taylor could take one hell of a beating but it looked like someone had butchered a couple of cows there. Whatever had happened, it couldn't have been good.

They picked up the pace to a fast trot, almost a jog, and he gave silent thanks that he'd been getting in better shape. Of course, Conrad quickly pulled out in front and, surprisingly, Presley wasn't far behind.

Riley offered a comment as he hustled along. "Some of that blood smelled really bad."

"One of Moswen's servants?" he asked.

"Maybe. Probably?" The fairy wasn't operating on all cylinders, so her senses may have been dulled.

For a moment, the two men slowed when there was a rumbling vibration somewhere up ahead.

"It's only a train in another tunnel, or perhaps a truck up above," Conrad suggested. He pressed on and the others followed closely.

"I think," Presley added, "that someone may be following us, however. It's difficult to tell with all the interference from the streets over our heads."

Remy's spirits sank at the thought of that. "Well, let's not waste time."

They'd gone only another fifty yards or so, though, when the two lycanthropes again came to a sudden halt. Before he could ask what was wrong, Presley held up an open hand for silence.

A narrow, perpendicular corridor branched off to the right ahead of them. The tunnel definitely rumbled. It was clearer now and in fact, it sounded less like a vehicle than it did like dozens of heavy, pounding footsteps.

"Oh, shit." His heart leapt painfully.

At least ten dwarves burst out of the corridor, streamed into the tunnel ahead of them, and spread into a skirmish line. All glared and brandished weapons. Their ranks were immediately swelled by two more waves of dwarves.

The quartet froze, all knowing they needed to act but not yet sure what to do.

Amidst the platoon of short, broad humanoids, one began to emerge slowly and towered over the others. His dark silhouette held a gigantic hammer.

"No!" Riley cried. "We can't fight him again. Not with all of them here."

A thunderous voice boomed out of the mass. "Yes, you can. And you will. Stand and fight. Fight!"

The dwarves hadn't attacked yet. Having cut them off, they seemed to be preparing to encircle them once all were assembled.

Conrad whispered to his companions. "Someone is coming from behind us, too. We walked into a trap."

"Well," Remy countered, "are we sure it's more dwarves? It might be a goddamn survey crew for all we know. Riley, go find out while we try to stall these assholes."

The fairy, her energy restored by the sudden danger, launched from his shoulder and darted back the way they'd come.

He cleared his throat. "Hi, Grayhammer! Sorry about the misunderstanding earlier, ha. We actually were only trying to...uh, pay tribute or something and propose an alliance to, you know, profit-share some of the—"

"Bullshit!" the dwarf leader roared. The investigator saw, with mounting terror, that a subtle whitish glow seemed to play about the surface of the dwarf's skin. "You're here to die!"

The three men began to back away and the dwarves

immediately started their advance. Glancing over his shoulder, Remy saw that Riley almost careened toward him.

"Well, that was fast," he said to her. "What—"

"Moswen's thralls!" the fairy shrieked. "They're coming around the bend."

He slapped his right hand directly onto his own face. "You have to be fucking kidding me," he mumbled.

At least the werewolves had already begun to strip their clothes off.

CHAPTER TWENTY-FOUR

Abandoned Subway Tunnel, Lower Manhattan, New York

The dwarves advanced at a fast march but not yet a full charge, almost as if they dared the four to try to run. Their heavy footfalls and disciplined formation seemed to be as much for intimidation as anything else.

Faintly, behind them, Remington could hear the other welcoming committee getting closer, a scrabbling, chaotic rush of bodies that tried to crawl over or around one another in a maddened frenzy.

Riley hovered in place over his head. The two lycanthropes were already hunched and hair sprouted from their bare backs. He noticed, with a curious amusement, that Presley's fur was a uniform milky white.

We are vastly fucking outnumbered. I don't care how kickass these two think they are, we cannot fight forty-some dwarves and deal with God knows how many vampiric thralls. If only there were some really clever way to—

"Uh," he said tentatively as the gears in his mind suddenly spun into action, "quick plan, you guys. How about we retreat and attempt a 'let's you and him fight' type of situation?"

If the fairy heard him, she gave no indication. Neither did his other two companions, who were halfway into their transformations. By now, he could actually feel the bestial rage rising from them both.

Do I have to do everything myself? They'll still try to protect me though, right? So all I need to do is lure the whole brawl back until it crashes into Moswen's merry band of dickheads, and—

"Slay them all!" Grayhammer bellowed.

Pandemonium erupted when the front line of dwarves attacked. They moved faster than such stumpy-looking creatures rightfully should have been able to, their axes, hammers, and maces raised in killing positions. None of them had guns or crossbows and Remy somehow suspected that their leader had insisted they die at close, intimate range.

At the same time as the dwarves attacked, the two werewolves pounced. The darker one—Conrad—surged into the fray and launched himself at the dwarf who blocked him from the cartel leader. His powerful jaws closed around his skull and wolf and dwarf went down in a tangle of violence.

Presley, on the other hand, kept lower to the ground, moved more slowly, and targeted a dwarf near the center of the formation who'd taken a step or two ahead of the others. The old lycanthrope bit his target's leg off and shoved him back to turn him into an obstacle which temporarily cut the dwarven lines in two.

"Riley!" Remy yelled when he realized that the butler

had perhaps bought them a precious moment. "Do something to slow those guys down. The dwarves on the left."

"Yes," she responded and elevated quickly, alert once again. Her hands flowed and twisted, and pale light shone from them to form a wall that became a wave. This tide of light engulfed the left half of the dwarven platoon and they all snarled and grimaced as their pace slowed to a crawl.

That left the right half, where Conrad had punched a hole in the ranks directly in front of their hulking commander.

"Hey!" Remy snapped. "You—the big ugly prick. Yeah, I remember you. What's with all the guys you have out in front of you? Are you scared to fight us again?"

Grayhammer's dark and smoldering gaze locked onto his face. "Die," he rasped. The battle had hardly begun but already, he looked on the verge of losing control. "You will die. Shut up!"

He shoved forward and his subordinates slowed and moved aside to allow him to pass.

For a brief instant, the investigator congratulated himself. Then, he realized that his success simply meant that a huge, angry, semi-invulnerable asshole was about twelve feet away from him and gaining.

He spun on one heel and bolted in the other direction at a full sprint.

"Nooooo!" Grayhammer's voice echoed. It was almost painful to listen to. "Come back. You have to stand and face what's coming." Already, his thunderous footsteps were in pursuit.

Somehow, he thought as the dark tunnel zoomed by

around him and his lungs filled with the fire of exertion, *I don't think that guy is a very happy person.*

He had almost forgotten how much distance he could clear when he ran at top speed, and in the thick darkness, his sense of space was distorted.

When he rounded the broad bend in the tunnel, he almost tripped over his own feet in near shock. He was, once again, only twelve feet from those who wanted him dead.

Moswen clearly understood the concept of escalation. From sending two thralls after him the first time, she had upgraded her second attempt to more like fifty.

"Merciful Buddha and Zoroaster," he sputtered, hopped in place to kill his own momentum, and tried to pivot more or less in midair.

The horde, having sensed the proximity of their target minutes before, had already worked themselves into a foaming frenzy. Dozens of human faces contorted with the same awful desperation and violent need to rend and tear that he'd seen in Alex weeks before. Not one of them would stop until he was dead.

He ran back toward Grayhammer and his army.

This is beyond crazy enough to work. It's more like plain crazy because we don't really have any other options, do we?

The massive dwarf boss barreled directly toward him. Drool streaked from his mouth to catch in his beard and his eyes almost shined with the prospect of revenge so close. His equally massive hammer made a low, unpleasant humming sound as it pulsed with dark energies, and his four magic rings glowed slightly even in the deep shadows of the tunnel.

Immediately behind him were two other dwarves, only slightly smaller than he. Something about the way they were outfitted and the general look of them suggested that they were elite bodyguards of some kind. Remy would be within pounding distance of all three of them within about two seconds.

At the same time, the vampiric thralls were gaining to the point where he could hear the projections of their breath in his ear and feel the slight disturbances of the air as their clawing hands reached toward his neck.

Riley fluttered toward him also and tried to shout something, although her high-pitched little voice was completely drowned in the echoing racket of the underground corridor.

"Here goes fucking nothing," Remy gasped.

Somehow, he pulled off a lightning-fast, three-point maneuver composed of stopping, darting a few inches to the side, and still retaining enough of the leftover momentum of his sprint to hurl himself forward again. He tumbled in midair and rolled ahead at top speed.

Grayhammer's raw-throated bellow and the thralls' compulsive howling mingled into a single horrific cacophony as the world spun. Thick hands and thicker weapons passed over his head or behind his ass and stumpy legs passed him.

Then suddenly—and almost miraculously—he staggered to his feet, half-balanced, with open black air before him. All of the violence and death lay a few feet behind.

"Remy!" the fairy yelled as she descended within shouting distance.

He lacked the breath to respond but motioned her to

follow him as he ran farther toward the other dwarves and, more importantly, toward Conrad and Presley.

A hasty backward glance confirmed that his effort had been rewarded. In a storm of cursing and incoherent shouts, Grayhammer and his two henchmen had bulldozed into Moswen's servants, and almost before either party fully understood what was happening, they had turned on each other.

Three or four thralls were already dead, and the dwarves seemed poised to claim several others, but the sheer numbers of the augmented humans gave them powerful advantages themselves.

He turned his head slowly forward in mid-jog and assessed the rest of the scene. First, to his dismay, some of the thralls had simply darted around Grayhammer to the sides and now scampered along the walls, trying to reach Remy.

Second, the werewolves were still on their feet and had rejoined each other and worked back toward him and the fairy. The remaining dwarves, however, had formed into two separate spearheads to attack them from both sides. The ones to the left lagged slightly behind thanks to Riley's slow spell, which already had mostly dissipated.

Unfortunately, everyone was about to crash into each other right in the middle of the tunnel.

"Riley—" Remy panted and struggled to get the words out quickly enough. "Disguise us—cloak—illusion. Get these assholes to all—fight—" He pointed the fingers of both hands at each other, twirled his arms in an inter-locking motion, and hoped she'd get the message.

Trick these bastards into killing each other instead of us.

It seemed, briefly, that the fairy squinted in bewilderment, but the basic facts of their situation were obvious enough that she must have understood. She shouted in a language beyond his knowledge, raised her hands, and worked her magic.

Total chaos engulfed them all once more.

Forms and light shifted to a background track of screams and growls and clanking weapons and somewhere amidst the battle, Remy was driven toward one of the tunnel walls by a rabid thrall.

It was a woman, jittery and lean and inherently scary in part simply because she looked ready to do anything to keep her mistress happy.

"Stay where you are," she hissed and lunged.

He caught her by the wrist and hair and dragged her forward, over his hip, and swung himself back as he flung her headfirst into the metal girders beside the wall. She squawked and crumpled.

As he turned out of the movement, Presley—surprisingly strong and majestic for an old, white-haired wolf—stood on his hind legs with a squirming dwarf in his forepaws. He growled and lobbed his foe into an oncoming battery of thralls, who tripped over the heavy body or were pushed aside.

A little beyond the lycanthrope, the darker, lither form of Conrad sprang again and again through the dim space, never in one place for more than a second. His fangs and claws rent the flesh of dwarf and enthralled human alike.

While Riley pushed their attackers into one another and manipulated appearances at will, dwarven axes descended into gibbering thralls' heads and thralls ripped out the throats of cursing dwarves.

"Damn." Remy breathed deeply. "We might actually get through this."

Remembering the electric baton he'd brought, he yanked it from his waistband, clicked it on, and drove it into the face of the next thrall to attack him, who shrieked and recoiled, his hair smoking.

He turned back to the fray.

"No!" a familiar voice thundered. "No, nooooo!"

He looked behind him.

Grayhammer had battered his way through half a dozen thralls and now shoved another aside as he strode toward Remy, crazed and murderous.

A white flash interposed itself. The investigator staggered back as Presley and the dwarf leader struggled, the werewolf's jaws and one front claw locked around the shaft of the accursed hammer.

Briefly, it looked like the two might be evenly matched but the lycanthrope began to shrink back and down. The sheer solidity of the dwarf's brutish frame and the pulsating dark magic of his weapon would crush the old lycanthrope in seconds.

Remy lurched forward and waved his hands and the baton in an effort to get the dwarf's attention. He succeeded.

With a sound like gargling rocks, Grayhammer shoved Presley aside and swung his weapon with unnatural speed.

"Crap!" Remy cried and fell back. The hammer missed his skull by about an inch. He crawled away on his hands and knees and noticed that both werewolves were moving toward him as well.

Much like it had been at the harbor, his only hope was to distract the dwarf leader enough to where the lycanthropes could kill him before he was aware of them. Riley's magic was useless against him.

"Uh," Remy shouted, not sure what to say yet, "Hammer guy! I fucked your girlfriend before we jumped you at the harbor. Yeah! Or your daughter, if you have one."

Grayhammer stormed forward and swung again. His terrible weapon crushed a heavy steel girder as though it were a whole-wheat cereal product. "Puling wretch. Miscreant dog, disavowed by all true men. Your words are as feeble as an old woman's piss!"

Conrad leapt out of the general melee and tried to bite into their adversary's neck from behind, but the towering dwarf knocked him away with a quick backhanded punch.

The other dwarves were converging. While there were still at least twenty thralls, Grayhammer's men were the more disciplined fighting force and were overcoming the chaos that Riley had helped create.

He tried not to despair, but things did not look good. The four of them were still outnumbered and they'd already spent most of their energy to simply survive for this long.

"Kneel!" the enraged dwarf commanded. Spittle flew from his lips. "Don't prolong this. Succumb, you piece of shit."

Suddenly, Remy had the odd sensation that someone was looking at him. Not Grayhammer but someone else. He looked up and down the length of the tunnel.

There, toward the end in the direction in which they'd been going before the dwarves had cut them off, stood a lithe black silhouette with one hand holding a sword. There was a lull in the fighting as all heads turned toward the new figure.

He would have laughed with relief if his lungs had been up to it, but all that came out was a feeble hacking sound.

"Well…" He gasped. "It's about frickin' time."

CHAPTER TWENTY-FIVE

An Abandoned Subway Tunnel, Lower Manhattan, New York

Taylor had not fully recovered and strenuous motions still caused some pain in her belly. The huge gash had closed, but the tissues within were not entirely mended.

But she could fight and she would.

It took particular types of sounds—or especially large amounts of deafening noise—to awaken her from slumber. Presley knew all the tricks and could rouse her in an instant if need be as he'd done earlier when Alex had called.

The distinctive signature of bloody combat was one such sound.

She'd woken in a state of brief disorientation, one which brought back dim memories of her distant life as a mortal when sleep was plagued with nightmares and fog. It happened sometimes when she was injured.

But her mind had not taken long to catch up. A battle raged almost directly outside her sanctuary. The implications of that were not lost on her.

She'd found her feet in an instant, drawn her sword, and climbed through the trapdoor, not quite sure what to expect but prepared to deal with it nonetheless.

Now, she stared at a whirlwind of carnage that exceeded anything she'd seen since the last major human war she'd dabbled in. Her brain processed and cataloged the information.

Remy and Presley had come looking for her, either in a misguided effort to protect her or out of a desperate need for her help. Unwittingly, they had led Moswen's thralls to her doorstep.

And Grayhammer, the head of the dwarven cartel whom the investigator had mentioned, must have gleaned the general location of her safe house from that asshole Surrly. Somehow, everyone had converged there at the same time.

She stood at the end of the tunnel and sent her will out to compel everyone to turn and look and notice her.

Then, she plunged into them.

Two yards away, a dwarf—seemingly an elite guardsman of some kind—struggled against two human fanatics enslaved to Moswen Neith. All three were momentarily frozen in indecision while their thoughts collided in a tangle and they attempted to decide which of them the vampire would regard as the greater foe.

She made no such discrimination. With a deft movement, she switched the sword to her left hand as she closed on them, pivoted to the side, and brought the blade up in an upward-arc backhand stroke. It cleaved through the bowels of the first thrall and slashed the throat of the great dwarf in the same motion.

As the two of them collapsed amidst spurts of their own blood, the second thrall tried to flee. She launched herself above him and impaled his head on her sword, wrenched him around, and flung him aside as she landed.

It had all happened in the space of about a second.

"It's Taylor. Ha!" Remy's voice wheezed.

"It's Taylor," another voice echoed and rose from a rumble to a crackle in only two words. "Get her. Kill her!"

She advanced and registered the presence of Remy, Conrad, Riley, and her butler, all struggling but still alive. Some of the thralls, still acting presumably on Moswen's command to capture Remington, ignored her approach and lunged at her partner.

The thralls closer to her, though, had little choice but to notice her. And Grayhammer and his dwarves had opted to give her their full attention. She repaid them in kind.

Heedless of the sting in her gut, she flashed into them. Her blade soared and struck to slice flesh and bone. The rapid motions severed entire bodies and she stepped between their ruined pieces and kicked open the wounds made by her sword before gravity could separate the tissues. Four thralls and five dwarves died in seconds.

Farther down the tunnel, Presley and Conrad flung themselves against the humans that targeted Remy, confident that Taylor would buy them time to fight their own battles.

On the other side of the battery of foes that Taylor efficiently dispatched, Starik Grayhammer stood, momentarily frozen with drug-addled hate bordering on awe, and decided to step up his game.

The vampire stabbed a hapless thrall and flung him

aside by his head. His neck snapped for good measure and she turned her focus onto the dwarf. He produced a glowing white syringe and plunged it into his own arm.

So that's Snow White, Taylor acknowledged as she brought her sword up to parry the clumsy ax-strike of a cartel soldier. *Let's see if she's as bad as everyone says.*

Her sword deflected the attacker's weapon and before he could react, her foot pounded into his nose and drove the bone shards into his brain. He stood dribbling blood from his nostrils for a moment, not yet aware that he was dead, before he fell.

As soon as Taylor had seen the huge dwarf called Grayhammer, she'd known something was wrong with him. It was clear that it wasn't only an imbalance of personality but also a willful disturbance of chemistry. The man was higher than a kite on some drug of preternatural origin.

Now, the second dose of Snow White had already begun to kick in. She could actually feel him descend into a psychotic maelstrom of white-hot rage. Every vestige of rational consciousness fell away like a cast-off robe and left only a rabid urge to murder.

Foam appeared around the rim of his mouth. His pupils were barely focused and like some sub-humanoid creature, she suspected he was losing the use of his vision while gaining augmented powers of smell, hearing, and proprioception.

Not to mention speed and strength. Even she might not recover from a single good blow from his hammer. Especially since it seemed to flow and pulse with a malign enchantment she could not quite identify.

Another dwarf, also a bodyguard type, stepped between her and his master. To her shock, Grayhammer brought his weapon down on the dwarf's thick head, all but obliterated it, and shoved the corpse aside. In his drug-fueled rage, he could no longer distinguish friend from foe and would destroy anything that got in his way.

Taylor surged toward the cartel leader, felt his eagerness to engage her, and darted to the side as his hammer moved to kill her.

The weapon cleared air far quicker than she would have liked, and she almost balked at the power the drug had given him. A bludgeoning tool like that should have generated far too much air resistance to keep pace with her.

Already, she had somersaulted back the way she'd come to complete her flanking maneuver. As Starik pivoted to meet her, the blade of her sword passed through his hip.

He ignored it and strode toward her.

"Shit," she muttered.

A miniature sonic boom resounded in the tunnel as the huge hammer thundered toward her head again and displaced air at unnatural speeds. The vampire vaulted upward and over the weapon before she forced herself down and sliced and hacked with her blade as she descended.

Blood welled from almost a dozen gashes that opened in Grayhammer's arms, shoulders, neck, and even the thick, almost concrete-like bone of his skull. He did not fall.

"You!" he roared. "You! You!" He hoisted the hammer

over his head and flung himself toward her. His onslaught seemed as if he no longer even tried to strike her and only aimed to envelop and crush her petite form with the mass of his body.

Among humans, Taylor recalled in the brief moment she had to plan, there were levels of adrenaline that ignored pain and even most types of damage. A person in such a state could only be brought down by force so massive as to short-circuit the body's bioelectricity or by dismantling those structures which it required to move.

She went down instead of up, ducked between Grayhammer's legs, spun, and swiped her sword through the bones and ligaments of both knees. He screamed, not in agony but in frustration at having again failed to kill her, despite the fact that both his legs fell aside and effectively crippled him.

He spun his torso and the hammer arced toward her face.

In response, she bent back, allowed herself to fall, and brought the sword up in time to intercept the blow. The blade of her weapon shattered and some of the shards left cuts in her body as they shrapneled.

The hammer, fortunately, did not strike her and she grabbed Starik's arm, broke it at the elbow with one twist and shattered his wrist with another. His accursed weapon clattered beyond his reach.

An easy vault landed her on Grayhammer's broad shoulders. She stared into his crazed, half-blinded eyes as she dug her claws into his neck. With both feet braced against his body, she tightened the firmness of her grip and launched upward with all the power she possessed.

Cracking and tearing like stone being demolished, the dwarf's head came off in her hands and ascended with her to the tunnel's ceiling. The hulking body finally toppled and thrashed a few more times as if to protest its own death.

The vampire descended, landed on her feet, and threw the huge head aside. It landed on the body with a thud, cushioned by its attached mane of hair but too blocky and heavy even to roll.

Her gaze assessed the scene. The werewolves, with some help from Riley—and to a lesser extent even Remington—had dispatched the last of the thralls. A few echoes of combat vibrations rippled down the length of the corridor before silence set in.

Taylor brushed herself off and noted, with dismay, that she would need a new sword. The one lost to Grayhammer had served her well while it lasted.

Gasping and near exhaustion, her four companions stumbled toward her. She nodded briefly to the fairy and the lycanthropes and focused her attention on the human.

"Remington," she said and employed her best tone of icy calm, "I have a question."

He simply stared and mouthed stupidly at her before the realization set in that they'd won and he was still alive. "Uh...yes?"

"Why," she grated, "did you bring a thundering cluster-fuck like this directly to the place I had specifically desig-nated as a safe house? This is one of those things that requires a supremely good explanation."

Remy hesitated and seemed to turn over a couple of possible responses in his mind. She imagined him considering some sarcastic bullshit like, *Well, I didn't want you to miss out on the fun, ha*. Or something similarly stupid.

Instead, he looked honestly happy to see her and said, "I thought I'd take you up on that offer of yours and ask you for a key." He cleared his throat and smiled.

CHAPTER TWENTY-SIX

Taylor's House, Harrison, Westchester County, New York

David Remington, whether known by his birth name or by Remington Davis or by Remy, had never been the type to forego a reasonable and generous offer made by good friends who wished him the best. No, he was the type to take full advantage of whatever was available.

"Make yourself at home," Taylor had said.

Therefore, he had. And already, Presley seemed to have developed a strange resistance to his employer's clearly stated wishes.

"Ah, sir," the butler called as their guest hoisted a big neon sign and carried it toward the second-floor staircase, "is that really necessary?"

"What? Why do you ask?" he retorted. "It's not as though all this ornamental stuff from the twelfth century you guys have is necessary, either. Besides, Taylor instructed me to make myself at home. Didn't you hear?"

The old man's jaw moved up and down for a second or

two but no coherent sounds emerged. Again, he took advantage of an opportunity as soon as it presented itself and started up the stairs.

"Sir," Presley said again and started after the younger man, "we do have…ah, power bills to consider. Wasting electricity on a neon beer sign is hardly what Ms Steele had in mind. Of that, I can assure you."

By now, he was already halfway up the stairs and the butler had barely reached the base.

"Oh?" he inquired. "Did you specifically ask her? Wait, don't bother. I'll do so myself after I get this set up. It's one of the few of my things that Moswen's thralls didn't smash into oblivion, so it has sentimental value besides. Maybe they thought it was beneath contempt?"

The old man started up the steps behind him and commented, "Yes, I'd say that's entirely possible. You don't plan to put that anywhere near the window, do you? Especially that brand? You might at least have gone with Newcastle Brown—"

Ignoring him, Remy carried the sign into the room that was to be his and decided that the best place for it was on an open space of wall directly opposite the window. He held it up in that location to confirm.

"No." Presley almost moaned. "Sir, you mustn't."

The elderly chap glanced also at the other things that littered the room, all objects he had salvaged from the ruins of his apartment. It was odd, really, that the thralls had mostly obliterated his classy belongings but left all the cheesy bachelor pad accouterments. Like his beanbag chair, his sports posters, or his gaudy neon advertisement of an iconic, if under-respected, US alcohol brand.

"Wellllll," he drawled, "I haven't made up my mind yet."

They descended together as he headed to the next load and paused briefly as they passed the sitting room where Taylor sat reading from a leather-bound tome on wartime economics.

"Remington," Presley scolded, "I simply can't allow this. It's true we don't have many visitors or onlookers, but there is still the possibility that someone might approach the house, look into the window and see...that. Glowing brightly, suggesting that persons in this household actually drink such rubbish."

He scoffed. "It's the sheer ironic kitsch appeal of it, don't you see?" he explained. "Everyone makes fun of it for being borderline tasteless and generically cheap, corporate, mass-produced, overly American, and so forth. Even though I think the brand was purchased by a company from...I don't know, Luxembourg or someplace a while ago."

The old man cleared his throat. "Belgium, sir. At least you were close."

"Right, Belgium. Whatever." He flapped a hand dismissively. "The point is, when a girl comes over, of course she'll make fun of it. I can then respond with a witty, self-deprecating remark and use that as a launching pad to make fun of her. It's all part of the gradual strategy of getting into her pa—er, I mean, into her good graces."

The butler, frowning even more deeply, looked at his own sleeve and brushed away a tiny piece of lint. "Whatever you say, sir. However, I don't think Ms Steele will approve of you trying to entertain young ladies in her home, even if your only purpose is to enter their 'good graces.'"

"Hmm, yes," Remy responded and placed his hands on his hips, "why don't we ask her? Straight from the vampire-horse's mouth. I bet, knowing me as well as she does, she wouldn't necessarily object to—"

Taylor looked up from her book. "No casual sex on the premises, please. It creates a certain smell that persists for far longer than you might think, depending on the sensitivity of one's olfactory receptors. Not to mention that I don't want to have to change your tires if they get slashed a week later." She turned her gaze back to her reading.

"Oh," he replied. "Damn."

Presley folded his hands behind his back and smirked. "There, you see? We have standards in this household, I'm afraid. And at the end of the day, sir, you're still a guest, which is to say you are dependent on our goodwill as hosts. Thus, you will abide by our rules while under our roof."

"I knew it," he muttered. "You'd get along great with my parents. In fact, why don't you apply to work for them? I bet they'd be thrilled to meet a genuine werewolf. My mother would have any number of questions about body hair and its proper care and removal. Meanwhile, I'll take over as butler here, I guess."

"Mm, no," the butler retorted. "You will recall that I trained for years at the academy for precisely this kind of duty. You're not qualified."

"Yeah, yeah." Remy picked up a two-foot square box filled to the brim with neckties. "That's what they all say."

Meanwhile, Riley had floated around outside and amused herself by licking the bases of icicles hanging off the eaves. She seemed fascinated by how long it took to get all the way through them so they would plummet earthward like vengeful spears of frigid death. It was good to see her enjoying herself at something other than bilking random men for clothes she'd never wear.

Now, she flew into the house.

"Is Remy almost moved in?" she asked the butler.

He spoke for himself before the old man could. "Yes, Riley, I'm almost done. I'll be here for a while, it seems. Not that long, but still. It's the same room we spent the night in a few months ago, in fact."

"I remember that," she quipped. "When you woke up, you had a—"

"Need for coffee." He cut her off. "Thanks."

"Well," she went on and her small face grew a trifle pouty, "if you'll be here all the time because it's dangerous, I should have a room here too. You know, to keep an eye on you."

Presley hastened up to them. "Another entire room given over purely to a single fairy is not very economical, sir. Might I suggest..."

After a few minutes of arguing, justifications, rationalizations, and thinly veiled threats, they all agreed that Riley could have a drawer within Remy's room all to herself.

The butler remained downstairs to clean up the mess created by the moving process. Remington and Riley went to the former guest room.

He sighed. "I suppose that with Moswen trying to draw

and quarter us and turn our skulls into teacups or whatever that it wouldn't hurt to have my own live-in bodyguard. There's no way in hell I'd let Conrad sleep in the
same room as me, after all."

The fairy smiled. "I'm glad to hear that."

"And," he added, "this way, I can keep an eye on you,
also. You know, paying attention to you and such. You'll
get enough attention, in fact, that you won't even want to
think about borderline-pornographic swimwear and the
imbeciles who are willing to shell out for it because a hot
girl asked them nicely."

"Yay!" She clapped her hands.

*She's starting to resemble her old self again. Perhaps the Fair
Folk recover from addictions faster than we do? It's a shame that
they're susceptible to them at all, to begin with.*

An hour passed, during which he arranged his things,
set his alarm clock, hung his clothes, and so forth. Here
and there, he spared a moment to look at Riley as she
wasted time and said pleasant things to her. Despite the
distraction, it didn't bother him too much.

Conrad called as he finished settling in.

"Sir," the werewolf asked, "will you need me today?"

"No, we should be fine for the moment, and you
deserve a day off." He took a deep breath and finally
continued with something he knew he ought to have said
before now.

"And, Conrad, well... I'm sorry about how I acted when
we first met and...uh, some of the shit I've said. It was...
uncalled-for. The BDSM shit, and the dog jokes. Wolf jokes
would have at least been more accurate. I was afraid, at
first, that you'd turn out to be another of those Ivy League

types who looks down their nose at everyone, especially me since I practically washed out of High Society. In fact, though, you turned out to be...tolerable. And you saved my ass a number of times. So, thanks. I'm not good at being emotional, but I mean it. Truly."

The lycanthrope was silent a moment on the other end, as though he hadn't expected to hear that.

"Well, sir, you're welcome, and thank you. I understand, but your apology is appreciated."

"Right. Maybe we can have a single beer together next time we meet or something. Enjoy your time off, talk to you later, and so forth."

Conrad said goodbye and hung up.

Soft footsteps ascended the staircase, and someone knocked gently on the door before they eased it open.

"Good evening," Taylor said.

Remington turned away from his tie rack to face her. "Good evening, although I'm fairly sure we already had that exchange when I first arrived. We won't keep going through the same formalities over and over again every time we bump into each other around the house, will we?"

The vampire almost smiled. "That ridiculous comment leads us directly into what I wished to discuss. Namely, the...ah, specific arrangements of our cohabitation. As Presley already said, this is my house. However, I'm willing to make a few small, reasonable compromises."

She glanced at his neon beer sign. "Since you won't be here long."

"Right," he confirmed. "This is strictly temporary. Too bad we have to leave it at a vague term like 'temporary' since that can mean…a while, but it's definitely not the same thing as 'permanent.' So there's that."

"Yes." She flicked her eyes to the side and drummed her fingernails against one arm. "You've arranged for your mail to be forwarded here until further notice, haven't you?"

He waved a hand. "I'll do that tomorrow. There's been enough horror and tribulation lately without having to go into the post office before it's strictly necessary."

"Do so," she instructed. "Also, speak to Presley about his schedule so that you can coordinate things like when to keep the noise down relative to each of your sleep times. I am virtually impossible to awaken via mere sound, so you needn't worry about me."

Remy smirked, sensing the irresistible opportunity for an incredibly lame joke. "So what you're saying," he began, winding up dramatically, "is that you sleep like the dead."

She rubbed her forehead as though afflicted by a sudden migraine. "Something like that, yes. Of course, I will also respect your privacy—within reason—and will expect the same from you in return. Over the course of this evening, I'll try to think of other things you should know, such as safety protocols, and write them down for you to study in the morning."

"Protocols." He sighed. "The fun never ends."

"Do recall, Remington," she added, "that this is only for the sake of your protection. Your apartment was attacked twice within less than the span of one full day. Not long ago you were…understandably offended at the idea that I was merely using you for bait." She frowned in what might even have been shame. "I hope that my inviting you here demonstrates that I...would prefer nothing bad happen to you."

She was, he realized, attempting to express something dangerously close to emotion. Never one to neglect an opportunity, he decided to see how she reacted to the unexpected.

He smiled with genuine warmth, stepped closer to her, and without even a trace of sarcasm in his voice, said, "Thank you, Taylor. Not many people have proven that they really care about me beyond what I can do for them financially or socially or whatever. You, however, have. I am grateful, and I mean that."

It seemed a perfectly natural gesture to put a hand on her shoulder.

Taylor took a step back and tensed and her hands rose to neck level in what almost looked like a defensive gesture. Her black eyes bulged with confusion.

"I—ah, you're welcome. Thank you. Yes..."

She's almost flustered, he marveled. *And for a split second there, it almost looked like she was blushing. I wouldn't have expected to see that in a woman who is kinda-sorta technically a walking corpse.*

In a moment, it passed and she was again cool and aloof, very much the mistress of the house. "You've earned the privilege," she stated, "since you've been most helpful to me and to the agency's goals. Of course, it will be important that you not impede my work while you're here."

"Oh, of course," he replied vaguely. "Very professional."

Again, it looked like she might smile, but she managed to stop herself beyond a barely perceptible softening of her expression.

"Although," she went on, "perhaps it...would not be so bad if we were able to spend a little more time together."

Now, he almost blushed as he hadn't expected to hear that.

"Perhaps," he said and wiped his palms off on the sheets of his bed.

EPILOGUE

A Hidden Location

Goran Petrović paused for a moment in the stone archway before the cavernous expanse of the chamber beyond. His host's environs were crude compared to what he was used to in Europe but by American standards, respectable enough.

Thralls formed a corridor leading from the archway to the throne at the far end of the room. They stood in two long ranks, motionless, expressionless, and deferential.

He nodded. Moswen Neith, unknown quantity that she was, had at least some notion of proper etiquette. He stepped into the chamber.

It was, however, a little disquieting since the Vampiric Order had not specifically mentioned that it would send a representative to New York. The idea had been to surprise her.

Two of Goran's own thralls followed closely behind him. He had possessed them for fourteen years each, a reasonably long time by human standards and enough to be sure of their reliability. They had also been empowered not only with his own strength but with part of the might of the entire ruling council of the Order.

In the luxurious chair across the room, elevated upon a low platform that rose from the floor, Moswen herself sat —or almost slouched, really. She appeared entirely at ease, relaxed and casual, and not even slightly shocked or flustered by his unannounced visit.

She was also tall and strong-looking. A vampire's physical appearance had little bearing on their power, but he had to admit that it gave her a regal bearing. Recalling the grievous injury done to himself and to all members of the Order by a certain other, less-intimidating vampire, he felt a renewed confidence that they had made the right decision in coming to her.

Halfway through the hallway of her slaves, he paused to announce himself.

To his surprise and slight perturbation, she spoke first.

"Greetings," she began in a voice that was resonant but with a curiously wispy quality like the blowing of dust in the wind. "Your arrival is not unexpected. I recognize you as the true minds and the true power behind the dwarven cartel overseen by the one known as Grayhammer, who was unfortunately destroyed so recently. I offer my condolences on your loss of a loyal ally."

Goran was not accustomed to having almost half of his own speaking points recited to him before he had even uttered them himself. He reverted to formality. "Greetings, Moswen Neith," he replied.

He then considered switching to another, more appropriate tongue, but the intelligence he had received suggested that Moswen, oddly enough, spoke only Hebrew and English, although one rumor held that she knew far more languages. Partially to play it safe, then, and partially out of politeness toward her residence in the United States, he continued to use English.

"I am Goran Petrović, ranking member of the Vampiric Order of Europe. What you have said is true and we thank you for your condolences. I have come to discuss the prospect of a mutually beneficial arrangement between us. Will you hear me?"

She smiled, and something about the expression reminded him of a fire spreading through desiccated brush.

"Yes," she declared. "I will. Come closer, Goran, and tell me your proposal."

He did as she said, although he wasn't sure he liked the implied presumption in her words. She was at once gracious and arrogant. Part of him bristled but there were more important considerations than mere protocol. Besides, she did not come from the European establishment. Customs in the Middle East and North Africa were expected to differ.

When he'd crossed the rest of the chamber, he decided to test the other vampire slightly. He stepped onto the raised platform and stood before her at the same level, although he remained at the platform's edge.

Moswen frowned. She did not otherwise react, but he had the uncomfortable sensation that she would remember that he had done this, possibly forever.

He began his pitch without further ado.

"We have all suffered from the recent foolhardy actions

of the rogue vampire Taylor Steele and her incorrigible servants from various lesser species. We understand that she has deprived you of your own servants, and this is in accordance with complaints we received some months ago by another vampire, called Gabriel, who attempted—and failed—to supplant her."

Goran ran a finger through his black beard and mustache and noted the way Moswen listened with a languid complacency.

"We have, until now, tolerated her illegitimate claim of New York City as her personal fiefdom due to her non-interference in our business. But now, she has annihilated the cartel upon which we relied for our profits. She could have made peace herself, even if Grayhammer was reluctant. But with his death in addition to Gabriel's, it is clear that she has succumbed to hubris. She will kill anyone who challenges her even slightly and considers herself omnipotent."

The woman smiled again and this time, her fangs showed. "She is not."

"Of course," he agreed. "Although neither is she to be taken lightly. She has threatened our continued prosperity and she has insulted our ancient honor and dignity. The vendetta that was Grayhammer's is now ours."

He paused for effect. "We want her eliminated."

The Israeli vampire folded one hand atop the other in her lap. "Good."

Goran raised a fist. "We make you this offer. Our complete support. All the resources at our disposal—everything we have available in America. Our full commitment to you, and to the cause of your usurpation. We would be happy to see you sit where she now sits in exchange for revenge. And the possibility of future business arrangements, of course. But first, she must die. No one has ever offended us to this extent."

A slight violet glow rose behind his eyes as he spoke, the indication of an age-old, bestial rage at even the idea of being challenged. His personal desire to dispatch Taylor to oblivion was no less than any other member of the Order. Their hatred had become a driving force, a pure and singular purpose

Moswen spread her arms and stood. She was slightly taller than he was.

"I accept your offer without reservation, Goran Petrović. Be sure to give my deepest thanks to the Order. We shall become great friends. All of us."

Something in her brown, almond-shaped eyes grew distant and faintly luminous. "Taylor will die, and I will rule New York. And beyond."

Look for book four in the series, Under Pressure, coming soon to Amazon and Kindle Unlimited.

AUTHOR NOTES FROM ISOBELLA CROWLEY (AKA ELL LEIGH CLARKE)

WRITTEN NOVEMBER 18, 2019

Thank yous

As always I'd like to thank MA for making this series happen. I've really enjoyed working on these characters, and MA is a fun collaborator. Plus, he let's me take the micky out of him without repercussion. Which is good, else I'd probably be in real trouble by now... :-D Thanks, dude!

Lots of people go into making a series like this happen.

I'd like to say a massive thank you to the team of suppliers who made this book possible: Brittany, Chiara, Nathan, Philip, Moonchild, and MA's editing team.

Thank you, guys. Your hard work, care and attention mean the world to me :)

Beta readers and JITers

Massive, and uber thanks also go out to our beta readers, led by Brittany, and MA's JIT team led by their high commander, Zen Steve. Thank you for all your hard work in making sure the words are right and inconsistencies slayed. You're the best <3

Reviewers

Mega thanks also goes out to our Amazon reviewers. It's because of you that we get to do this full time. Without your five-star reviews and thoughtful words on Amazon we simply wouldn't have enough folks reading these space shenanigans to be able to write full time.

Truly, thank you... As of writing we have 20 ALL five-star reviews on book 1. You're the best <3 Look out for your name and our thank yous on the fb page. You have no idea how much this means to me. <3

Readers and FB page supporters

I'd like to also thank *YOU* for reading this book. Your enthusiasm for the worlds and characters we come up with is heart-warming. Thank you for being here, for the giggles and interaction, for reading, and reviewing.

You rock.

And feel free to join the fun over on fb: www.facebook.com/ellleighclarke

We have a fb page as Izzie too: www.facebook.com/IsobellaCrowley

Or the mailing list, for more fun and frolics into paranormal fantasy: www.isobellacrowley.com

If you'd like more of the insider lo-down, feel free to join us over at Patreon too.

We have a few things like a movie watch in the pipeline for all patrons... https://www.patreon.com/ellleighclarke

Why did he slit his writs?

So I finally asked MA about his new slap-dash approach to author notes. You'll probably have noticed how this series instead of writing his own, he's taken to just commenting on mine.

His response was something along the lines of him not having the fucks to be able to do it. Poor guy. He works so hard and apparently he's handed multiple sets of author notes for all the books each week… He just doesn't have it in him anymore. :-(

Maybe that will change with our next series? But for now, he says, and I quote:

"Why did he slit his wrists? No More Author Notes!!!! I'm done." – MA.

I get it. It takes a lot to keep up with the wit and humor I lay down… And if you don't got it… ;P

So, for now, you'll just have to contend with me… and MA interjecting now and again.

This is probably a bad time to tell him that I've been told that people don't read his notes anyway…

…

…

…

Hahahaha. I'm kidding, Anderle.

Seriously, I'm pulling your leg… (Man, I'm probably going to get some flack in his comments for that…!)

So you have to imagine how this is working. What happens with the ANs is that I write mine, normally several days ahead of publication. (I'm cutting it tight today though. Steve pushes the button tomorrow morning.)

Then I send them to MA, and he comments in them, and then he sends them all to Steve.

Steve then reads them.

I hadn't realized that this means Steve ALWAYS reads them... I thought it had meant that now and again Steve might cast his eye over some section of them, and that's how he stays in the loop.

Nope.

It's way more systematic than that. On his last podcast recording Steve confirmed that he reads every word.

Every word!

So I'm wondering... maybe Steve should start writing author notes for this series... Just while MA catches his breath?

Just a suggestion, Steve ;)

<Steve Note 1: Not happening ;)>

MA: "So you're a publisher now?"

As we began our call the other day, MA commented that he'd seen an email from me. "So you're a publisher now?" he asked.

If you're on my mailing list you will have seen the same email where I explained a few changes that have been going on for me.

I'd already explained in a previous message about how wearing spaceships on my t-shirt helped me overcome feeling like an imposter.

All in all, it took about a year before I really started telling people I was an author.

The readers who were around during that era REALLY helped: reading your 5* reviews and comments and banter on my Facebook page... you helped me get through some of the toughest challenges I've had to face.

Not that calling myself an author was a massive road-block – but it was a psychological sticking point that was holding my back, keeping me playing small.

Once I got through that though things were great. For a few months.

I embraced my quirkiness and accepted myself as a writer of stories.

I even grew in confidence to take on other writing projects.

But then, the landscape started to shift again.

With all the new projects I was working on, and new series I was leading, when people asked what I did, my "I'm a sci-fi author" response didn't feel authentic anymore.

At this point I was also creating stories in Urban Fantasy. But – hey, your Lyft driver doesn't care about that level of detail, so I either felt I was getting it wrong again, or... I turned into a babbling idiot trying to explain exactly what I did!

Additionally, I had already started transitioning into publishing and series *creation* rather than just writing. Subtle difference, but I was working on more stories, with other collaborators, than I put my name on.

Plus, I was kinda shy.

And being British, I didn't need to be braggy, or have my name on the books. After all, why does it matter if I get credit for it or not?

Well, it doesn't. That part is still true.

But the real way I've messed up is not letting you guys know that there are books here that you'd enjoy because even if I didn't write every word myself, I've been running the team – kinda like a showrunner would run a writers room.

Not that I'm anywhere near the levels of story-genius my heroes: Stephen Moffatt and Josh Whedon are just amazing!

But they have influenced a lot of my thinking on how to get more stories out there, and how to think creatively.

During my most recent episode of "downtime" I realize that I've again, been hiding too long.

It's time to come out of the closet and start acting like a publisher/ showrunner, rather than an author.

Over two years from when I started, I really need to make this transition.

As such I'm going to bring everything I've been involved in (contracts allowing) under the brand of Ellieverse Publishing. At the very least, then you'll know that there are stories I've had a significant hand in.

It's a quick way for you to see that if you've enjoyed my other series, (like Molly and Bentley), you'll also probably like some of the other series I've been working on. I do believe that Brittany has finished getting the website up.

You can check it out here: ellieverse.com

(UN)Conferencing in Florida

This is un-conferencing. Not as in the United Nations of conferencing…. Although that would be amazing to be a part of!

If you follow me on The Facebook, you'll have seen I posted a few pic about my fun plane ride across Florida and being at a swanky beach resort for a conference. The conference is called NINC. Don't ask me what it stands for. I think the actual name is something like Writers Ink, so some people spell it Nink. Anyway, I didn't care enough to investigate it, and it effects nothing ;P

<Steve Note 2: Ninc is a shortened version of Novelists, Inc.>

All I cared about was finding the best source of coffee for the duration, and trying to deal with the craziness of being in such an intense environment. Psychically and psychologically there is so much going on at these things that it can be pretty overwhelming.

So anyway, it would be remiss of me to not explain a few things about this conference. It's been going for a looong time. It's an off-shoot of the romance writers conferences, so there are a lot of romance folks there – and everyone knows each other. On top of that, there is a qualifier to get in. You have to be making a certain amount of money form your books sales to go – so that means that there are no newbies. I like the concept, because it means that the talks and conversations can assume a lot more. Some folks take this as an indicator that they can let their inner elitist dangle out... which can be kinda gross to watch. But all in all, most people were super down to earth and friendly.

I found a good bunch of friends – who didn't feel they always had to talk about books(!) - and we had a blast, often not turning in until the wee hours.

During this week, I realized something about myself. And anyone who has seen me at conferences has probably already noticed this.... I don't do well sitting in the room. I get bored and fidgety – so I naturally have a resistance to going in. I tend to do what we call "unconference" – where we hang out at the bars and just socialize. I also realized that my only reasons for ever going in the room were to support my friends who were speak.

Feel free to replace the word "support" with "heckle". It was a small enough conference for it to be appreciated… and heard. **Some places it's pointless because no one hands me a mic for the purpose of heckling.**

(Hint, hint, Michael….)

We have Vegas 50 books coming up… #justsayin'

MA also suggested I tell you about the tiki bar. (MA went a previous year so he knows the drill.) After a certain time of day, when the sun is over the yardarm, everyone filters down to the tiki bar to continue the conversations and drinking. The tiki bar is almost on the beach with lots of tables around for sitting and talking, and the water just a short walk to dip one's feet. This is where the real conferencing happens.

Also, the tiki tends to be open until fairly late – something that we count on, because who wants to go to bed when you're in paradise and don't have to get up and write the next day? (Okay, *some* diligent souls would get up and write each morning, but I justified it like so: I should probably be in the conference from 9am, so I wouldn't be writing anyway. And I don't sit in conference rooms anymore, so I'll just be socializing. No one else will be up to socialize at 9am, so I may as well take my time wandering down in the morning. Ergo, staying up all night is a totally legit choice.)

Needless to say, the last night I didn't sleep at all… And

was still dashing to get my gear packed up for my trip to the airport.

I could tell you about how when the tiki bar closed, we trekked down the beach to another resort to carry on the party. I could also tell you about a certain rep that had to be deposited at his hotel and taken up to his room by the group because he was so drunk... I could tell you a whole lot more about the tiki bar soap opera antics from the week.

But just like Vegas, what happens at Ninc, stays at Ninc.

And I fear I may already have told you too much.

Mum and my Car Insurance Company

I feel there is a wealth of information I need to share with my mother at some point. She's not exactly receptive though... so I'll tell you, just to get it off my chest.

Mum called me the other day.

"Do you want the good news or the bad news?"

My heart sank. I'd asked her to call my car insurance company to pay another bill. I'd recently changed the address the car was being kept, and while they could update the address over email, they wanted more money and I had to call them.

Except, I have no cell signal in my apartment, and they don't accept voip calls... meaning I would have to try and do the call from a noisy café which is never ideal.

So, I asked my mum to make the call for me, and sent her all the information she'd need and my card details.

Two days later I'm making my second coffee of the morning and my music in my headphones stops, and a call from my mum comes through on messenger.

"Give me the good news first," I tell her, bracing myself. At this point I'm calculating that maybe the good news is good enough to cancel out the bad.

"Well, I've got you a rebate."

Huh? "But they wanted more money, and I've just renewed. I don't understand."

"Well, I did everything you asked," she explained, "and it all went through. They've updated your card on the system like you asked… and then I said to the girl… That's kinda steep, isn't it? 700? I'm sure I can get it cheaper if I just ring around."

I put down the coffee pot and continued to listen. Now bear in mind my mum has fallen for a total of 6 or 7 scams in the last ten years. That's just the big ones, that I know about. That's not counting the everyday scams and ill-advised purchases… Like expensive rugs on her trip to Morocco, or a ridiculously priced sky package full of stuff she doesn't watch. So forgive me if I'm more than a little impressed with her negotiating on my car insurance! I mean, she has no dog in this fight… And she'd done the task she'd agreed to do – call them, pay the money on my card. It was finished. But yet she asked that question.

More than a little impressed.

"So she said, *hang on just a minute*," she continued clearly enjoying the telling of the story. "She put me on hold for a minute, and came back… and she said she could take off ninety quid, if we didn't want the breakdown cover. Since you're not using it and if I use it it's covered by my break-down service, I said we could get rid of that. If you come back and want to drive it, then I can add you onto mine."

Smart thinking, Hubbard. "Great! Yeah sure… thank you!"

"Hang on, there's more…" she pressed.

There is more. You still need to tell me the bad news. I mean, 90 quid back is fab, but it's not going to change a lot. Especially not if there is bad news yet to come. I find myself still bracing. "Uh huh?"

"Well then I asked her what else she could do?"

Color me super impressed at this point! She's going for it!

"And?"

"Well, all in all instead of you paying an extra two hundred and something, you're going to be getting a forty pound rebate."

Wha… why?

Because, I asked if she could do any better and said I'd ring around and get a cheaper quote. She knew I could. That's it. They just gave it to me.

OMG. Hubbard!

"That's amazing! Thank you so much! I can't believe you pushed them… I thought you'd just pay it and be done with it."

"Well, I thought it was a lot to be paying for a car you don't drive. And it was pretty steep…."

I had to ask. I was feeling pretty nervous still. Last thing I needed was another thing to sort out on a car in another country. "So what was the bad news?"

"Oh, there isn't anything. I just said it."

"Mother! Omg seriously? I've been bracing myself all the time you were telling that story… waiting for the bad news."

"Oh, well. No. just good news then."

"Okay, thanks pet..." We chinwagged a little more and then hung up.

Here's what I would have liked her to know when using the *good news, bad news* phrase....

ONLY USE THAT IF THERE IS SOME FRIKKIN' BAD NEWS!

I would have enjoyed this a lot more if I wasn't waiting for the other shoe to drop.

But thanks for negotiating me a better rate on the car I don't drive ;)

Rex and Hexe

My deal friend and I have just started releasing his new series Hexe.

Volume 1 is now out on Amazon. It's called Chosen for Power, and has his name, Rex Baron, on the cover.

Hexe: Vol 1, Chosen for Power

https://books2read.com/u/b5QzwG

Here's the skinny:

Magic... when ruthless ambition is not enough.

Lucy has it all.

A blossoming singing career, the looks for the silent movie business, and a lover to die for.

All is unfolding swimmingly until she is confronted by a young actress who is well versed in dark magic and her sights set on stealing everything from her.

Having denied her own birthright as witchcraft, Lucy has to protect her career, relationship and ultimately, her life.

Before it's too late.

Surrounded by a world of glamour and wooed by a leading matinee idol, Volume One: Chosen for Power follows Lucy in a sweeping tale of obsessive love, witch-craft and retribution.

This spellbinding eight-part historical fantasy drama is set in four different eras spanning the course of a century. Beginning in 1921, *Hexe* tracks the dark magical exploits of four women joined by the thread of destiny.

If you read it, hit me up and let me know what you think. I loved this series and I'm so excited to see what happens with it.

Note, all of the spells inside are real, but they've been tweaked slightly so that folks can't cause any damage with them! Just FYI ;P

Okay, I'm up to my word quota for the back of the book notes. Thanks again for reading, and for your 5* reviews on the Zon. You really are the best. I'll see you in book 4, which should be out in just a few weeks after this one goes live.

Ellie/Izzie x

AUTHOR NOTES FROM MICHAEL ANDERLE

NOVEMBER 19, 2019

Thank you for reading both this series, and these author notes.

H#ly C43p Ellie's notes are ... *long*. I didn't see a lot of good places to interject, so I'll just post something way back here in the back, in the dark, where no one goes...

HA!

Ellie wrote her author notes before 20Booksto50k® Vegas and I am writing mine after. It was a fantastic event and my head is still a bit foggy from it all.

During the event, a metric buttload of authors (closer to 1,000) have all sorts of conversations, meetings, events, games and general merriment and recklessness (as authors have done through the ages.)

This conference was spawned out of the 20Booksto50K® Facebook group which was created as a way to give back. To share the ideas and tactics that help authors get a leg up and a hand up in their author career.

During the event, one of the authors came up to me as I was standing on the stage (the presentation was over) and I sat down to chat with him. He handed me a book, and explained I had paid for the cover and he wanted to share. I accepted the book, but then he reminded me why I did that.

At the time he reached out to talk with me on social media, he was homeless. Due to some strings I pulled, I was able to procure him a cover (as that was the best item to help him sell his books he lacked.) He had to create the story, acquire the proofing etc. himself.

I asked him where he was living now – "What is your situation?" I asked.

"I'm in a small trailer and I have five books out, now!"

That man made me feel 10 feet tall. He not only went on to publish that first book, but he published four more books and got himself a place to live. That was work and effort on his part, not mine.

And some people wonder why I don't get more upset with Amazon when things go wrong?

It's because without KDP, we wouldn't have stories like this.

Amazon has changed the world for the better, and I'm a huge supporter.

Ad Aeternitatem,

Michael Anderle

with Michael Anderle

Darkest Before The Dawn (3)

Dawn Arrives (4)

Interplanetary Spy For Hire
with Michael Anderle

Expelled

Deuces Wild
with Michael Anderle

Beyond The Frontiers (1)

Rampage (2)

Labyrinth (3)

Birthright (4)

The Sword-Mage Chronicles

Awakening

Taken

Heist

Resistance

Legba

Storm

CONNECT WITH MICHAEL ANDERLE

Michael Anderle Social
  Website:
  http://www.lmbpn.com

Email List:
  http://lmbpn.com/email/

Facebook Here:
  www.facebook.com/TheKurtherianGambitBooks/